Bottom-Tier
Character
TOMOZAKI
Lv.9

YUKI YAKU

Illustration by
Fly

"So you're a masochist, Rena-san?"

"H-hya!
...Huh?"

CONTENTS

Hanabi Natsubayashi

Design Yuko Mucadeya + Caiko Monma (musicagographics)

Bottom-Tier Character TOMOZAKI

Lv.9

Yuki Yaku

Illustration by Fly

YEN ON

New York

Bottom-Tier CHARACTER TOMOZAKI Lv.9

YUKI YAKU

Translation by Jennifer Ward
Cover art by Fly

JAKU CHARA TOMOZAKI-KUN LV.9
by Yuki YAKU
© 2016 Yuki YAKU
Illustration by FLY
All rights reserved.
Original Japanese edition published by SHOGAKUKAN.
English translation rights in the United States of America, Canada, the United Kingdom, Ireland, Australia, and New Zealand arranged with SHOGAKUKAN through Tuttle-Mori Agency, Inc.

English translation © 2023 by Yen Press, LLC

Yen On
150 West 30th Street, 19th Floor
New York, NY 10001

Visit us at yenpress.com
facebook.com/yenpress
twitter.com/yenpress
yenpress.tumblr.com
instagram.com/yenpress

First Yen On Edition: January 2023
Edited by Yen On Editorial: Anna Powers
Designed by Yen Press Design: Wendy Chan

Yen On is an imprint of Yen Press, LLC.
The Yen On name and logo are trademarks of Yen Press, LLC.

Library of Congress Cataloging-in-Publication Data
Names: Yaku, Yuki, author. | Fly, 1963- illustrator. | Ward, Jennifer, translator.
Title: Bottom-tier character Tomozaki / Yuki Yaku ; illustration by Fly ; v. 1 - 8.5: translation by Winifred Bird ; v. 9 translation by Jennifer Ward.
Other titles: Jyakukyara Tomozaki-kun. English
Description: First Yen On edition. | New York : Yen On, 2019-
Identifiers: LCCN 2019017466 | ISBN 9781975358259 (v. 1 : pbk.) | ISBN 9781975384586 (v. 2 : pbk.) | ISBN 9781975384593 (v. 3 : pbk.) | ISBN 9781975384609 (v. 4 : pbk.) | ISBN 9781975384616 (v. 5 : pbk.) | ISBN 9781975384623 (v. 6 : pbk.) | ISBN 9781975320386 (v. 6.5 : pbk.) | ISBN 9781975333461 (v. 7 : pbk.) | ISBN 9781975335502 (v. 8 : pbk.) | ISBN 9781975338404 (v. 8.5 : pbk.) | ISBN 9781975338411 (v. 9 : pbk.)
Subjects: LCSH: Video games--Fiction. | Video gamers--Fiction.
Classification: LCC PL877.5.A35 J9313 2019 | DDC 895.63/6--dc23
LC record available at https://lccn.loc.gov/2019017466

ISBNs: 978-1-9753-3841-1 (paperback)
978-1-9753-3926-5 (ebook)

10 9 8 7 6 5 4 3 2 1

LSC-C

Printed in the United States of America

Bottom-Tier

Lv.9

CHARACTER TOMOZAKI

Characters

Fumiya Tomozaki
Second-year high school student. Bottom-tier.

Aoi Hinami
Second-year high school student. Perfect heroine of the school.

Minami Nanami
Second-year high school student. Class clown.

Hanabi Natsubayashi
Second-year high school student. Small.

Yuzu Izumi
Second-year high school student. Hot.

Fuka Kikuchi
Second-year high school student. Bookworm.

Takahiro Mizusawa
Second-year high school student. Wants to be a beautician.

Shuji Nakamura
Second-year high school student. Class boss.

Takei
Second-year high school student. Built.

Tsugumi Narita
First-year high school student. Easygoing.

Erika Konno
Second-year high school student. Queen of the class.

Rena
Twenty years old. Likes to drink.

Ashigaru-san
Pro *Atafami* player.

Common Honorifics

In order to preserve the authenticity of the Japanese setting of this book, we have chosen to retain the honorifics used in the original language to express the relationships between characters.

No honorific: Indicates familiarity or closeness; if used without permission or reason, addressing someone in this manner would constitute an insult.

-san: The Japanese equivalent of Mr./Mrs./Miss. If a situation calls for politeness, this is the fail-safe honorific.

-kun: Used most often when referring to boys, this indicates affection or familiarity. Occasionally used by older men among their peers, but it may also be used by anyone referring to a person of lower standing.

-chan: An affectionate honorific indicating familiarity used mostly in reference to girls; also used in reference to cute persons or animals of either gender.

-senpai: An honorific indicating respect for a senior member of an organization. Often used by younger students with their upperclassmen at school.

-sensei: An honorific indicating respect for a master of some field of study. Perhaps most commonly known as the form of address for teachers in school.

1

If you walk around while poisoned, eventually you're going to pass out

When you've done something that hurts someone unintentionally, and when the person you've hurt is someone important to you—how do you make up for that in a way that's sincere to both them and yourself?

All I could do was just stand there in the classroom after school. Guilt and regret were clenching around my insides near my core. I'd never experienced this feeling before, having lived most of my life on my own.

There was a suggestive message from Rena-chan showing on the screen of my smartphone. After seeing it, Kikuchi-san had dashed out of the library. I had to get going right this minute, but it was like black ivy was tangling around my thoughts, slowing me down. I didn't know what it really was, but I knew it was reaching up from the depths of my heart.

I'd made a choice, acted on it, and then failed. This was my own fault. But the one who got hurt wasn't me. I'd been changing myself on my own until now, but this was fundamentally different.

This was all still nothing but unknowns, but I didn't know how to confront them. I mean, it's literally impossible for me to take responsibility for the shifts in someone else's heart, yet right that moment, it was unmistakable that Kikuchi-san had been hurt.

So of course, my only option was to throw myself into doing what I could for now.

"...!" I realized I'd been biting my tongue, and I picked up my bag and dashed out of the library.

I just focused on moving my feet as I detangled the vines from my thoughts and considered what I should do. As I passed the other students who were walking down the hall in the same direction as me, I hoped that I was getting closer to Kikuchi-san, though I didn't know where she was. I pulled my shoes out from my cubby by the front doors of the school and put them on, wiped the cold sweat off with my sleeve, and pulled my phone out of my pocket.

When I opened LINE, that message from Rena-chan was displayed at the very top. I tried not to look at it as I tapped my chat with Kikuchi-san.

[*Sorry, I want to talk. Where are you now?*]

Tucking away my phone, I resumed striding aimlessly around the school. That message Kikuchi-san had seen was the sort that would cause misunderstandings, but it wasn't like anything had actually happened. That didn't mean I hadn't hurt her, but I could talk to her and share the truth. That was about all I could do now.

After a while, I reached the front gates of Sekitomo High School. If Kikuchi-san was still at school, she'd go through here eventually; if I found out she'd left, then this was the fastest way out of the school. That was why I was standing there, but I wasn't sure how logical I was being. If anything, I had the feeling I was just rationalizing.

The January air was freezing, and at our school, which was atop a hill about a ten-minute walk from a rural train station, the cold was piercing.

Clusters of students were passing by. There were groups bursting with energy as they walked home, as well as intimate-looking couples, and seeing them stirred up feelings inside me. If I hadn't screwed up so bad, would I be walking with Kikuchi-san just like them right now? Had these couples made mistakes like I had?

I waited five minutes, then ten, but there was no response at all. I opened LINE again, but there wasn't even the "read" notification there from Kikuchi-san. I was stuck.

"...Oh yeah." After racking my brain, I eventually remembered something. If a gamer can't resolve a situation alone, the next step is to look to someone for help. That's what I've always done. I've started to get used to clearing these hurdles in life, but I'm still basically an amateur when it comes to romance. If I wanted to proceed, I should obviously do the same thing.

I swiped down my chat column list to search for the right person.

Most likely, Hinami wasn't the best for times like this—

"Whoa?"

I suddenly got a notification on my phone. It was telling me about a new message on LINE—but it wasn't Hinami, or Kikuchi-san, who I'd been hoping to hear from.

"...Izumi?" Displayed there was a familiar username: "Yuzu-san."

Izumi and I would rarely ever chat for no reason, so this was unexpected. But based on the message in the chat, I could basically get what was going on.

[*What're you doing, Tomozaki?!*]

This text, and its message, had reached me in a very timely manner.

Which meant she'd probably heard something from Kikuchi-san. While this wasn't at all a solution, maybe this could get me in contact with Kikuchi-san. It was a sign of progress. Clinging to that thin thread of hope, I opened the message. And that was when—

"Ack!"

Just as suddenly, the whole screen switched without my input, and Izumi's icon of a selfie was displayed on my phone screen. Having experienced it a number of times, I knew what this was. The call screen. I'm still not used to it, even after all this time, so I wish people would let me know first before they make a call.

I swiped the green button with a trembling finger, and then when I took the call, the voice of a slightly angry Izumi came out of the receiver. "Helloooo?!"

"H-hey. Hello?" I made an effort to speak calmly as I kept my heart from beating out of my chest. I felt confusion, bewilderment, and shock all at once.

"What's going on here?!" Izumi cried out. She sounded emotional, but it was an incredibly vague question. In context, she had to be talking about Kikuchi-san.

But I didn't know how to reply. "Umm...?"

"Don't just 'umm' me! Answer the question!"

"*Was* that a question...?" I was confused, but she was probably upset by the situation. It seemed like it would be best to sort out this conversation first. "...This is about Kikuchi-san, right?"

"Of course it is!"

"Is it that obvious...?" As she tried to drag me headlong into this topic, I was actually calming down. Times like these, it really helps when the other person is worked up. "So this means you heard what happened from Kikuchi-san?"

"Of course I have! What the heck, don't avoid this!"

"*Am* I avoiding this...?" We weren't quite on the same page with this conversation. But this wouldn't go anywhere if she just kept snapping at me. For now, I decided to wait for Izumi to say what she wanted to say.

"I misjudged you, Tomozaki! Cheating?!"

"Uh, I didn't...," I denied vaguely, but since I didn't know what she heard from who, I didn't know where to begin explaining. But given the situation, Kikuchi-san must have turned to Izumi to ask for advice. And if Izumi was saying that—it meant Kikuchi-san had gotten that impression, too.

"Um, sorry, but just so you know, I didn't cheat on her or anything. But I do think I did something that would cause misunderstandings, so...I want to sit down and talk with Kikuchi-san," I said, endeavoring to make my tone as calm and collected as possible.

Over the phone, Izumi's voice stopped for a while. "...I'm suspicious. That's what boys always say."

"What's that supposed to mean...?"

"Anyway! Come over here for a bit!"

"C-come over?"

"Agh, good grief, you get what I mean!"

"I-I'm not sure I—?"

"I'll send it now!"

"O-okay…"

Though Izumi had totally steamrolled me for the whole conversation, I waited for her message.

* * *

And now I was taking off my shoes to kneel on the booth bench at a family restaurant near the school. Sitting before me was Izumi plus one—Nakamura.

"…So that's what's happened," I said, hanging my head as I explained the situation to them. I was kneeling in a show of penitence, waiting for word from the two gods towering over me.

"Hmm." Nakamura seemed bored as he watched me, tossing back a glass of ginger ale. This was a drink bar in a family restaurant, so it was the sweet kind—although the way Nakamura drinks it, you'd think it was the dry kind.

Beside him, Izumi studied me with serious eyes for a while before letting out a little breath of understanding. "Oh, so that's what happened."

"Yeah…"

I'd explained that I'd started going to offline *Atafami* meetups, that I'd met a woman there named Rena-chan who was actively pursuing me, and that while I was gently distancing myself from her, she was still flirting aggressively with me.

And that was when Kikuchi-san had seen that message from her on LINE.

"Well…that's very you. Right?" Izumi drew her eyebrows together with a sigh, glancing to Nakamura for his agreement.

"Uh-huh. You're so dense," he said.

"Wha…?" I was shocked. Nakamura was dense. The dense one was *him*. The guy was dense incarnate. He used to flat-out ignore all the interest Izumi showed, which had been so obvious that even I could tell, and now he was saying this.

"B-but I was trying to do things right…," I stammered.

"Looks like Kikuchi doesn't see that, though."

"Urk…" Getting lectured by Nakamura on this was a shock to my system, but when I actually thought about it, he had been dating Izumi for a few months. And just based off the rumors, he'd dated a number of girls before, so he was obviously a few levels above someone like me. But that didn't mean I had to be happy about it.

"And, like, did you actually talk? The only way you resolve these things is by having a fight and then sitting down for a real talk," Nakamura said with real emotion in his words.

"...Yeah." I was convinced. You can tell how powerful he is just from his scary looks, but I was forced to agree entirely with his point. Frustrating.

But I'm sure it was actually just as Nakamura said. All I could do now was speak with her.

"Umm, why do you two know about this...?" I voiced the doubt I'd been feeling.

"Ahh, about that...," Izumi said. "I talked lots with Fuka-chan before, during New Year's, right? And since then, I've been chatting on and off with her on LINE."

"Ahh." I remembered. In the winter when we'd first started dating, Kikuchi-san and I had visited Hikawa Shrine together on New Year's, and we'd bumped into Izumi and Nakamura. Back then, I'd thought that Kikuchi-san and Izumi had been surprisingly friendly when talking together, but I hadn't imagined they'd still be connected on LINE.

"She asked for advice." Nakamura bluntly explained. "She said she's not good at this stuff and was asking what she should do."

"O-oh, okay..." But well, that's how it is with a couple. If someone was asking me for relationship advice, I think I'd ask Kikuchi-san for her opinion, too.

"But then is that really all it is in your mind?" Izumi looked up at me inquiringly.

"What do you mean? You think there's more?" I answered back.

"That girl wasn't the only thing as far as I could tell. There's, like, lots more other stuff, from what I heard."

"...Lots of stuff," I repeated as I thought back on recent events. The Rena-chan thing was the definitive incident, but it was true there were minor misunderstandings before that.

"Like how our schedules clashed a lot...and we couldn't make much time together?" I said.

Izumi wrinkled her nose. Apparently, I was half-correct?

Why does she seem kinda exasperated?

With a glare, she said, "Well yes, but the important part is what exactly?"

"...Umm?" I still wasn't getting her point.

"Agh." Izumi sighed. "Like when you guys went to go hang out at Tama-chan's house, or how you apparently talked to Mimimi about lots of important stuff." And then still apparently annoyed, she continued, "Or how you went together with Aoi to that meetup."

Instantly, a cold sweat ran down my spine.

The last item was just one of many on the list, but I felt something like a chill across my mind. *Oh yeah, I guess I did.*

I'd wanted to avoid hiding things as much as possible, so I'd told Kikuchi-san that I was going to an *Atafami* meetup, and I'd also mentioned Hinami would be there. That wouldn't be enough for her to know about Hinami's hidden side, but she'd still sensed that something was up.

"Y-yeah." I nodded, smoothing over my tone of voice.

"Hey, do you understand what the problem is here?" Izumi pressed, sounding accusatory.

I guess everyone had accepted by now that I was friends with Hinami and her whole group, so fortunately, Izumi was just moving on without picking up anything as odd.

But that made me understand. Even if we were dating, maybe it wasn't a good idea to tell Kikuchi-san everything. I didn't want to go exposing my and Hinami's secret with some slipup.

Need to be a little more careful. I sucked in a breath and mentally nodded to myself before returning my gaze to Izumi. What was important now was talking with Kikuchi-san.

"...You mean that I left Kikuchi-san on her own and hung out too much with other friends, huh... So she felt lonely, I guess," I said, tracing back over what Izumi had said.

She sighed for some reason, and Nakamura frowned. "How stupid are you?" he said. "You really are dense."

"Wha...?!"

For the second time that day, Nakamura was ripping into me for being dense. What's more, Izumi was nodding along vigorously. My guilt here was unanimous.

"Hmm, like, you're not quite there," Izumi said, "or that's sorta not enough? Put yourself in her shoes."

"Uh, how?" I looked up for a moment.

Izumi leaned forward over the table to peer at my face. "If Fuka-chan, like, starts telling you she uses the same station as a guy...yeah...," she said, as if she was sharply testing me. "If she walked back *with Tachibana* all the time, then what would you think?"

"—!" Her emphasis made me finally understand what had been happening from Kikuchi-san's view.

"Geez, you finally get it?" said Nakamura.

"...Uh-huh." Yeah, duh.

In my mind, everyone I hung out with really was just friends, nothing else. But that was ultimately in my own head.

"You mean that from her point of view, they seem less like friends, and more like other girls...," I said.

That comparison to Tachibana instantly cleared up what the problem was. From Kikuchi-san's view, what I was doing was not her boyfriend going to hang out with friends. And my behavior had wounded her at the worst time.

"Well, at least you get it. Then handle the rest yourself," Nakamura said.

"How...?" *Right now, I can't even get in contact with Kikuchi-san to start handling anything*, I started saying, but then I realized they were looking at something behind me. And they were also kind of smirking.

Feeling skeptical, I turned around to see—

"K-Kikuchi-san...?!"

Standing there was my girlfriend, watching us awkwardly. *Hey, what's with this sudden turn of events?* I'd been thinking maybe I could talk to her a bit somehow, but coming face-to-face with her with no warning, I didn't know what to do anymore.

I looked back to Izumi and Nakamura again in a panic and saw they were eyeing each other with the smugness of a plan well executed. *Ah. They set me up.*

"T-Tomozaki-kun...?" For some reason, Kikuchi-san was surprised to see me, too. Which meant that she hadn't been informed that I was here, and that the two of us had been caught in the same web.

So this was Izumi and Nakamura's scheme. Since it was kind of hard for us to meet, they'd created a situation for us to face each other without either knowing the other was coming... *Huh? For a moment there, I was ready to tell them off, but they're actually helping me out, aren't they?*

I was staring at Kikuchi-san in confusion when I heard little clinks of metal behind my back. I turned around to see Izumi and Nakamura placing small change and bills on top of the table and standing up.

"Then we'll get going," Izumi said with a smug smile, waving a hand as she vanished into the distance, while Nakamura's smile looked somehow amused as he gave me a big whack on the back.

"Just do it, man."

"Ah...uh-huh."

Their plan was successful; I was alone with Kikuchi-san.

* * *

The two of us sat opposite each other in a four-seater booth, silence hanging between us.

On the table were two empty glasses of ginger ale and iced tea, plus the two glasses of water Kikuchi-san and I had grabbed.

What should we talk about? What should I ask? I definitely had to untangle this misunderstanding, but I shouldn't be wimpy and make excuses for myself, either. Izumi had said that this wasn't just about that message on LINE. There was more I had to fix.

But what should I tell her? How should I change our relationship to make up for this? And how did I want to move forward? I didn't have any answers to those questions.

Unsure of what to say, I was sorting through my thoughts when suddenly—

"I'm sorry!" she apologized, but I didn't know what for.

"…Huh?" I started blinking so fast, even I noticed. "Hold on, why are you apologizing…?"

She hung her head awkwardly. Eventually, her gaze started flicking over to me, and her lips parted slightly. "Um…whatever you were saying on LINE…I think I shouldn't have looked without your permission…"

"—!" Intense guilt welled up in my heart. *First, I made Kikuchi-san upset, and now she's apologizing? What the heck am I doing?* "No, no, no, hold on. I'm the one who should apologize."

"Oh, no, I was also…"

"No, I mean I was the one who made you anxious in the first place…"

"But…"

We argued back and forth like that for a while from opposite ends, each of us insisting we were the one at fault.

Then I remembered. Nakamura and Izumi had both said that we just had to have a proper talk if we wanted to fix this.

"Okay." I held my palm up at Kikuchi-san to put a stop to this. Her eyes widened in puzzlement as she gazed at my palm.

We'd gotten this far with our relationship. It's not like I fully understood Kikuchi-san yet, but I had been involved with her more deeply than anyone else.

So I was sure she'd understand what I should say. This was between us.

"You're right, I agree that it's not good to look at someone's phone without their permission… I'll give you that." Since we were arguing from opposite ends, what popped out of my mouth was the opposite point, an acknowledgment that she was at fault. But I don't think this was wrong.

Kikuchi-san seemed confused, but she was meeting my eyes. "Mm-hmm. That's why I…"

"But…you've apologized for that, and I've already forgiven you. So now it's over and done with." I put a smile on, but I didn't beat around the bush.

If I'd said something wrong, then I should talk it through and apologize, and once we were both satisfied, it should be forgiven. Though, maybe that's an expression of my desire to have her forgive me for my mistake.

"I—I understand… If you forgive me for it, then…" Okay, she accepted that.

"So next is my turn." When I'm talking with Kikuchi-san, the best thing to do is to spell everything out in words, lining it all up one after another in the direction that seems closest to ideal as possible. I think that communication style suits both of us, which is why we were able to connect.

"I feel like it wasn't good of me to make you lonely while I was going out and having fun, either…" If we took care to eliminate these issues directly, then this falling-out would be slowly resolved. "If there's anything else…anything that bothered you, or anything that was on your mind, I want you to tell me."

I wanted to know what had been uncomfortable for her, and what she wanted me to do—what I should change.

Of course, it would probably be best if I could figure that out on my own, but only masters in dating like Mizusawa or Hinami could pull that off. I'm such a bottom-tier dater, I'm sure thinking about it alone wouldn't get me anywhere with my skills. So there was nothing for it but to really talk it out, picking out items as cautiously as if I was going through some safety protocol.

"…Um, I…" Kikuchi-san looked down and to the side, but I could see the earnestness on her face. It was probably very difficult to say. I mean, it was basically laying her wishes bare. But I could tell from her face that she was really trying to take this seriously.

But then what popped out of her mouth was unexpectedly positive. "I…want to support you, Tomozaki-kun."

"Support me?" I thought this conversation was about a fight between us, so what did this mean? With no idea what would come next, I stayed silent and waited for her to continue.

"When you went to that offline meetup, and when you went to Hanabi-chan's place…I did miss you. But I understand that you're thinking about your future and about your goals…and even if I'm wrong about that, I'm glad that you're actively expanding your world, too."

"…Thanks." She'd spoken her mind, but still been respectful.

"So I don't want to get in the way, and I want to support that...u-um... as your...girlfriend." With that combination of bashfulness and honesty, she had my undivided attention.

"Y-yeah."

"I'm sure your world is bigger than the fireling lake where I live. So the time you spend with other people is important to you, too."

"...Right. The firelings," I echoed quietly.

When we'd written the script for that play, that had been a key creature during our discussion about Poppol and Kikuchi-san's values.

They're a closed-off species that can only live in a certain environment.

"That's why...I didn't want to destroy your world by being selfish." Kikuchi-san's white fingertip traced the rim on the glass in front of her. A droplet of condensation fell to the table, leaving a crooked trail along the glass's surface.

"Because you're not a fireling... You're Poppol," she said. "And I think it's wonderful for you to broaden your world for the sake of your own path." She looked up at me once more with dewy eyes, slightly unsteady and filled with urgency. "You and I are, um...dating, but...I do try to remember that we don't live exactly the same lives. So I knew I had to respect that, too." Her voice held a mix of frustration, loneliness, and lots more, but it still came straight to my ears.

"But..." Then Kikuchi-san's eyes lowered, and as if she was making sure of something, she licked her lips.

"...I got...just a little lonely."

She said it with a self-deprecating smile.

That expression was heartrending to me. A weight dropped into the pit of my stomach, heavy enough to punch right through me.

"Sorry," I said. "I should have invited you, too."

But she smiled slowly and shook her head. "No. I don't think that's right, either."

"It's not?" I asked back, and she nodded.

"I mean, you're the one who told me not to force myself," she said, smiling gently, "and that it's okay for us to live in different environments. And that I should just look for friends in the lake where firelings are."

That struck me. "...Oh."

Those were my own words.

When Kikuchi-san had been unsure and wondering if she had to change, that was the answer I'd offered to her.

If the school environment didn't suit her, there was no need to force herself to fit in there. It wasn't like there was only one way for someone to live.

That's why I'd pointed out the idea of searching the world of social media for people who shared her interests. That had helped Kikuchi-san decide she was going to be a writer, and she was now making progress toward that goal.

If deepening her world on her own was comfortable for her, then there was no need for her to change who she was just to accept others.

"...You're right," I said, "I still think changing yourself isn't the only right answer." That was why after the cultural festival, I hadn't tried to drag Kikuchi-san to karaoke or the class get-togethers after that. I hadn't wanted to force her out of her lake.

Kikuchi-san clasped her left hand in her right, rubbing it anxiously. "I think it's natural for me to watch from the lake as you broaden your world, Tomozaki-kun..." The voice that spilled out from her trembling lips really did seem lonely. "I... When I accepted this relationship, I knew I would be a fireling with Poppol." Her hand stopped and squeezed her fingers tight with emotion. "—But then watching from afar how much fun you were having, I still found myself feeling jealous."

Jealous. That word made something cool pass through my chest.

"It's not that I'm suspicious of you, but I'm still anxious. It makes me want something I can believe in... My feelings just get further and further away from my ideal of what I think I should do."

As Kikuchi-san's emotional confession reached me, the words we'd exchanged in the library back during the cultural festival returned to my mind.

"You mean...," I began.

She nodded. "It really is about ideals and emotions."

"…"

The ideal that you want reality to conform to, and the emotions that well up in your heart.

A contradiction.

I don't think people live on one or the other—only correct logic or emotional impulses. That's why those forces will contradict inside you, sometimes bind you, and those chains will occasionally hurt you or others.

I'd given meaning to that by saying that she should pursue both, despite the contradictions, and found a reason for us to be together, since we were both going about the same thing from opposite ends—and then I had chosen Kikuchi-san of my own will.

But what about this time?

"Tomozaki-kun, you chose a fireling…but I can't leave the lake."

This contradictory relationship had been given a reason with words to tie it together, but if something was beginning to bleed out of the seams—

"And if that's all, then I should just accept that world. If I can just find the right words, in the world where I can live, this can be resolved."

If the contradiction isn't simply in yourself—if it's in your connection or relationship with someone—then what should you change, and what should you keep?

Kikuchi-san seemed unusually restless, stirring her straw around in the clear water of her glass. She sounded frightened as she spoke again. "But—"

The water swirled around with no exit and eventually became still again, like a toy that had run out of battery power.

"—the fireling can't leave the lake, and Poppol can make friends with any species. But if Poppol winds up with a fireling—then what should each of them do?"

That was our relationship in a nutshell.

After some thought, my doubts about the issue between us were visible. This problem would be more difficult to resolve than I'd assumed.

I desperately racked my brains.

What should I say now? What should I change?

Kikuchi-san's eyes held loneliness, mingled with the various apprehensions and anxieties that had built up over these past few months.

"Kikuchi-san." I made an effort to keep my voice steady. It was a technique I'd trained myself to learn, but right now, I needed it to communicate my feelings honestly.

After Izumi and Nakamura gave me what for, and then Kikuchi-san told me what was on her mind—

—I wasn't going to claim that I understood everything in her heart. But I did my best to imagine it.

Feelings were most important right now.

"I'm sorry for making you lonely." Then I met her eyes. "And for making you feel anxious. And for not explaining properly."

I have absolutely no dating experience, so I don't know what to say at times like these. But the sorrowful person before me right then was not a fireling or Kris—it was Kikuchi-san. She was the one who needed me.

I've always been good at just saying what I think. So if I was going to show care to someone important to me, then that was all I had to offer.

"...Mm." Kikuchi-san accepted that with a sincere nod.

"I want you to feel better... Um."

I wanted to eliminate all her anxieties, so I would put my feelings into words—

"You're the only one I like."

After I said that, time came to a momentary stop.

"U-um...! A-a-ah...!" Anyone could hear the panic in her voice. Her face turned such a bright red that I could almost hear steam coming out of her ears, too. "Th-thank you so much...!" She was her own heat source now.

"Ah...mm..." Before I knew it, the warmth was transferring to my cheeks, too. Or maybe they'd been warm for a while.

Soon, the heat we'd both generated washed away and cooled, slowly pushing away the stagnant air that had been hanging over us—at the very least, that vague apprehension that things would fall apart was no longer sneaking up from below.

Our hearts were racing after that expression of our feelings. Being a beginner at romance, I wasn't sure how to take it, but for now, the warmth was holding.

* * *

And so we came to Kita-Asaka Station, which was the one closest to Kikuchi-san's house.

"Um...thank you for coming all this way," she said.

After I'd made that embarrassing admission at the family restaurant, we'd talked for a while, searching for a way to bridge the rift between us, and we'd decided to increase our time together as much as possible to compensate for our recent conflicts.

Along those lines, since it had gotten dark out and my personal idea of romance was the typical "walk her home" thing, I suggested giving that a try. Actually, the fact that I'd never even done that before might have been the problem.

We got off the train, and when we approached the ticket gates, Kikuchi-san suddenly stopped. "Th-this this is far enough..."

"...Huh?"

"Um, you walked me back to my station, so...," she said hesitantly, sort of fidgeting and staring at the ground. Hmm.

But I wasn't about to turn back here. "I came this far, so I'll walk you up to your house...um, as long as you don't mind..."

"I—I don't!" Kikuchi-san said, head jerking up before it gradually drooped once again. "I don't mind... I'm actually glad, but..." Her sentence got quiet at the end. She wilted even further, eyeing me with some reservation.

But I had a good guess what she was thinking—after all, this was something we had in common. "...You'd feel bad?"

"Um...y-yes."

She had to have largely been on her own until now—so she tended to resist someone doing something for her with no expectation of reciprocation. Accepting charity means putting a level of burden on the one giving it.

"It's fine. Um...ah," I tried to say what was on my mind one more time—but before I could, just thinking about the implications made me too shy.

I mean, it sounded too dumb, or just too direct, I suppose. It was like a scene out of some romance novel. Just kind of embarrassing.

"...What is it?" Kikuchi-san waited for me to continue, her eyes filled with expectation. Maybe she'd already guessed.

"Um..."

"Mm-hmm," she answered like she was pressing me.

Why do I feel cornered now?

There was no point getting all flustered. *Okay!* I took a deep breath and just translated the thought into words.

"I—I want to...be with you for as long as I can!"

"...! Th-thank you very much..."

And then we were both bright-red heat sources again. *First, I'm saying weird stuff at the restaurant, and now on the way back from the station... What the heck are we doing here?*

"S-so, um...let's walk back together...all the way to your house," I said.

"O-okay."

And so we left the ticket gates and started to walk along the road at night.

* * *

It was late January. The sinking of the sun recalled the freezing cold of winter, but I could hardly feel the chill with someone next to me.

In Saitama, you can't see many stars at night. The few that were visible shone with an achingly beautiful light only on that day, at that time.

As the night wind nipped at my cheeks, we walked along the sidewalk in Kita-Asaka. After so much sharing of feelings, the silence was peaceful and not uncomfortable. It didn't feel like we were tiptoeing around each other on our walk together. That sense of comfort was really important to me.

"Tomozaki-kun...why did you choose me?" Her question sounded like a secret slipping out of her into the silence.

I wanted to handle that question with care, so I paid close attention to how I spoke. "What do you mean?"

"Um...I wondered why it would be me when there are so many attractive girls around you."

"Umm, well..." I pondered a little and eventually reached a single answer.

We'd talked about it in the library that time.

"Between the contradictions of like...masks and honesty, ideals and emotions, we were coming from completely opposite directions. But then when I considered it, we were the same... It seemed so special, almost like a miracle... I think that's why."

Kikuchi-san looked up at me, but her face wasn't content. "And that counts as a reason our relationship is special?"

"Huh? Is that weird?" When Hinami had told me to select someone, I'd searched for a reason to begin a relationship with the one I'd chosen. Of those options, I'd been drawn to Kikuchi-san, and I'd told her that after the play.

Was that not enough?

"It's not weird, but, um..." Kikuchi-san shyly looked down and to the side, touching the fingertips of her hands together and fidgeting. "Why you would choose *me*, I mean... Why you, um, like me... That's what I wanted to know."

"Why I'd choose you?"

She gave two tiny, anxious nods. "I think I assumed that reason and your personal feelings are two different things..."

When she said that, I understood.

The reason that I'd come to was ultimately a post hoc explanation to make our relationship something special—a reason to create an ideal. My feelings were not the reason I'd been drawn to Kikuchi-san.

So what the heck was it, you might ask? Well, that would be rather difficult to explain.

"I dunno... We made the script for the play together, and then..."

There were few cars on the wide road as we headed upstream, the cold breeze off the water ruffling our hair. The sky and surface of the water were both the color of night, and it was like the tranquility after the fireworks show in Todabashi.

"I came to see you because of that story...and that drew me to you, and um...it made me...want to protect you." I recalled the important times we'd spent together. "You were so sincere about everything, so positive as you worked to overcome a difficult problem for you, and you seemed, like, really radiant..." The more I talked, the shyer I got. Honesty'll do that to you.

Kikuchi-san probably sensed my sincerity, as her face was getting redder and redder. "O-oh..."

"And part of it was that we thought in similar ways to begin with... That's why I could understand what you were worried about and sympathize. Seeing you overcome that made my heart race..."

"Th-thank you..."

Both our faces got even redder. The residential area didn't have many streetlights. The bridge over the wide river was calm, while the two of us were fidgeting.

"So then before I knew it...u-um, I was thinking about how...I care about you...or, I mean, I...l-like you..."

"—!"

Her eyebrows shot upward, and she stopped right on the spot. I couldn't say which words had provoked that reaction.

"U-um, I—!" Kikuchi-san said in the middle of the sidewalk, her volume suddenly jumping several notches. Startled by the sound of her own voice, her shoulders cringed inward. "Whenever I see you, you're always moving forward and broadening your world, and I've always respected you for that..." Her head was tilting downward as she peeked out from behind her hair, but her tone of voice was straight and direct. "And that's also why...I took your hand when you offered..." The babbling of the clear river filled up the silence between her words. "So I don't want you to stop broadening your world… I don't want you to stop being Poppol."

After she opened up to me so much, I found myself getting shy again. She didn't want me to stop being Poppol. She was validating me being me.

"Um…th-thanks." I took a few deep breaths as I came up by Kikuchi-san's side again.

Once both of us fell silent, for the first time I noticed my own heart racing—but I hoped she was the same. The beams of some headlights *vroom*ed by, but that driver would know nothing about our embarrassing conversation.

Side by side, we passed over the bridge. About three houses down, we reached Kikuchi-san's place.

"Thank you very much…for walking me all this way today." There was still heat in her voice as it reached my ears. Warm light was seeping out through the curtains of the house in front of us.

"No, no. I'm the one who should apologize for being so clueless for so long."

"…Oh, no, I'm the one who's sorry."

And now it seemed like we'd wind up each trying to give way to the other again, but Kikuchi-san appeared to notice it, too. When our eyes met, we giggled at each other.

"…Good night," she said.

"Yeah. Night."

Kikuchi-san turned away from me and walked off to her door. Once she opened it, she turned to me again to give me a little wave before stepping fully inside.

I felt shy but waved back, gazing at the door as it shut with a *tump*.

I was left by myself in some place I didn't know. But I didn't feel lonely at all as I walked back to the station.

* * *

That night.

I was typing a message on my phone aggressively, almost angrily.

This was the message on my screen.

*   *   *

[*Stop randomly sending me messages like that.*]

Of course, Rena-chan was the recipient. You might think, *Hey, isn't that rather harsh?* but really, she was the one who'd suddenly brought up sex with me, and she was also the one to send me that message that started all this: [*I'm sorry for bringing up sex out of the blue the other day.*] I think I have the right to be angry at her.

I pressed the LINE SEND button with a bouncing tap, then whipped my phone onto the bed like a shuriken. If this had been the Edo period, the futon would have detransformed to reveal that I'd taken out an enemy ninja.

Shortly after that, my phone vibrated.

"...Mm."

I went to grab the phone on the bed more timidly this time to check it, and I found it was Rena-chan.

[*Oh, sorry. Were you at school or something? Did someone see?*]

"Hmph..."

Rena-chan was the type to do what she pleased, so I was expecting a reply like *I don't care.* Her unexpectedly forthcoming apology cooled down the ninja blood inside me. I put away my metaphorical caltrops as I calmly looked at the screen.

"Well...I guess we're good, then."

Figuring that continuing to talk would be a bad idea, I just sent, [*Kind of, yeah! It's fine so long as you don't do it in the future!*] However she replied, it would be best to end the conversation there.

I hadn't meant to hurt anyone, but misunderstandings happen. I'm sure a lot of it came down RNG elements that I wouldn't be able to entirely control myself. To minimize those elements, I had to make sure to check for traps each step along the way before proceeding forward. Maybe relationships are just hard and unfair sometimes.

Thinking these thoughts as I lay on my back, I gazed up at the ceiling.

* * *

The morning of the next day.

"Ohh, lovey-dovey first thing in the morning, huh?" Mizusawa teased me and Kikuchi-san as we walked to school together.

He was smirking. I glanced at him, then sighed. "The most annoying guy just had to find us..." I felt something plunge into the pit of my stomach.

Mizusawa grinned gleefully. "Ha-ha-ha. So what's up? You guys decided to go to school together?"

"Y-yeah, basically."

Yep. After walking Kikuchi-san home the day before, I'd sent her a message on LINE about what we could do to have more one-on-one time, and so we'd decided to head to school together that morning. Incidentally, I'd also made sure to let Hinami know and arrange things so there was no meeting that day.

Then once the two of us walked out together from the station that was closest to the school, we were immediately found by Mizusawa.

"...Hmm, well, at least you guys seem happy."

"I didn't need your input," I said lightly, and Kikuchi-san glanced at Mizusawa from behind me.

Mizusawa noticed that, and when his eyes met with hers, he smiled gently. "Morning."

He was so practiced at that, I kinda wanted to be like, *Hey, don't try to seduce her.* But actually thinking about it, he's just saying hi. He had an alibi, so I was forced to accept it.

"G-good morning...," she stuttered back.

This was quite the unusual crew, or at least a rare set of people together. Not many kids would bother to meet up in the morning to go to school as a group, either, so we were a fairly conspicuous trio. Apparently, the rumor was going around that Kikuchi-san and I started dating from working on the script and directing that play, so I was sensing some attention from others in our school year.

Mizusawa must have picked up on that, as he took a step away from us.

"Well, I don't want to be a third wheel, so—," he began when a cheerful but accusatory call reached us.

"Ohh! Everyone's going to school all together!"

I turned around to see Izumi swiftly approaching us from behind, and as Mizusawa moved away, she came in between him and me. Now we were attracting even more attention, but the group was so large that it might as well happen.

"It's unusual to see you guys all walking to school together!" she said. "What's this? Strategy meeting?"

"You don't like it?" I joked back.

Izumi gave a lethargic *ah-ha-haah*, then flicked me and Kikuchi-san a look. "Oh! You made u...make such a nice couple!!"

"W-well, thanks to you."

Izumi was probably trying to be considerate since Mizusawa basically didn't know what had happened, as she avoided bringing up the fight. She'd made a nice dodge and recovery on the "you made up." That was some normie-level social competency.

"A nice couple, huh..." Mizusawa eyed us with a little suspicion. Did he notice something was slightly off just now, or had he pinged on something else?

Regardless, Izumi was trying her best to cover it, so I was planning to play along and change the subject. Before I could, Izumi turned back to me and Kikuchi-san as if she'd just remembered something. "Oh, so Tomozaki and Fuka-chan!"

"Uh-huh?"

"Y-yes?!" Kikuchi-san's reply sounded incredibly tense, coming at the same time as mine. I could understand her anxiety, suddenly having her name called when she was surrounded by normies like Mizusawa and Izumi. I'd been like that before, too.

"This is perfect! I wanted to ask you a favor—do you mind?!"

"What kind of favor?" I was used to normies, but it was unusual for people to ask me for things. And if I was a set with Kikuchi-san, too, I couldn't imagine what it could be.

"So look, there's a send-off for the third-years coming up, right? I'm on the event committee for it."

"Huh, really?"

The third-year send-off is like the final party for the graduating class. I think you also call them graduation parties.

The current first- and second-years would see off the departing third-years with an event. The Sekitomo High School send-offs are more casual compared with other events like the graduation ceremony, and volunteers from clubs and the organizing committee and whatnot would put on plays to entertain them and stuff. The seating order was ostensibly by attendance number, but people were allowed to move around freely so long as it wasn't a disruption.

Of course, that freedom had been the deadliest knife to me last year, and I'd survived by taking the ideal position: one of the folding chairs at the very end of the row. What even was that party?

"You don't know, Tomozaki?" Izumi said. "We present these mementos."

"...Mementos?" I knew what the word meant, but I didn't really get why she was bringing that up now. I doubted they were gifting something super fancy and expensive, but nothing else made sense.

"Ha-ha-ha. You really didn't interact with anyone at all last year, huh," said Mizusawa.

"Wh-what do you mean?"

"You really haven't heard about it?" Izumi gushed, her eyes suddenly getting sparkly.

"—It's the school badges of destiny!"

I'd never heard that term once before in my life, but Mizusawa was nodding along, and even Kikuchi-san had reacted with recognition. Odds were I was just out of touch.

"Umm...did you know, Kikuchi-san?" I checked with her, just in case.

Kikuchi-san nodded a little hesitantly, like she was really trying to be considerate of me. "Y-yes...I've heard of them just a bit."

"Hmm." She was definitely trying to avoid offending me. The story must have spread far enough in that time before May of my second year, when I'd totally been a shadow, that it would be weird not to know. Great.

"...What is it?" I asked Kikuchi-san, since things were leading that way.

Izumi interjected with a "Well, um!" from the side—guess she wanted to take care of it. Based on the romantic-sounding name, she probably wanted to inform me about it herself. "Sekitomo has that old school building that isn't being used anymore, right? The place with the cooking prep room and Sewing Room #2 and stuff!"

"Y...yeah, I know." Though I was surprised to hear about that familiar place in this conversation, I indicated I was listening.

"Apparently, they used it all the time until about ten years ago, when they switched to the current school building. That's also when they updated the uniforms and school badges—even the school name."

"Ohh... I think I have heard about that. Something about how this was a different school until not that long ago."

I'm told there was a big reform movement about ten years back. This school wasn't really university-oriented—based on the grade averages anyway. And then they transformed absolutely everything: the name of the school, the uniforms, the school building, and even the school badges, changing them from the common cherry-blossom motif to a pen motif. It was all part of the shift to a focus on academics. In less than ten years, they brought the school up to be one of the top three prep schools in Saitama Prefecture...or I think I heard a story like that back at the original school information session.

"So," Izumi continued, "at the send-off, there's a presentation of mementos from the second-years to the graduating students, with one representative for the boys and one for the girls, and they give them a plaque and a bouquet—but when the teachers aren't looking, the third-years also hand things over to the second-year boy and girl."

"...Ohh."

So that meant...

"And that's the old school badges, from before we got the current ones.

The old school badges of destiny," Mizusawa slipped in to say with incredible smugness.

"Hey! You stole my thunder!" Izumi shot back.

"Ha-ha-ha, I know. That's why I said it."

"You're terrible!"

"Thanks."

The two of them quipped back and forth, casual and fast as ever. I've gotten used to normie conversations, but when I get pulled into the fast lane, I'm just not used to keeping track.

I got the gist of this story, though. "So basically...two former school badges from ten years ago are passed down for just one moment at the send-off?" I said.

Izumi nodded. "They say the school badges will carry happiness all the way until graduation for the pair who accept them...and then after graduation, they'll have a special relationship like no one else's!"

"...Ohh, I see." I nodded, but my mind stuck on just one word of that statement.

That word had come up when Kikuchi-san had been talking about our relationship, too.

"And apparently, the two third-years really are going to go to the same university and be living together," Mizusawa said, adjusting his schoolbag on his shoulder.

"Oh, yeah, yeah!" Izumi jabbed a finger at him excitedly. "They're saying it's just a countdown until they get married!"

You could say it's one of those local customs that's common enough in schools, but these were school badges that had changed ten years ago and been secretly handed down all this time. I understood how you'd find meaning in it. And the number of people who did find it meaningful meant it had a real effect on relationships.

While I was reflecting on all this, I shifted my gaze to the left—and saw Kikuchi-san touching her right palm to her chest as if holding something back, her lips parted just slightly.

The words spilled out of her with a white breath. "What a romantic tradition."

"Ah-ha-ha. Yeah, it is like out of a story," I said softly, and Kikuchi-san closed her lips and smiled with a slow nod. Feeling eyes on me, I turned to the right to see Izumi and Mizusawa smirking and watching. *Guys.*

—That was when I realized.

"Wait...so then your request for us was..."

"That's right!" Izumi chirped. "We were thinking you and Fuka-chan could accept the badges!"

"U-us...?!" Kikuchi-san cried in surprise with a blush. I'm sure that meant she was glad, but there was a hint of uncertainty in her eyes.

Was it simply the pressure of standing in front of others, or was there some other reason?

"It's an honor for sure...but why us?" I asked. There had to be other people better suited for this, like an official school couple—and I'd told Izumi about our falling-out, too. That was another reason I was unsure if it should be us.

Then Izumi started off again. "Well, about that! Look, you guys are officially recognized as the couple who made that play for the cultural festival, and I think you're perfect for a job like this! And everyone at school knows about this. It really feels super special, right?!"

"Special...huh." I was glad to hear her repeat that word, but I still couldn't help but think of our falling-out the day before. My bad feelings about that were fading, yeah, but I still wasn't sure we'd managed to resolve everything that had caused it.

If the relationships of those couples who'd inherited the old school badges before had become special—if they were able to have a relationship that *they* thought of as special—then what about the contradiction I'd felt then? Could I say with confidence that we could have a relationship that would be on par with theirs?

"...I wasn't totally sure before," Izumi said in a hushed voice, "but seeing you guys walk to school together today made me think, yeah!"

"Ohh...so that's what you mean," I replied.

"Ah-ha-ha! Look, I also want you guys to stay together!" I figured this was her way of showing her consideration after that whole falling-out.

"Well, thanks. But, um..." I hesitated.

"You're not into it, Fumiya?" Mizusawa said, sounding cool and whatever about it. "If you're not gonna do it, then I'll take the badges."

"Huh?! You've got a girlfriend, Hiro?!" Izumi cried.

"Nah, but I'll go all-in on nabbing Aoi by the time of the send-off," Mizusawa said like he was looking for a challenge.

"That's one heck of a declaration!"

Mizusawa was acting like it was a joke, but this guy does walk the walk.

I was unable to quite come up with an answer, so I looked over to Kikuchi-san to see unease was showing stronger in her eyes than before as she looked at me.

...But yeah. Of course.

"Sure, I'll do it," I said.

"!"

"...Are you okay with that, Kikuchi-san?" I asked her, and she responded with a "Y-yes!" Although, it would've been hard to say no.

"Thanks, you guys! So then we're counting on you!" Izumi said, and I smiled back at her.

When I glanced back at Kikuchi-san again, she was looking down, but the glimpses of her reddened cheeks behind her hair put me at ease.

There was no point in being wishy-washy now. I'd only just told her my feelings again and renewed our relationship the day before, so giving her more anxiety over something small like this would make me a failure as her boyfriend. And besides, Izumi had gone to the trouble of coming up with this for us, too.

And that was when I realized something.

"...Wait. What about you and Nakamura?" I asked Izumi.

Now that I'd heard about it, wouldn't any couple want to do it? And Izumi was the type to be into romantic events, so it seemed to me like she'd want to nominate herself for this.

Izumi pouted with a complicated expression. "Well, I would like me and Shuji to accept them together and do the whole 'let's be together till graduation' thing, but..." She touched her fingers to the hole on her blazer where the school crest was pinned. "...I doubt he'd be able to hold on to something that small for a whole year without losing it."

"Wait, that's it?"

Her very final remark was so completely unromantic, I just about fell over.

* * *

Break time that day.

As I was putting away my textbook from the previous class, Mizusawa slid on over to me to talk. "'Sup."

The corner of his mouth was raised in a smirk. When he came to talk to me with that expression, it was generally safe to assume I was in for some teasing. He'd also helped me out a lot, but I doubted that was the case right now. He'd probably come to give me a hard time for walking to school with Kikuchi-san or about the old school badges thing.

"What is it...?" I groaned—I wanted him to know I was super done with this. *C'mon, can you see I need a break?*

"So, Fumiya." But Mizusawa totally ignored that as he popped up one eyebrow in his usual manner. After a slight pause, he asked, "Things okay, accepting the badges?"

"Things...? What things?" His unexpected question confused me.

Expression unchanged, Mizusawa said, "Oh, I wondered if maybe you had a fight with Kikuchi-san or something."

"Huh...? Why?" I asked back, surprised.

I mean, Mizusawa had literally just seen Kikuchi-san and I walking to school together, and then we'd promised to inherit the old school badges of destiny. So I'd assumed he'd be teasing me and wolf-whistling or something. Why was he assuming it was the opposite?

... There definitely is something more to this.

"Did someone tell you?" I asked.

Nakamura's face immediately came to mind. Izumi had done a good job hiding it before, so the odds were low it was her. Problem is, the information hotline in normie groups comes with the label *I'll only say it to someone I can trust*, so when someone tells you a secret, you take it for granted that each person will tell one or two more people, until everyone and their mother knows.

"Nah, nobody told me anything," said Mizusawa.

"Really? Then why did you ask?"

"Oh. So then I'm right, huh?"

"Urk... You play dirty."

He'd used my little slip of the tongue to fish for info easily. You could argue that it's my fault for being terrible at hiding things, but I've learned the hard way that at times like these, Mizusawa figures it out no matter what I say. If I try to hide it, then it winds up backfiring, so I decided to just be straight with him. "Agh, yeah, you're right. We fought. How'd you know?"

Mizusawa's eyes did a scan around the classroom. He must have been checking that there was nobody nearby to hear—or was he looking for Kikuchi-san? Whatever the case, once he was satisfied, he grinned once again. "You guys came to school separately before, and now you're suddenly coming together. I figured that might be it," he said. That was even more confusing

"...What's that supposed to mean? Doesn't walking to school together mean you're close?"

Mizusawa chuckled, then wagged his finger in a *tsk, tsk, tsk* kind of way. It was a good look on him, especially paired with that mean expression, but being the one on the receiving end kinda sucked. *Jerk...*

He started to lecture me with his trademark arrogance. "Listen, Fumiya. When two people in a relationship suddenly start fixating on formalities like that, it means they're trying to make up for things not going well."

"Urk..."

"Nail on the head, huh?" Mizusawa said. His tone was detached as usual, but he'd instantly slid right up to find the truth. He pointed a finger at my chest, slick as always. "My guess is you were like, *Sorry for making you feel lonely; let's walk to school together from now on so we can have more time together.*"

"Huh? Were you listening to us?" He was so on the nose, I shuddered. Did he have a hidden camera or a mini-mic in my bag or something? "Well, ding-ding-ding, you're aaaabsolutely right! Congratulations, you win, Mizusawa-san," I said with as much sarcasm as I could muster.

But my acerbic reply only made him stronger, and I couldn't do a thing to him. "Ha-ha-ha. I know," he said. "So then what happened? Give me the deets."

"…Well, since you already know." I decided to shift this discussion to the corner of the classroom and tell Mizusawa everything that had happened.

"—Well, sounds like you had a fight coming," Mizusawa commented lightly after I told him the same stuff I'd discussed with Izumi and Nakamura. "This stuff happens all the time."

"I—I mean…I'm serious about this, though…" The difference in the way we were taking this left me nervous.

But Mizusawa laughed. "Ha-ha-ha, I know, I know." Then he raised an eyebrow like he always did. "But, like…just listen," he said. That level of confidence forced me to follow behind him.

"O-okay."

Mizusawa spread his arms out to lecture me. We were just conversing by the wall in the classroom at break time, but something about his posture or tone of voice made it feel like we were talking all alone together in some kind of pocket dimension. *Ohh, so this is how he always seduces girls, huh.*

"For starters," he began, "this is your fault for hanging out with other girls when you're dating Kikuchi-san."

"Th-they're not *other girls*…"

"Ha-ha-ha. What else would they be?"

"Well, technically, but…" It's true that if you took the phrase at face value, then they would count, but it's about how you say it.

"No 'but's. Girls care about formalities like that."

"Formalities…" I muttered that word back, and Mizusawa smiled silently and nodded. *I guess he wants me to think about it myself now. He's a hell of a teacher.* "You mean like how actions speak louder than words…?"

"Mmm, close, but not quite. You should get it intuitively, too."

I was confused. "Huh?"

"I mean, you're the one who decided to make it up to her with couple-y things like walking to and from school together, right?"

"...Ah," I said out loud when I figured it out.

Mizusawa was somehow acting even more full of himself. "Which means...?" he prompted me.

I gave him my answer. "You mean that basically, we're performing the formalities of dating right now...?" *Why does this feel like I've lost? Well, maybe because I have.*

"Exactly." Having easily guided me to the answer, Mizusawa cackled childishly.

It was true, now that he was pointing it out to me. I was doing "couple-y things" like this to make up for making her feel lonely. *Formalities* was a good word for it.

Mizusawa grinned like the cat that got the cream as he continued his smooth talk. "When you're dating a girl, you've got to throw her a bone once in a while and go through the motions. So what you're doing is the right choice, in a sense."

"Seriously, dude...? What is she, a dog...?" I argued back.

But Mizusawa did that *tsk, tsk, tsk* finger wag again. I think he was having fun. "But that *is* what you're doing, isn't it?"

"...Yeah, maybe, but..." Depending on how you thought about it, coming to school together that morning would also be a formality, huh.

When I agreed with him, Mizusawa grinned in amusement and silent approval.

It's true that that was basically what'd happened. I'd inadvertently made her feel lonely, then compensated for it in another way to close the rift between us. I could understand intuitively that it was a bone—a formality.

When I fell into thought, Mizusawa's smile settled down as he looked me in the eye. "But you know—that's the right choice, but it's not very you."

It was as if he was seeing something about me that I couldn't.

That was what made me want to listen to him a little more. "...What do you mean?"

"Hmm. How do I put it?" Then he scratched under one ear with a finger and did another scan around the classroom again.

A couple dozen students were here. I'm sure they all had their own worries, sometimes letting others lead them along or occasionally change their opinions, living in their own small worlds.

Were they conversing for fun or just for conversation's sake? Whichever it was, I couldn't tell if they were keeping up appearances with masks or showing their real faces to express themselves—it was the usual scene that I was completely familiar with.

"Formality is ultimately to keep up surface appearances; it's not how things really are."

He said it almost like an indictment. He was still smiling his unreadable smile, but his eyes were serious.

And then his smile faded as he quietly pushed it down, his eyes shifting from the classroom to the window. Out there was the sky with the cold and quiet breeze winding around. Nobody could predict where that wind would blow next.

"Well...I know that," I said.

"Of course you do."

I thought back on summer vacation—on what Mizusawa had confided to Hinami.

About superficiality versus your truth, and the perspective of the player versus the perspective of the character.

Maybe it was because Mizusawa knew about fighting your own mask, or because he knew someone who was continually fixated on her superficial mask more than anyone else. Whatever it was, I got him—he was thinking about those things, too.

"So I don't think like a shallow player anymore, just assuming putting the formalities in order is all it takes...though it's a work in progress," he said with some heat in his voice. "But what you're doing, Fumiya, is just slapping a Band-Aid on it. I mean, no matter how many bones you offer afterward, it doesn't change that you're still gonna go to meetups and hang out with friends, and Kikuchi-san isn't the type of girl to do those things."

"...Yeah." I nodded, remembering the day before.

Kikuchi-san had said our relationship was like one between Poppol and a fireling.

"I thought you were really particular about that stuff, so it was kinda strange to see from you. I'd assume you'd be like, *Then I'm just not going to any offline meetups* or something." He was speaking at a more relaxed pace than usual, as if he was gathering his thoughts as he said them. I dunno—something about it was more vulnerable than the usual Mizusawa.

Watching each other's reactions as we deepened the conversation felt comfortable to me.

"Oh, not that I think that's the right way to resolve this, though," he continued. "Just that it's what I've learned to expect from you."

"Yeah..." Now that he pointed it out, my solution this time had been uncharacteristic—it was kind of relying on how I imagined a relationship to be without necessarily resolving the fundamental issue.

But I'd still chosen the formality, and not a way that would upend everything from the root.

Why was this the one time I'd chosen that?

After I asked myself, I could feel the words coming out slowly. "I think...it's that these gaming meetups are connected to my future, and they're not just about spending time with people I get along with. I always have fun there, too... Hanging out with people who might become my friends is something I want to do to get more out of life." What came out of my mouth was the plain, unvarnished truth.

"Ha-ha-ha. What was that? An essay from a third grader?" Mizusawa said teasingly.

"Sh-shut up," I hastily shot back. "Honesty tends to sound like an elementary-school essay."

Then Mizusawa laughed loud, smacking my shoulder in amusement. "Ha-ha-ha! Yeah, maybe." And then his chuckling continued to linger.

Uh, did I say something funny?

"Agh, whatever! Basically, that's how I thought about it, and I decided to approach romance as romance. I think."

Mizusawa's laughter gradually settled down. "I see," he commented quietly. "Uh-huh. What you said just now was probably everything," he said. He always did this, acting like he was one step ahead. His wording kept me in suspense.

"...What do you mean?"

"Fumiya. You're not just trying to do whatever to fake your way through a relationship—"

And then with that same lonely smile, he said:

"You think about your future, and your friends, and dating... Everything has the same weight."

My mouth remained open, and I couldn't say anything.

I mean, he'd totally hit the nail on the head.

"You're right... I want my time with my original friends, the things that will expand in my life in the future...and my time with Kikuchi-san all to have just as much priority." Maybe some people will tell you to put your romantic relationships first, and some people might tell you to make your future number one. But in my mind, there was no ranking on any of these.

"Yeah." Mizusawa nodded.

But I didn't know how to think about this. "...Is that not a good thing?" I asked.

Mizusawa raised one eyebrow. "Dunno. Like, there's no right or wrong with this stuff, y'know?"

"S-so then is this really—?" I tried to get his approval.

But Mizusawa pointed his palms upward with a cool expression. "Well, here's the thing..." He closed his hand around some invisible object as he grinned.

"You don't have all the time in the world, so I don't think you can choose everything."

*   *   *

"…"

He was indeed entirely right, but what I'd been trying to do…

"If you're going to take things seriously, you're going to have to choose only the things you really want. And you're not even trying."

"H-hey…" I couldn't argue that.

Mizusawa pointed at me. He was getting into this. "And so right now, Kikuchi-san is about to slip through your fingers."

"Urk…"

Yeah, this was probably the core of it.

I'd expanded my world and come to face lots of things. And then just like unlocking the hidden characters and stages in *Atafami*, I'd come to have a lot more options.

Those had started to surpass my capacity, so the things at the edges were spilling out from my grasp. In this case, he was saying this was Kikuchi-san.

I imitated Mizusawa and held my palms out, staring at them. "…You mean if I choose too many things, eventually, I won't be able to hold on to everything," I said.

Mizusawa nodded, then paused for just a moment's thought. "So like. If I put it in your words—don't you think that's not being sincere?"

Unfortunately, that wasn't enough for me to clearly understand what he was trying to say.

"…You mean that it's irresponsible to let things slip when I chose them all myself?"

"No, that's not what I mean," Mizusawa answered instantly.

"Hmm?"

"This isn't just about Kikuchi-san." Mizusawa spoke with heat, eyes shifting upward, and he gathered his thoughts as he went. His expression seemed full of life as I watched him patiently. "If you choose too much, and then something spills out of your grasp—"

Then he tilted his cupped palms diagonally like he was dropping something he'd scooped up.

* * *

"—that means you're only choosing what to take on. *You're not choosing what to throw away—just leaving it to circumstance.*"

He had correctly guessed at my hidden hypocrisy.

"...You're right, I've never considered that," I said.

"Yeah? I only just thought of it now, too."

"Hey."

Mizusawa laughed breezily with an almost childlike smile.

"So you're saying if I'm going to abandon something, then I should try to actually make that choice myself...?"

"Yeah, yeah...and, I guess I also mean that just continuing to take on everything isn't sincere."

"...I see." It was true—his words were like a knife inside me.

"Hey, do you know what Yuzu meant when she wanted to pass the old school badges to you guys?"

"...What do you mean?"

Mizusawa sighed again. "Yuzu is like... She believes that you guys will still be dating after a year."

"Oh..."

He had a point—I'd also kind of put two and two together.

The school badges would be handed from a graduating couple to a couple who were currently in school to pass it on.

That meant that next year, the same pair would be passing it forward again.

"So if you're not sure about that, Fumiya, it also takes courage to refuse."

"...I'll give it some thought." I sucked in a breath and squeezed my fists tight.

I reflected again on the things I was carrying now.

I was playing the game of life; I had a number of friendships, a romantic relationship, and *Atafami*, and—

If I kept coming up with things, there would be no end to it. Even if it wasn't right now, I'm sure the day would come eventually when I'd become unable to prioritize everything, and something would slip.

"Choosing one thing means abandoning something else, huh..." I considered this earnestly.

Mizusawa gave me a fixed look and started teasing me again. "Why're you trying to say it all cool?"

"Hey."

I thought we were having a real heart-to-heart here; don't tease me and ruin it. Agh, he really is annoying. Mizusawa comes off as so detached, but he won't hold back when he offers his opinions. I still felt like a weight had been lifted off, even after the teasing.

"Formality versus following your heart," I muttered to myself. "I guess it's like...logic versus feelings."

This was just like always.

When I don't know what to do in life, and when I discover a contradiction in my behavior—those have always been the two things standing before me.

This time was no different.

I'd mull it over, and I'm sure that was where I would find the answer.

"...Thanks for the advice. You've helped a lot," I said honestly.

Mizusawa raised another smug eyebrow. "You're *very* welcome." And then with a *hup* as he came off the wall he'd been leaning against, all the tension seemed to fall out of him. He pulled out his phone.

Now that we were done with an important conversation, it was time for a break and a switch to mundane chat—or so I thought.

But then he asked nonchalantly, "So did you not ask anyone for advice before things got like this?"

"Well, I did, but...," I said as Hinami's face rose in my mind.

"You did? Then that's strange."

"What's strange?" I asked.

Mizusawa's tone was still light. "I mean...as relationships go, this falling-out was the basics of the basics. I figure anyone would've told you things were going bad."

"..."

Was I anticipating trouble, or was this just a feeling it was unlucky? A shapeless haze that I didn't even understand myself spread through my chest.

When I'd asked Hinami, she had told me to keep going, since there weren't really any problems. But she should have been able to see what Mizusawa called "the basics of the basics."

"Wonder why they didn't help you correct course," Mizusawa said. It was like he'd put the discrepancy into words.

"Yeah…," I answered.

He fell silent for an instant, then gave me a dubious look. I don't know what he saw on my face. But whatever it was must have been different from usual. "…Well, I'm not gonna butt in and ask who you talked to…"

And then with a cutting look, Mizusawa did a horizontal slice through my weakest spots.

"…but don't look to the wrong person for advice."

2

Often, you only realize how important your friends are once they've left the party

It was after school that day in Sewing Room #2.

"So I hear you're going to be accepting the 'badges of destiny'?" Unusually, Hinami was asking me a question about something other than her assignments.

"You always hear about things so fast..."

It was a little surprising she'd bother bringing up the subject with me, though. I mean, I'd assumed Hinami would say something like, *That's all just superstition; it's dumb to believe in it.*

"The student council is involved, too," she explained. "Didn't know you were the type to believe in romantic traditions."

"Well, it just sort of happened. It's kinda exciting to be part of a ten-year tradition, and Kikuchi-san seemed into it, too," I said, though I remembered what Mizusawa had said to me that morning.

There was that falling-out with Kikuchi-san—I had to ask Hinami about this.

"...So, um. Can I ask you something?"

"Hmm? What's up?"

I kind of saw this less as a question, and more like just checking. "Hinami, did you not notice...that my relationship with Kikuchi-san had been going south?" I asked cautiously.

After some silence, Hinami said grumpily, "...I don't really get what you mean."

"I mean pretty much what I said. I updated you several times on the situation, right? I was wondering if that never occurred to you when I brought it up."

There was what Mizusawa had said—and the doubts I'd had then.

I had the feeling I was trying to peer through a hole at something I shouldn't see. But I had to check. "I want you to give me an honest answer."

I was determined to swim into deeper waters if I had to.

But for some reason, she just sighed and scowled as if this was tedious to her. "...Ugh." And then she spoke indifferently, like it was obvious. "Of course I noticed. I was thinking you were definitely going to mess things up if you kept going like this."

"...!" That was an upsetting thing to hear.

It wasn't like I wanted to blame her for my relationship problems. But something like anger or sadness was prodding me—even though some part of me had been bracing for this.

"So why didn't you tell me?" It was like I was trying to shine a light through that hole, and her answer sort of gave me a hint.

Hinami seemed annoyed by the prospect of explaining. "Even if you are dating, that's no guarantee of security. You'd wind up fighting eventually anyway."

That was the same Aoi I knew, building her correct logical proofs.

"But still, you deliberately did nothing to prevent it...," I cut in. I was putting my hopes on this.

But she continued explaining. Her expression didn't change at all. "The thing you most want to avoid is wrecking things to the point of a breakup. Having your first fight is practice, in a sense. There's a clear reason, it's easy to resolve, and it's best if it's actually a misunderstanding where you haven't actually done anything, right? So I figured it would be most efficient for you to get that early practice in with something easy. Ergo, I chose to do nothing."

Hinami lined up her logical and well-thought-out reasoning, as always. Now that I was listening, she had no ill will. Just logic for reaching a goal in the shortest possible distance.

"And then you talked, and you made up. Don't you think that enabled you to cultivate a relationship where you can be open with each other? Plus, Yuzu asked you two to inherit the old school badges, right? Your relationship has progressed a lot in just these past few days."

It was true that since then, Kikuchi-san and I had managed to communicate our feelings, and Izumi had even arranged the romantic-relationship event out of concern for our falling-out.

If you looked only at the string of events, that did spell out progress.

"I understand what you're trying to say. But…" There was just such a lack of consideration for our feelings.

All that was inside her was her usual cold, hard logic.

"Please never do something like that again." I was almost losing my grip on myself, and my voice trembled a little. But I wasn't angry about the whole mishap.

It was frustrating and sad to me that Aoi Hinami was like *that*, after all.

"Listen," she said. "Getting a girlfriend was ultimately just a mid-term goal. If you want to efficiently fulfill an even bigger goal—"

"Hinami." I cut her off. "…I'm sorry. Just stop it." I couldn't take this discussion anymore. This felt too much like summer vacation—that good-bye at Kitayono Station.

"…What do you mean?" Hinami's eyes were cold.

"It's not that I'm rejecting your values." This time—it was more like self-defense.

"Then what is it?"

It wasn't like I was trying to invalidate her. After that farewell at Kitayono Station, I'd decided that I'd take those cold and stubborn parts of her, too, when I was with her. Of my own will, I'd declared I'd teach her how to enjoy life.

In a way, it was unavoidable when she applied that cold correctness to my and Kikuchi-san's relationship, too. I'd accepted that these were her values right now.

But…

"If I hear any more, I might actually start to hate the way you do things and the way you think…so I don't want to hear any more right now."

I just told her what I thought.

I get that Hinami has her perspective. I do understand her point.

And I've personally experienced many times how, from a certain angle, this way of thinking is always right.

But…

"Even knowing your way of doing things is *correct*, I'm worried I'll come to hate it, because of how I feel," I explained with some difficulty.

I wanted to know her. I really, truly wanted to understand her. But if I kept on getting drenched in her cold correctness—if that kept getting applied to how I acted toward the people I cared about—

—I knew that understanding her would be out of the question before my heart could meet her halfway. I'd wind up hating her.

There's more to people than logic.

"So I need to protect that part of myself. I don't want to hear you say anything else."

At least not right now, when I was feeling on edge from this issue with Kikuchi-san.

"…Hmm." As expected, Hinami answered without any change in her expression. I'd told her my feelings with a willingness to expose everything in my heart, and I couldn't even tell how she had taken what I'd said.

That seemed unbalanced to me. Now that I was actually thinking about it, maybe that's how it had always been.

"Hey, Hinami," I said, trying to get a little closer to her.

I didn't mean this as a rejection at all.

But maybe this wasn't what I should prioritize right now.

"How about we not have meetings for a while?" I said.

Hinami's eyes widened for just a moment. "…Why?" It was rare for her to ask for my reasoning.

So I told her how I felt, trying to keep it honest. "One reason is that I'm scared that I'm going to hate you if I hear any more. And the other reason is"—the sad face of the girlfriend I cared about crossed my mind—"I want to have more time with Kikuchi-san."

Now that I thought about it, I had meetings with Hinami in the morning and after school, and on weekends, we went to the offline meet-ups together—I might have wound up spending more time with her than with Kikuchi-san.

Of course, I don't think that the amount of time spent with someone directly relates to the depth of the relationship, but still, if I'm dating a girl—if I want to take good care of Kikuchi-san—

If I'm going to be ready for us to inherit the ten-year tradition of the old school badges...

I wasn't quite ready to drop something for it, like I'd talked about with Mizusawa, and maybe this was just going through the motions. But at the very least, I needed to sort out priorities.

After listening to me, Hinami was silent for a while before giving just the slightest nod. "All right."

Her expression was hard as iron, unsurprisingly, and I couldn't even guess as to what feelings she was trying to hide. Or if she was feeling anything at all.

She never talked about her emotions; she never even dropped any hints that would let you see inside.

"So from now on, our meetings will be irregular. I'll leave it up to you how to handle the assignments I give, and we'll just come here when we both want to come. Are you okay with that?" she said without any hesitation, and I nodded silently.

"Okay. Then let me know if there's anything else." Hinami's tone of voice didn't show even a slight reluctance to part. It stung a little, the way she didn't resist my proposal at all, but that was nothing more than my own selfishness.

"Yeah. Then...see you around."

Hinami's back was receding without any hesitation, and even though I was the one who suggested it, I somehow felt like she was the one who had left me.

I'd thought I was comfortable here, in the atmosphere of the old school building.

But right now, in this one moment, that atmosphere was hopelessly lonely.

* * *

The sky was now orange, glowing over the students walking home from school.

The same old smell of dry grass and earth was on the wind that blew around us as the seven of us walked to the station.

Hinami was diagonally ahead of me, her earlier iron face nowhere to be seen as she teased Takei and laughed with Tama-chan. Slightly ahead of them was Mizusawa, who I'd spoken with during the break that day about my feelings. He was talking casually about his current dating pursuits while Tachibana and Mimimi made fun of him.

The more I looked, the more it was all just formality. Far as I could tell, nobody there was expressing anything substantial or heartfelt.

I filled the empty moments with normie-like smiles and listening remarks, which I could now do completely automatically. But I felt left behind, all alone. The more I became used to this space, the more I felt like I was going to be swept somewhere far away.

"Heeey, Farm Boy, heads-up!"

Along with the sudden call of that nickname I'd never agreed to, a schoolbag flew at me. I saw it coming, but my body didn't move.

"Ow!"

I took the bag to the face, and it thumped heavily to the ground. Everyone else walking home with me who saw it burst into laughter, but how much of that was out of real emotion? I awkwardly wrenched my face into a smile, chirping "Sorry, sorry" as I picked the bag off the ground. It looked like Tachibana's.

"Nice face-catch!" That was Takei, sounding amused. He was always loud and annoying, but the obvious fun he was having somehow put me at ease.

"How was that a catch?!" My chipper comeback made everyone laugh. These days, I can pretend to be a normie out of habit. That's exactly what makes this time feel empty.

I returned the bag to Tachibana and faced forward again. My facial muscles have gotten way stronger, so smiling doesn't ache anymore. But if I kept smiling like this, something else would start to hurt.

"Geez. Give him a break, okay?"

"Next is Takei's turn, hyah!"

The voices were close, but they sounded far away. I was staring at some vague place between the earth and sky, joining in with everyone with mixed feelings. I still had that smile and a certain tone of voice. The more I stared, the more I could tell the visual resolution of the world was decreasing.

Could I still see a colorful world right now?

"—Brain!" The voice that reached my ears was boundlessly bright, as pleasantly clear as the blue sky.

"…Huh?"

"Slow on the uptake as always, huh, Brain?" That tone was teasing and mischievous, but also kind.

When I looked over, Mimimi was wiggling her eyebrows and peering at my face as I rubbed my nose where the bag had hit.

"…Sh-shut up!" I fired a comeback at her surprise attack. My extensive practice had turned it into reflex, and my body reacted regardless of whether I actually wanted to do it or not. That's important in fighting games, but in real life, it feels like being controlled by someone else.

Mimimi laughed through her teeth as she popped up from her bent-over posture. "Ah-ha-ha! You really do have your head in the clouds!"

"Huh? D-do I?" I thought I'd been managing things as usual, so I was surprised. Had I messed up somewhere?

"Yup! Since we did that comedy routine, I can tell! Your timing was just a liiiittle too late!"

"…Ha-ha-ha, you got me there." Though my smile was strained, I was kind of glad. There was someone who would notice even such a slight change in me. That had to be a good thing.

"What's wrong? Did you have a fight with Fuka-chan? Or are you hungry?" she pressed me jokingly, making me flinch.

"Umm…well."

"'Well' what?"

"Well, um…uhh."

"Out with iiiiiiit!" And then Mimimi's usual Mimimi Slap came flying at my shoulder. It was so predictable, I could have avoided it, but Mimimi was right: I should be out with it. I decided to just take it.

But one thing was unexpected. The angle of her hand was not perpendicular to the ground like always, and what hit my shoulder was not the flat of her palm—this was not a Mimimi Slap, but a Mimimi Chop.

"Ah... Ow!!" It hurt five times more than I'd imagined, and I yelped ten times harder than expected. Of course, since we were all walking together as a group, everyone turned toward me. *Stop, don't look.*

Mimimi laughed. "Ha-haa! Ohhh! Now you're away!"

"You really are acting like a muscle-brain!"

She gave another piercing laugh. "All right! Now we've got the usual Brain comebacks again!" She took my complaint as a comeback and cackled cheerily. Mimimi is so Mimimi, and sometimes, I get caught in the cross fire.

"Agh..." Though I was sighing in exasperation, it was starting to seem funny. Mimimi always sweeps in to put me right where she wants me. But that's what she does—fooling around until you can't help being in a better mood.

"So what is it, what is it?" she asked me. "A fight?"

"Agh, geez, yeah. Yeah, we had a fight," I said carelessly.

"Now you're being forthcoming. Very good." Mimimi puffed out her chest with a smug chuckle, followed by genuinely satisfied *sh-sh-sh* laughter through her teeth.

"How could you tell?"

"Huh? Well, Brain, you had girl trouble written all over your face!"

"Really...?"

"Also, didn't you have some deep conversation with Takahiro today?"

"S-so you were watching that..."

It's true that we did talk in a corner of the classroom like we were having a super-secret meeting... And this time wasn't just about dating woes, but a broad span of relationship concerns that included Hinami, too.

"So then what's wrong with our star Tomozaki? Share it with Big Sis!" Mimimi said as she pointed that weird key chain at my mouth. I still had the same thing in a different color on my bag—I also had the matching amulets I'd bought together with Kikuchi-san.

Though I felt a prickle of something like guilt, I told her, "Umm... So we had a fight—or like a falling-out. I did my best to try to make up for it, more or less...but I feel like I haven't managed to fix what caused it." I searched for the words as I spoke, while Mimimi listened attentively.

"Umm…so there's the old school badges of destiny, right?" I continued.

"Ohhh, yeah, yeah! It's just about time for that, huh!" She immediately knew what I was talking about. I guess I was the only one out of the loop after all.

"Izumi asked if Kikuchi-san and I would take them…"

"Huh?! *You're* getting it, Brain?! Th-that's not fair!"

Ahh, so that would be unfair, after all. Now I'm even more unsure.

"But I was wondering if we should accept them when we haven't even resolved our conflict."

"I gotcha…but then what was the cause of your fight?"

Now that she asks, it's a little difficult to put it into words, I thought, but I tried to explain. "It's like…Kikuchi-san and I can be total opposites, right?" The story of Poppol and the firelings came to my mind.

"Total opposites…" Mimimi considered a bit, then nodded. "Oh! I see! You mean like how you're trying to get along with everyone, but Kikuchi-san isn't like that, right?!"

"Ohh…you got it."

"I did it! Eighty points!"

"I dunno, isn't jumping right to eighty too high?" *Mimimi's getting a high score for no reason, but it's not messing up the conversation. I'll let it go.* At least she understood my point. "…But I'm impressed you got it right away."

"Huh, you are?"

"I mean, Kikuchi-san and I are both kind of nerdy introverts… Most people probably wouldn't see us as opposites."

Mimimi snorted a smug *hmph.* "Well, that means my eye for people is just that good!"

"Ha-ha-ha, is it?" I said, but I was kind of glad. I mean, she'd seen a part of me that was a little more hidden, and she'd told me how she felt, too.

"Hmm. The more I think about it, the more I see you really are total opposites."

"The more you think about it?" I repeated, puzzled.

"You want to expand your world, while Kikuchi-san's, like…observing other peoples' worlds."

"…Ohhh." Hearing her point that out, I couldn't help but be impressed.

Someone who expands their world, and someone who observes the world.

I had used a relatively vague expression—"total opposites"—but when you put it like that…

"It's true, we are on the reverse ends of the spectrum in that way."

"Right?!" Mimimi said eagerly. "Hmm…then that's what caused your fight?"

"Well…broadly speaking, yeah."

Mimimi tap-tapped her chin with her index finger and stuck her lips out. "But, like…doesn't that also mean that you're compatible? It means you each have something the other doesn't. It makes you feel like, *Yeah! That's the couple that should get the badges!*"

"Well, sure, but still…" I did actually agree.

The mask and the truth behind it. Ideals and feelings.

Kikuchi-san and I had worried about those things from completely opposite directions, and we'd resolved each other's problems with words from opposing perspectives.

That was exactly what had convinced me that we'd found the "special reason" it had to be Kikuchi-san and me. When we shared our feelings in the library—that moment was one of a kind.

Problem is, situations and feelings can also change that.

"But that's actually been creating, like, jealousy and conflict…," I continued.

"…Jealousy, huh," Mimimi muttered, sounding surprised, but she was warm enough to keep from prying too much.

I started to worry that maybe I was sharing too much of Kikuchi-san's secrets, so I shifted the topic slightly away from that. "Ahh, umm…the main reason was kinda like, um, me going to offline *Atafami* meetups, and going to hang out too much without her…"

Mimimi's eyebrows furrowed. "Ahh…," she said in an implicative tone.

"But I do want to go to meetups, and there's other things I want to do, too… I was thinking like, if I'm hurting Kikuchi-san every time, then just talking about our feelings may not be enough…"

"Well, yeah. That's just cheering her up after you've made her lonely."

"Urk..." She hit me right where it hurt, and I almost fell forward. Mizusawa had told me something similar.

My leg swung in a kick as I walked, knocking a rock on the ground into the roadside gutter. Like it was running away from me.

I hung my head and let out a sigh. I had no idea what to do.

"Mm-hmm, so if I've got this right, you thought that being opposites was exactly what made you compatible, but it's actually caused a falling-out?" Mimimi was like the detective revealing the truth, and I was like the culprit confessing to the crime.

"That's it exactly..."

"But I understand how Kikuchi-san feels. Girls tend to get anxious easily..." Mimimi feigned sobbing, then stretched out with *boing* like a spring. "Well, that's just the eternal theme of love between guys and girls!"

"O-oh, do you think...?"

Hearing all this now, everything was starting to feel too hard. Could a romance-level-one guy like me even solve this? But I didn't want to make Kikuchi-san sad, so I had to fix this issue.

"Hmm... What do you think, ace hitter Tama?!" Mimimi suddenly whipped around to ask Tama-chan, who was walking behind us. Tama-chan and Hinami had been messing with Takei, and Takei was happily chattering away. But when Mimimi turned to her, Tama-chan readily walked up to us, leaving Takei teary-eyed and watching her back. Getting to hear Tama-chan's view while also being able to protect her from Takei's clutches—two birds with one stone.

"What do I think about what?" Tama-chan asked bluntly.

Mimimi hugged her arm. "How you and I could be together all this time when we're total opposites!"

I listened blankly to Mimimi's question, but then I got it. "Oh! You've got a point... I'd like to know." Now that I thought about it, Mimimi and Tama-chan also had attributes as people that were totally opposite, too.

One girl couldn't have confidence in herself but was great at social situations and accommodating others, while the other girl had baseless confidence in herself, but she was awkward and bad at accommodating others.

Tama-chan had gained some skills through the Erika Konno incident, and she'd changed her situation quite a lot, but she was still fundamentally the same. She and Mimimi still had a relationship where they both made up for each other's weaknesses.

But not only did they not have fights, they also fell deeper in love every day... Well, okay, that's misleading, but you could say they continued to maintain their relationship as a widely acknowledged duo.

Just what was different about their relationship of opposites and mine?

Tama-chan made an unaffected *hmm* and then eventually gave a nonchalant answer. "Isn't it 'cause you're so clingy, Minmi?"

"Gagh!" The merciless bullet shot Mimimi through the heart.

Fare thee well, Mimimi. Leave the rest to me.

"Ngh...still safe."

But Mimimi was so strong, she could take losing a heart or two. She tugged herself up from her stagger and said with wibbly valor, "I can't believe it... If I wasn't so clingy, then Tama-chan would leave me..."

"Hmm. I wouldn't say that," Tama-chan said plainly. "But you give us lots of opportunities."

"Tama...my bestest bestie." With just that one remark, Mimimi's expression did a one-eighty. She gazed with sparkling eyes at Tama-chan, who ignored her.

"Yeah, yeah."

"...But you two do seem to be offsetting each other's weak points," I said from the side.

"Right?!" Mimimi pointed a finger at me happily. "In other words, it's Tama's unconditional love!"

"You are so annoying."

"Gagh?!"

This time, Tama-chan sliced her clean in two at the torso, but Mimimi looked glad. Love takes many forms.

"Wait, why are we even talking about this?" asked Tama-chan.

"Oh yeah! Okay, you field this one, Brain." Mimimi tossed everything in my lap, like always.

"Ahh...umm." That really was the obvious question. If anything, she was being too nice by waiting this long to ask.

And so I decided to summarize my situation to Tama-chan as well.

"...And that's what happened."

"Oh, really? Hmm..." After listening, Tama-chan started giving it some serious thought. She never lies, and I think she might actually use a hundred percent of her brainpower to ponder things for me. What a good person.

Eventually, it seemed she'd mentally sorted out the situation. "The difference between us and you guys...is probably that I don't get jealous, right?" She was holding nothing back.

"What the heck, Tama?! What's that supposed to mean?!" Mimimi pressed her for details.

But as the one in the middle of all this, I got her point. "You're right... If we're comparing with you and Mimimi, then Kikuchi-san is like you, Tama-chan."

"Mm-hmm." Tama-chan nodded simply.

Yeah, not actually saying anything feels very Tama-chan.

And maybe because of all the explaining, Mimimi also seemed to get it, and her eyes lit up as a light bulb went *ding* over her head. "Oh, I get it! You mean how Tama has her own world like Kikuchi-san, while I'm on the other end, making friends with lots of people?" Mimimi said.

I nodded. "Yeah, that's what I mean."

"So I was the Brain?!"

"Nah."

"Huh?! Now *you're* being mean to me, Brain?!" Mimimi's eyes and mouth widened in shock. Tama-chan and I looked at each other and giggled. "It's true, if Tama started hanging out with other girls all the time like Brain does, then maybe I would get jealous!"

"Right?" Tama-chan just took that statement. She really is such an accepting and openhearted person. Then she glanced over at Mimimi. "I think maybe when you have two people, one will be leaning, and the other stands on their own...and when the one who stands on their own goes off everywhere, the other person can get jealous."

"Ahh...I see." I pictured it in my mind like a board and a stick that supported each other. "I'm leaning on them, but then if the other person leaves and goes around somewhere else, I'll fall over."

"Yeah, yeah."

"Ohh, that's true!" Mimimi said, apparently convinced. "You're so smart, Tama! And great!"

"I know."

"You knew?!" Mimimi was struck with shock again. Tama-chan's method of ignoring her has only gotten more powerful.

While pointing at herself and Mimimi, Tama-chan continued, "But we're the other way, right?"

"...Ahh." Mimimi made a reconsidering sound, as if that also made sense to her.

But I didn't get that immediately. "What do you mean?"

"...Umm, so look. I do lean on Tama, but..." Mimimi seemed to be having more trouble talking about this. "It's like I'm going all over the place and dragging Tama around with me."

"Ohh...so that's what you mean." I got what their relationship was. Tama-chan's the one who standing strong, while Mimimi is the one who gives Tama-chan the opportunities to broaden her world. It really was balanced.

"With you guys, it's the opposite," said Tama-chan.

"Yeah! With us, Tama's strong, but she has the tendency to live in her own world, while I'm delicate and cute and the most beautiful girl ever, but I'm expanding my world with my own two feet, right?"

"Well, I won't make any quips here."

"Hey, you!" Mimimi shot me a look and continued, "But, like, in your guys' case, Kikuchi-san is weaker and tends to live in her own world—"

Then she looked at me with a faint, ephemeral smile.

"—but not only are you standing on your own, you're also expanding your world on your own, too."

Mimimi's smile was lonely, and the emotion in her words felt real, somehow. "I do understand feeling jealous about that."

I'd never been that aware of it, but now that she was pointing it out, I was forced to agree.

Tama-chan smoothly put forth her conclusion. "So maybe that's why it's not really balanced?"

"Yeah…" What she was saying weirdly made sense to me.

I'd felt something was off when I was speaking with Kikuchi-san, too.

We'd both worried about the opposite things and given each other the opposite words to reach a resolution.

That had seemed like a miracle to me, so I'd called it our "special reason"—but for exactly the same reasons, you could also call it a contradiction. An imbalance.

If this was because we were different species at our core, then we—

Mimimi pointed her gaze diagonally up with a *hmm*. "It's true that I don't really see Kikuchi-san hanging out with people besides you that much, Tomozaki."

"…Yeah," I agreed wholeheartedly.

Since I'd been getting the strategy guide to life from Hinami, I'd changed the way I looked at the world, and I was continuing to broaden it. Meanwhile, Kikuchi-san looked to the things that she loved, and she was deepening herself in the lake where she'd always lived.

It really was like the relationship between Poppol and the firelings.

"I was originally from a lake, too, where I did nothing but *Atafami*… but I left there."

"What lake?" Tama-chan gave me a puzzled look.

"Oh, no, never mind." I hurriedly took that back. The usual fireling comparison had popped out of my mouth, but of course she wouldn't get that.

"Hmm…" Tama-chan didn't really get hung up on what I'd said and moved on. It's a relief that she's the way she is; it really helps me at times like this. "So then maybe all you can do is just tell her it'll be okay?" she said.

Mimimi agreed brightly, too. "Oh, true! Ladies want to talk about everything!"

"Talking…" That was a lot like what Mizusawa had said.

I guess that is a thing, but is that really all it is? Something still seemed off.

I considered their proposal just a little. "I do more or less feel like I said it in my own way...," I replied as I racked my brains, wondering what to do.

"Oh, really?"

"What did you say to her?!"

With the two of them cornering me, I realized: This wasn't good. I'd said too much. "Uhhh, um! No, it's nothing." I panicked and took it back, but this was the perfect example of *too little, too late.*

"Hey, Brain? We're trying to offer you advice, so you've got to give us answers, or we can't do anything for you."

Tama-chan also smiled like she was enjoying herself, giving me a mischievous look. "Yeah, Tomozaki. You've got to tell us."

"Y-you too, Tama-chan...?" *Oh no. I don't want to see Tama-chan using that acting-cheerful skill for evil.*

But the smirking pair were locked on me and wouldn't let go.

"Urk..."

"C'mon, Brain! Time is money!"

"Yeah, yeah."

"...F-fine!"

They had me where they wanted me. I had no choice but to just tell them.

"Umm—I said she's the only one I like."

Then Tama-chan burst out laughing, and Mimimi slapped my shoulder.

* * *

Less than an hour after I totally embarrassed myself, I was with Mimimi at Kitayono Station.

We split with everyone and got off the train, and once the two of us came out of the ticket gates, Mimimi seemed a little uncomfortable as she lowered her eyes.

"...What's wrong?" I asked. She was acting completely different from her earlier fun vibe; her smile was kind of hard and awkward when she looked back up at me.

"So, Kikuchi-san! She was jealous about you going to meetups and hanging out and stuff, right?"

"Mm, yeah," I agreed.

Mimimi pressed her lips tight a moment, like she was bracing herself, but her tone was still bright and cheery. "Well, then! I figure we shouldn't walk home together today, either!"

"...Ah."

Yeah. I was unsure about what to do about that fact.

One of the things that had hurt Kikuchi-san was that Mimimi and I occasionally walked back from the station together. We'd been doing it since before I'd begun dating Kikuchi-san, but speaking in terms of formalities, this might be one of the things you should avoid when you have a girlfriend.

To be honest, I didn't think it would be a problem so long as I kept a firm head on my shoulders, and my time with Mimimi was important to me. But...

...it wasn't like Mimimi had only ever simply been a friend.

"Yeah, you're right, actually...," I said. "Umm..."

Mimimi smiled. "What're you apologizing for?! Or are you prepared to accept the school badges with me instead?! You got a girlfriend, so take good care of her!"

"...Yeah. But sorry."

"Like I saaaaid! It's fine, it's fine! Actually, it sounds like I'm one of the causes of your issues, so I'm sorry!"

"Well, I wouldn't say that..."

We wound up apologizing to each other like Kikuchi-san and I had done before, and for some reason, I felt a sense of loss.

"Oookay, then I'll be off!" Mimimi chirped.

"...Yeah."

"Don't get lonely and cry, Brain," she said as she spun away from me.

"Sh-shut up, don't *you* cry." I gave back what I got, and her shoulders twitched just a second.

Then she turned around. "Heh-heh-heh. Customarily, the one who's left behind is the one who gets lonely."

"Huh, what? Th-that's not fair."

"Bye! See you at school!"

And then Mimimi zoomed off. With the orange sun lighting her from the other side, her back got smaller and smaller in the blink of an eye.

And as it did, I felt like I was slowly letting something important slip from my grasp.

"...Is this really for the best?"

This loneliness right then really was a complicated feeling, like I'd indeed been left behind.

* * *

The morning of the next day.

"Actually...I've been thinking about posting a novel online," Kikuchi-san said with determination.

"Oooh!" I brightly showed her I was listening.

We were in the library that morning, just like the day before; we had walked to school together in order to have more time as a couple.

"I was thinking that might help me get used to people reading my writing."

"Mm, I get that."

I was glad to hear about it. It's not like I know a lot about those communities, but if you were considering it experience, it couldn't be a bad idea to make your written work public in a form anyone could read. At New Year's, Kikuchi-san had said that she would be submitting her next work to a publisher's writing competition, and posting online would be a great first step to that end.

As we talked, the "unbalance" that I'd discussed the day before with Mimimi and Tama-chan crossed my mind. But right now, I wanted to hear about Kikuchi-san.

"I think that's a great idea," I told her. "What are you going to post?"

"Umm, it's difficult to explain, but..." Her gaze drifted up as if she was tracing her thoughts or even daydreaming. Her expression when she was considering her novel was gentle; I could tell she enjoyed thinking about it a lot.

The morning air in the library was very still, as if each one of the books would absorb the sound and light, but it didn't seem dim. It was more as if faint light was hanging there.

The atmosphere really did suit Kikuchi-san.

"I was thinking about making it like a combination of the themes in the play we did, *On the Wings of the Unknown*, and *Poppol*."

"Ohh!" Of course, she'd need to elaborate. But I was really looking forward to seeing what she'd do with the script she'd worked on so seriously. "I think that's a great idea!"

But she was even grateful for my vague encouragement. "Tee-hee... Thank you very much," she said. The air around her was gentle, not even a hint of sharpness. "After writing *Wings*, I realized there were still things that I hadn't managed to include in that play, so I was thinking about writing that in this story."

"Things you hadn't included? Like what?"

For some reason, her smile turned a little sad. "...*Wings* wound up being a story about Kris, right?"

"Mm...yeah, that's right," I said, remembering the performance of the play.

That story had been for Kris—for Kikuchi-san.

"The girl who was cooped up inside a little garden... And then she eventually realized she was keeping herself there. After that, she chose herself and the center of her world and found a way to take flight outside the garden... I feel like that's the story it became."

I nodded again.

Kris had chosen to become a creator of the flower crowns she loved, and Kikuchi-san—

"It was about creating a connection with the world through making what you want to make," I said, wording it to be a general *you* that could mean either the story or reality.

Kikuchi-san touched a hand to her chest and smiled with a polite nod.

"Back then...I'm sure that was what I had to write. That's why my current goal is to seriously pursue being a novelist...and that's why you and I..."

"Y-yeah... We could start dating," I said, mustering my courage to say it out loud.

"...!" Though I'd thought Kikuchi-san had turned from fairy to human, she invoked a blazing flame spell. By the way, I was also emitting what they call in *Atafami* "Fire Breath." Generally not a good idea to do that at the library.

And then both our fires combined into an advanced spell.

"S-so...um...!" Kikuchi-san dithered around for a bit.

"...Mm."

"Um..." Eventually, she paused for a long moment and said, "...Where was I again?" The heat must have burned up the rest of what she'd meant to say.

"Come on," I said with a wry smile. "You were talking about what you hadn't managed to include in *Wings* with Kris."

"Oh, that's right..."

We both looked at each other, then giggled.

Even while I was prompting her to explain, I kinda did understand.

That story had become about Kris, so there was something she hadn't written about yet.

Which means. "You mean you haven't written about the other characters aside from Kris yet?"

"...Yes."

If we wanted to get specific, I knew who she was referring to. "I see... We did do those interviews and stuff, huh."

Kikuchi-san nodded.

Yeah. When Kikuchi-san and I had been writing that play, we had gone out to interview a certain someone in the hopes of depicting a character more deeply. Then, assuming she hadn't offered anything real to us, we even went to ask her old classmates.

That had all been for the sake of writing the interiority of another heroine.

"...You mean that you're not finished writing about Alucia," I said.

About Aoi Hinami.

Kikuchi-san had only depicted Hinami's darkness halfway. There'd been a sharpness to it, like she was shining a harsh light on Hinami's motives and values; knowing her secret side myself, it had been deeply fascinating.

"Yes... Though, there are many areas that are difficult to touch on..." Kikuchi-san's gaze wandered around as if she was struggling to find the words.

It's true that Hinami's past and true self was still largely a black box. And I had the sense that if I took one wrong step, I'd wind up touching something I shouldn't...like the matter of her younger sister.

"Um, the rest will be in the story..."

"Yeah, okay. I won't pry, then."

Maybe it was just something she was particular about in writing a book, but it seemed Kikuchi-san didn't want to discuss the themes any further.

Kikuchi-san was normally the type who wouldn't assert herself, but she would sometimes take on the disposition of an artist. She'd done it during the play, too; she'd kept tweaking the script right up to the last minute, even considering things like making the stage background go from black and white to color. I'd seen that side of her as a creator a number of times.

At times like that, she would think up amazing ideas I wouldn't even expect, so I figured I should let her handle things how she wanted. "I'm rooting for you."

"Thank you very much. Though, it's still one step forward and one step back." She smiled like she was enjoying herself, until eventually, a serious expression came to her face. "Tomozaki-kun...you're aiming to be a pro gamer, aren't you?" she asked, apparently trying to be careful about it.

For a moment, I wondered why she was asking, but I immediately figured it out.

I think the profession of pro gamer is generally viewed as an unrealistic choice, or seen maliciously, it would even appear ridiculous. Touching on it had to seem almost taboo, or at least difficult to approach.

"Yeah. That's my goal." That's why I acknowledged that clearly and with confidence. "I want to be a pro gamer." And then I smiled for her.

No matter how you look at it, this is a path of thorns, but there are already people who are active in the field, so I'd gotten a vague sense of how to get there.

There were thorns, but it's not at all impossible.

"That's very difficult, isn't it?" she said.

"Yeah. But I think I have the skills… Well, maybe not quite…"

Seeing Kikuchi-san tilt her head, I probed the reason for my own confidence.

I didn't think I would be able to make it as a pro gamer the way I was now. Even just from what I'd heard from Ashigaru-san, it seemed like I was lacking in a number of specific areas, and I had actually lost to him in a first-to-three.

So that wasn't the reason for my confidence.

"Even if I don't have what it takes now," I said, "I feel like I can learn in the future—I guess that's my idea."

Kikuchi-san examined my face closely for a while, and then she smiled with some relief. "…That seems very you."

"Huh? What's that supposed to mean? Is that a compliment?"

"Tee-hee, I wonder," she said as she turned to look away. "But I am complimenting you." Then she flicked a sidelong glance at me and smiled.

"Th-thanks."

Her profile was cute—like a young girl enjoying mischief.

"But still, it's not like I'm just blindly chasing that and only that—"

I talked more about myself, as though Kikuchi-san was drawing it out from me.

I explained the ideals I'd decided myself and reality; though I was aiming to be a pro gamer, I also planned to go to university, and to that end, I wanted to study hard as well as practice *Atafami*. I also talked about how I couldn't just improve my game, but that I also had to consider strategies on how to make a living.

"Wow…just hearing about it kind of gets me excited." Kikuchi-san was as glad as if it were about herself, her cheeks pink with heat. And then in a serene tone of voice just like a hug of validation, she said, "That seems really difficult, and I think it will be a struggle...but I bet you could be okay."

"...Thanks," I said shyly, and she eyed my expression before finally giggling. "What?" I asked.

She nodded happily a bunch of times. "When you're talking, you seem like you're really having fun."

Fun.

That remark, and Kikuchi-san's beautiful smile, made my breath catch. "...Yeah."

It's a simple word, but I think it's very important.

That was exactly why I'd wanted to teach that to a certain empty someone.

"I'm rooting for you, too," Kikuchi-san said in a voice like tinkling bells, then examined my face with mild concern. "Umm...so then you'll still be going to those offline meetups?"

"Ahh...umm."

There, I found myself a bit unsure.

I did want to go to the meetups. But right then, Kikuchi-san had to be thinking about Rena-chan, who'd been one of the reasons for our falling-out.

I remembered what I'd talked about the day before, after school.

Mizusawa had said that if you're going to choose something, then you have to abandon something else.

Mimimi had said that the two of us were unbalanced.

"Yeah...I'm thinking I want to go," I said.

Kikuchi-san's eyes darted around just as I had expected, like she felt lost. "Yes, of course."

"Um...partially because I decided that I would become a pro gamer. There's a person who helped me make that decision, and I want to tell him...and I have a lot of questions about the pro world, too."

"S-so then next time is...," Kikuchi-san said, sentence wilting at the end.

"...This Saturday. I was invited to a game night, and I'm planning to go." I didn't soften it at all, and Kikuchi-san's whole body twitched. The guilt came rushing back.

"Um, will that person from LINE be...?" She had to mean Rena-chan.

"I'm not sure...but I think she'll probably be there."

"O-oh..." Kikuchi-san hung her head uneasily. The way she bit her lip looked so fragile.

"...It makes you nervous, doesn't it?"

"U-um..." She didn't say so, but that was basically a yes. I could feel the prickling of stabbing thorns inside me.

Kikuchi-san's attention eventually shifted to someone other than Rena-chan. "For game night...Hinami-san has been with you every time, hasn't she?"

"Huh...?" The question had snuck up on me, and my guard was up. If I said something wrong, I'd wind up in territory that would cause trouble for Hinami.

Kikuchi-san would probably accept my game nights if it was because I'd decided to be a pro gamer. I'd been playing this game enough to be the top player online before any of this started.

But Hinami being there with me every time would be hard to explain.

"...Yeah," I acknowledged, but I didn't know what else to say.

I'd already told Kikuchi-san that Hinami was into *Atafami*, and if it that was all, you could just barely explain it away by saying it was both a competitive game and a party game with mass appeal. So her coming with me out of curiosity that first time hadn't been that odd.

But there was an actual pro gamer there, plus the high schooler with the number one winrate who was aiming for pro, plus a commentator duo who were pretty competent, and a mysterious adult woman. Hinami continuing to join in with this unique lineup, and even fit in, would make you think something was off.

Yes, Hinami can get along with anyone, and she can do anything— but sheer curiosity wasn't enough to explain this.

I doubted it would lead to her getting exposed as NO NAME, the number two in Japan, but Hinami wouldn't want even something close to that getting revealed.

"Umm...uh..."

But.

Kikuchi-san's next words were once again not quite what I'd expected.

"Is Hinami-san someone special to you...?"

I sensed jealousy in both her tone and her expression.

The word *special* had certain implications, and not just from her play-script. It was also based on that discussion of the old school badges that we'd been asked to inherit.

"...What do you mean by 'special'?" I pressed her for details.

Kikuchi-san looked up at me with worry. "...I understand that you chose me, Tomozaki-kun, but..." And then like it was a little hard to say— "I feel that you and Hinami-san really are like a key and keyhole..."

"You said that before..."

"...I did." Her voice was wavering.

Kikuchi-san had talked about her ideals of the world during the play, too. This could become a real problem.

The relationships I'd built and my actions had once again unintentionally wound up hurting Kikuchi-san, bringing the guilt back.

"I've become...more and more anxious," Kikuchi-san said. "Can I really say that our relationship is special? ...Should you and I really accept the school badges?"

"..." That sounded a lot like what I'd talked about with Mimimi and Tama-chan, and Mizusawa and the others.

When Izumi had asked us to take on the old school badges, I'd thought I'd seen a ripple of uncertainty in Kikuchi-san's eyes. This reminded me of that.

"I've been scared that our complementary viewpoints don't really make for a special reason... That maybe we're just opposites."

It felt ominous that Kikuchi-san had arrived at that doubt at the same time as me.

"Isn't the real special relationship—?" Kikuchi-san gently touched the collar of her blazer. "Shouldn't the ones to succeed the story that has gone on for ten years be...you and Hinami-san?" she asked once more, and I considered.

To me, Hinami was a classmate, but more importantly, she was my teacher in life, and my competitor NO NAME.

She was an important friend to me who I was personally involved with, and I wanted to teach her about how much fun life could be.

If you wanted to call it special, then yeah, but it was special in a way Kikuchi-san didn't know. And there was inevitably a big wall getting in the way of explaining that.

"...Sorry."

That's when I realized something.

This was just between me and Hinami, so I wasn't allowed to breach that territory. I couldn't do anything selfish that would cause trouble for her. But...

If I could get permission.

"I'll give you the whole story...so could you wait for me for just a few days?"

If I could just do that...

For the first time, I thought that maybe I could tell someone about my and Hinami's "special" relationship.

"...I understand." As expected, there was mixed indecision and trust in Kikuchi-san's expression.

"So then are you okay with me going to the meetup?" I tried asking her again directly. Then...

"Um..." She hung her head in hesitation.

But...even as I said that, I couldn't even understand my own feelings anymore.

If...

If right that moment, Kikuchi-san were to say, *I still don't want you to go*, then what would I do?

*　　*　　*

After the silence continued for a while...

Kikuchi-san opened her mouth hastily. "O-oh, no! ...Um, I don't want to interfere with your future, so..."

That tone, that expression.

I could tell even as she said it, she couldn't shake off her reserve.

She was clearly forcing herself, and she was shoving down her own feelings—her eyes were wet, her focus was wavering, and her fingers on the desk were trembling weakly.

She seemed so insecure that it would be weird not to touch on it. It was painfully obvious that I was hurting her right this minute.

But in spite of that...

"...Yeah, thanks."

I just accepted what she'd said.

After all—I wasn't sure.

Right then if she were to honestly plead me not to go...

...if someone I cared about were to deny the path that was important to me, this thing I wanted to do that I'd finally found—

—I had the feeling I wouldn't be able to say yes.

I was surprised that such feelings were inside me, but I still didn't know how to face them right now.

"...Sorry," I muttered quietly enough that maybe Kikuchi-san couldn't even hear—like an atonement, like a compensation.

I figured my voice reached her, but she didn't hear what it meant.

The imbalance in our relationship—did it make us special? Or just incompatible?

I had the feeling that the answer to this question was slowly becoming more pronounced.

A hero with both physical attacks
and healing can adventure alone

Saturday. The morning of the *Atafami* meetup.

I was in my room, eating breakfast in front of my computer.

On the screen was cold and impersonal writing software. Typed out on it was this:

Short-term goal: beat Ashigaru-san in a tournament-style first-to-three.
Mid-term goal: win at a major tournament of S-tier or higher.
Long-term goal: become the top player in the world according to overall tournament ranking.

These were the *Atafami* goals I'd settled on when I'd decided I was going to be a pro gamer, and I was doing it in the same format as my life-strategy meetings with Hinami. I wouldn't say I was emulating her way of doing things, but rather that I'd set goals like that to begin with as a part of my ongoing practice at *Atafami,* so it would be accurate to say I was just taking that further. Meaning from here on out, I was taking on new challenges. Clicking the mouse, I opened up another tab.

Written on this one was the following:

Short-term goal: find a special reason for my relationship with Kikuchi-san and accept the old school badges together.
Mid-term goal:
Long-term goal: become a "character" in life and have a fun life.

*   *   *

Those were the life goals I'd assigned myself now that I'd put my sessions with Hinami on pause.

Though I'd told her we wouldn't meet for now, that was ultimately just because I wanted to stop following strategies that were geared toward what she thought was a fulfilling normie life. As nanashi, I'd always taken a game seriously once I got started, and I'd come to believe that the game of life was a masterpiece. So there was no reason to stop goal-setting.

"Hmm..."

The mid-term goal was still empty. I was honestly worried about that. Hinami had said that the mid-term goal was the most important, but the difficulty level here was actually really high. Maybe my problem was that the big goal, which was supposed to help me decide that, was overbroad to begin with. But when you're honest with your feelings, it really does wind up sounding juvenile.

But that makes me think...

For the big goal, I'd set *to have a fun life*—what you'd call a life concept.

"So to Hinami...that was *becoming a normie*, huh."

Was that a strength, or was it more a form of weakness?

Thinking about that suddenly brought back the question that had come to me in the hallway.

It was what I'd felt when Hinami had levied her "punishment" on Erika Konno.

I'd experienced a lot of things in the past six-odd months. But I hadn't often felt a strong, concrete desire to do something in particular .

So then *that* had to be the goal that was most important to me.

—*That's a hell of an idea.*

Mid-term goal: know Aoi Hinami.

And so I closed the laptop, which kept the record of my goals.

* * *

I left the house a little early and got on the Saikyo Line from Kitayono Station to head to the game night.

I was taking the train in the Tokyo direction. I generally always ride the train going toward Omiya, so it felt a little adventurous to travel this way. It's exciting. I was a little worried about the possibility of getting assassinated as a traitor by Kobaton, our mascot who always watched over the people of Saitama Prefecture, but I figure Kobaton probably can't go over the prefectural border. If I can get as far as Ukimafunado Station, I can probably get away.

Right as I was thinking that, my phone vibrated in my pocket.

"Hmm?" I pulled it out to find a notification showing new messages on LINE.

"…Whoa."

It goes without saying, but that reaction was because the sender was Rena-chan.

This was the first message I'd gotten from Rena-chan since that day when I'd made up with Kikuchi-san and complained to Rena-chan herself that night. By the way, my message that I had sent her at the end that day with the intention of ending the conversation—[*Kind of, yeah! It's fine so long as you don't do it in the future!*]—she'd never replied to. Which is fine, but it kind of made me wonder what was up.

"What's this…?"

There were two messages on LINE from Rena-chan, and when I swiped, all I saw was [*you have received an image*] and [*hey look what I bought*]. Since I couldn't see images from the notification screen, I couldn't tell what she'd sent.

I wasn't sure whether I should put the "read" notification on it, but when Ashigaru-san had contacted me, he'd said Rena-chan would be at the game night…so I had to open it by then. If I didn't look, and then at the apartment, she was like, *Hey, did you see my message?* that would probably be trouble.

So while I was on the train, I opened up the chat screen with Rena-chan—and then.

"…?!"

I just barely restrained my instinct to yelp. There was an outrageous sight on my phone screen.

The image she'd sent was a mirror selfie of her in slightly see-through pajamas that were wide open in the front, revealing her underwear.

Her fitted sweaters had alerted me to her figure before, but the parts to emphasize were emphasized there, and the other tight and seductive curves stood out. It wasn't just a shot of her in her underwear—the slight concealment made the whole thing feel weirdly raw, as if I was sneaking a peek at her. The eye-catchingly deep and vivid blue gave it an allure. And the fact she was the one sending it to me made it feel strangely naughty.

I immediately closed the chat screen and turned around to check to see if anyone was looking—not too fast to keep from seeming sketchy. I got no sense that anyone had seen my screen just now or had been suspicious of my smothered cry, but the photo had been powerful enough to instantly flip the switch in my body.

Wh-what is this about?

I wasn't sure what I should do. If I replied, the image would stay on screen as I typed, and that glimpse would be dealing constant psychic damage. Since I was on the train for Tokyo on a holiday, it was decently crowded, and the difficulty level of doing that on a train seemed kind of high.

I closed my eyes to regain my cool for the moment. But once my eyes were closed, the image rose up behind my eyelids. "…Ngh."

I had utterly failed at clearing my mind of all thoughts—in fact, my face was even hotter now, so I just opened my eyes. There was a man who looked in his fifties standing right in front of me, and staring at the end of his nose helped me calm down. Our eyes kinda met for a second, and he gave me a suspicious look, but you can't solve a problem without making some sort of sacrifice.

"…Okay." Now having regained my composure, I gave up trying to respond to that message and decided to focus on the event and whatever came before that. *It'll be okay. If I focus on* Atafami, *I should be able to manage somehow.*

But...Rena-chan's at the meetup, huh. If one photo had this much of an effect on me, what should I do if she pulls something on me in real life? I've just got a bad feeling about this.

* * *

A half hour or so later, I was at a café in front of Itabashi Station.

"I'm glad you actually came," I said.

I was alone with Hinami as we sat in the counter seats by the window.

"...I mean, I said I'd come," she responded a bit huffily.

Hinami was sitting sharp beside me in refined attire that made her stand out from her surroundings. Just seeing her sit there, she had such an aura—that had to simply be her foundation of "posture." Meanwhile, I was beside her feeling uncomfortable as I nervously sipped at a latte. Of course I'd look bad next to Hinami, but that wasn't what this was about—

"You said you're putting life-strategy meetings on pause, but you'll still invite me to meetups, huh?" she said like a stab to the gut.

I stuck out my lips idly as I just said what I thought. "Well...life strategy has nothing to do with *Atafami*."

A few days earlier in Sewing Room #2, after checking with her about telling Kikuchi-san her secret, I'd invited Hinami to come with me to the *Atafami* meetup.

"Hmph...," Hinami said as she set her phone on the counter and checked her Instagram feed, choosing a few fancy-looking posts to like. *I guess knowing how to choose that stuff is another necessity for maintaining the perfect-heroine image. There are a lot of clothes and fancy household items and stuff there—does she go equip herself with all that later?* I wondered, but then a heartbeat later, she started snapping photos of the cheesecake she'd ordered from fashionable angles. *No rest for the wicked.*

"That's no reason to invite me, though. Weren't you about ready to hate me?" she said expressionlessly, without meeting my eyes.

But I wouldn't be discouraged. "Well, yeah. If we'd continued meetings regularly like that, maybe I would have."

"Why would you go to the trouble of inviting someone to a meetup with you if that's how you feel?" Hinami said as she flicked a glance at me. Her eyebrows were knit in displeasure.

"I still have a problem with your cold approach to everything. You only seem to care about being right, and you don't consider people's feelings."

"If that's your problem…"

"Have you forgotten?" I cut her off, drawing in a breath.

I'm sure this thought was an important impulse—this was feeling over reason.

"I said I'd teach you how to enjoy life."

Hinami's eyes flared wide.

"I want to put a pause on our meetings, but I never said I wanted to stop that part."

The muscles of her face didn't even twitch—the only change she revealed was in the movements of her eyes.

I hoped that it was her true self peeking out from behind the holes of her mask, but I was using my face to reflect my own self, this time as a smile.

"Because—this is what I want to do."

Saying that with pride, I didn't look away from her.

"…I see." She did another big blink. I have no idea what it meant. But for now, I was okay with that. "…Well, I love *Atafami*, too, so it's fine."

"Yeah, I thought you'd say that."

An irritated crease formed in Hinami's brow. "I don't like being so predictable, so maybe I'll go home after all."

"H-hey, don't do that."

Seeing me get flustered, she sighed again. "Agh…what you really want to do, huh?" She raised her eyebrows and gave me a sidelong look. "You're not…planning to prove anything else now, huh."

"…Anything else?"

Without giving me a reply, Hinami turned away and gazed at the people walking outside the broad windows.

I couldn't tell what she was thinking, after all.

* * *

"…I see." Hair swaying in the winter wind with the scents of downtown, Hinami scowled.

"That's the one thing I just can't explain," I said. I was telling her about how Kikuchi-san was confused by my relationship with Hinami, and about how I wanted to tell what I could to her about our history—about how I had met Hinami offline as NO NAME, number two in Japan, and how she had been offering me advice for the game of life. That way, I could clarify the connection through which we were going to these meetups.

"When you really think about it, it's hard to explain the reason that you're going to these meetups every time, but I can't hide that we're going together, either… And even without that, our relationship is kinda special, isn't it? …Huh? Which way are we going?"

Hinami nodded like this made sense to her, but her brow was furrowed. "Well, I suppose when you're dating, some people will worry you. And it's left."

By the way, I was leading Hinami based on the address that Ashigaru-san had sent me, while Hinami had opened up a map. It was highly likely that she didn't trust my guidance. I'd say that was wise.

"…And she's even worrying that maybe it would be better for you and me to accept the school badges instead," I said.

"Well…that wouldn't make sense to the people watching, so we can't do that."

"Um…okay, that's true. But I mean feelings-wise."

As usual, Hinami was incredibly correct—she was looking straight at reality.

"…I remember you've told her that a 'certain someone' was helping you with a strategy guide for life, right? Also, red light."

"Whoa!" The triple task of checking the map, talking to someone, and also watching out for traffic was apparently too heavy a burden for me; Hinami was giving me constant heads-ups. She was easily juggling all three.

"Umm, yeah. I've told her about the life-strategy part."

After the fireworks festival during summer vacation last year, I parted ways with Hinami. And then when Kikuchi-san opened up to me about her problems, I told her that someone was teaching me, though I hid who that was.

"Frankly...this being Fuka-chan, it wouldn't be strange for her to have deduced who that someone was. Even if she's not quite certain," Hinami said calmly.

I nodded. "Well, she's picked up on the fact that we don't have a normal relationship...so maybe she does know."

Hinami sighed in resignation, then tugged my arm to clear the way for a vehicle coming from behind. *Thanks.*

"You can tell her, you know. It's not like it was absolutely not allowed for anyone to find out in the first place anyway."

"Really?" I asked back.

"The coolest girl in class gives advice to a classmate who doesn't fit in, to help him get along with everyone, and succeeds amazingly," Hinami continued smoothly. "That's not really something that would hurt my reputation, is it?"

"Well...true."

"What's more, said boy took charge of the cultural-festival play, inspiring the whole class to make it a big success, and then started dating the pretty girl who wrote the script. Now he's saying he's going to become a pro gamer and starting to actually sound like the number one *Atafami* player in Japan. At this point, my reputation might even improve."

Though I was nodding along, I was once again impressed by how well her life strategy worked for me. I mean, I'd gotten that far in just barely over six months.

"But it is thanks to you that I could get that far. You deserve an improved reputation," I said.

But Hinami didn't seem to care. "...Hmm."

Huh?

She continued to explain. "I've already thought about it, and I figure if you drop your phone and someone sees your LINE, or someone figures it out from a slip of the tongue, it's fine."

"You're assuming I'd be the one to let the cat out of the bag, huh?" Though she was probably right, I did make a token resistance.

"Of course. I already regularly erase your messages to me on LINE, so I'm fine there."

"Hey, that kind of hurts." I smiled wryly, but what she said made sense. So sad. "So it's okay for me to tell her?"

"Sure. I don't mind. But..." The dry winter wind must have gotten to her, as her tongue ran over her unusually dry lips. It was a more restless gesture than usual.

"Of all people—Fuka-chan, huh."

Brown, dead leaves rustled as they danced around her.

"...What's that supposed to mean?" I asked.

Her next comment wasn't much more of an explanation. "It seemed like she was...investigating me."

"Sure...I guess," I agreed, hesitating a moment before I continued, "...You mean for the play?"

Hinami nodded, and the fallen leaves crushed under her black heel crunched in protest. "Fuka-chan is kind of...different from the people I've been involved with before."

Looking at her unsure expression, I thought back on the depictions in Kikuchi-san's play.

Hinami's emptiness, and her fixation on climbing.

It was true, there couldn't have been anyone before who had tried to dig into her mind with such sharpness and coolheadedness.

Since I know her hidden side, I feel like I know Hinami better than anyone else, but even I don't have the confidence to go there. Mizusawa told her his feelings, so he's probably prepared to dive into the deep end, but I don't think he knows about her hidden side as well as I do. Still...

...Kikuchi-san plunged into something with her clear eyes, claiming the necessity of it for writing, and she had to be trying to delve somewhere neither I nor Mizusawa could.

"So I don't really like the idea...," Hinami said. "But if you're telling me not doing it would cause problems, then it's fine."

"Yeah...it would help."

And so our talk wrapped up nicely, but I was also surprised by what she'd said—*"Of all people—Fuka-chan, huh."*

It meant that she felt wary, and the implication was that Hinami found her threatening. I'm pretty sure I'd never seen that from her before.

* * *

Eventually, we reached our goal: the foot of the apartment building where Ashigaru-san lived.

"...I-it's here?" I said, looking up from the street.

A black high-rise apartment building towered over us, and through the glass doors in the lobby, I could see a subdued brown sofa and a strange, geometrically shaped art piece, giving the place a high-class feeling. I have no idea what the heck that thing was, but the fact that they had a decoration with no practical function just left a stronger impression.

"Whoa, this place is nice," I said.

"...He has a day job, too, right?"

"Yeah."

Hinami was probably thinking that rent here looked expensive, so could he afford this apartment with just pro-gamer work? Having an interest in that career myself, I wanted to discuss those practical issues. According to what I'd seen online, Ashigaru-san had a day job in addition to being a pro gamer, but I still didn't know at what level you had to be as a pro gamer in order to make a living. And those questions are hard to ask.

"Anyway, let's just go in," Hinami said.

We buzzed his room number on the panel in front of the building, and then we went inside.

We took the elevator to the thirteenth floor. The simple black door at the end of the hall opened up, and Ashigaru-san poked his face out. "Oh, welcome. Come in, come in," he beckoned.

"Pardon me!" Hinami said smoothly, with no nastiness, while I was less accustomed to the rituals of visiting people's houses.

"P-pardon me."

There was a clear difference of tone in our greetings, but well, that's just our difference in experience.

When I came into the entranceway, a woody but refreshing scent wafted over to tickle my nostrils. Those little things really make you realize it's not your own house, and it gets me a little nervous.

We used his sink to wash our hands, and then Ashigaru-san showed us in to the living room.

* * *

A few minutes after we settled in the living room...

"...Huh, so you've already made up your mind? You're unusual, nanashi-kun."

I'd immediately told Ashigaru-san about my decision.

"Yes. I've considered it a lot since then, and I figure that's my only option."

There were six people present: me, Hinami, Ashigaru-san, Harry-san, Max-san, and Rena-chan.

In the living room, there was a green sofa, a largish TV with a game console attached, a black low table, and some tall lighting and other things. Overall, there wasn't much random stuff in the room, and it didn't feel lived-in.

Beside the sofa, there was a dining table and chairs for four people, where me, Ashigaru-san, and Rena-chan were sitting. By the way, Hinami was sitting on the sofa in front of the TV playing a match with Harry-san, with Max-san watching.

"I don't think that's your only option, though," Ashigaru-san said, sitting across from me, though he smiled like he was amused. Having a predecessor hear about my decision and implicitly welcome me honestly made me happy.

Incidentally, Rena-chan was sitting beside me; after getting that photo that morning, just having her close by made me incredibly fidgety.

"But I've made up my mind, so…I hope you'll teach me lots," I said.

"Sure. It means you've got to take things even more seriously than you have been before. Both practicing *Atafami*, and with other strategies, too."

"Right." I nodded, smiling back.

"Wooow. It feels like Fumiya-kun is going far away," Rena-chan said in a syrupy, nasal voice. *I'd really like her to stop calling me Fumiya-kun in front of everyone. But I doubt she would, even if I asked.*

"…Uh…it's not like I was really close to you in the first place, though," I said, closing the gates to my heart.

For some reason, she seemed tickled. "Aww, you're so mean, Fumiya-kun!" She grinned, touching my shoulder flirtatiously.

Hey, stop that. I'm genuinely telling you off; don't act like this is some intimate banter.

I'd smelled Rena-chan's sweet scent before, and now her coming this close was sending whiffs of that smell up my nose. My gaze was drawn toward her almost irresistibly, and my eyes met with hers. The photo she'd sent earlier loomed in my mind.

"Urk…" *This is bad.* Having her right in front of me made me imagine it even more vividly—and her clothes were already kind of revealing, so it was just total overkill. What the hell? Was this her strategy?

Rena-chan wore an enchanting smile and something like a sweater that was divided into two parts. One was a sleeveless top, and the other was shaped to leave her shoulders wide-open. Even putting the two together still showed all her shoulders—is she not satisfied unless she's exposing some part of her body? By the way, the sweater was short, of course, revealing lots of leg, too. She's always doing that, so maybe she sees flaunting her legs as kind of like manners. So does this count as her formal dress?

As my thoughts spiraled into nonsense, I averted my eyes, but my attention still kept getting sucked toward her every few seconds. Geez. Her grab range is too wide. It really seems like she'll do a back throw.

"Tee-hee, what's up, Fumiya-kun?" Rena-chan said as she stretched her arm underneath the table to brush my waist for just a moment. *Hey, isn't this sexual harassment?* A ticklish feeling ran up my body, and it reminded me again of the photo she'd sent me. I wished she'd stop.

"There's! Nothing! Up!" I said with firm intention, pulling back my chair to place myself a ways away. As a Found player, this was outrageous in terms of spacing, but Rena-chan's incredible range attacks made this distance necessary. Rena-chan giggled, watching me. *God, she's scary.*

"Really?"

"Ha-ha-ha. But it's true that he might go far away surprisingly fast," Ashigaru-san said, returning to the original rails of the conversation. I guess he had no idea of the psychological battle going on.

Umm, I got knocked off course by Rena-chan's shock-wave attack, but this is about me becoming a pro gamer, right? Even though not much time had passed, it felt like a topic from a few minutes ago. Rena-chan is a fearsome foe.

"I think you can do it, too," Rena-chan said. "You're good-looking, being a high schooler is sexy, and having the number one winrate—all those elements could make you famous."

Aside from that one random part of Rena-chan's remark, I actually kind of agreed. *Isn't it kinda sketchy for a twenty-year-old to find high school boys sexy?*

It's true that I had the number one online winrate in the game with the most Japanese players, even if offline was where the pros were. That alone made me a pretty scarce commodity. Then I was also in high school, I had polished up my clothes and hair enough just from putting in little effort, and I was decently okay at talking, based on what I'd heard from six months of my recordings…so at this stage, it seemed like I could be successful as a spectacle, at the very least. Well, for everything aside from *Atafami* skill, it's just some six months' worth of minor growth, though.

"Ohh…well, I guess," I said.

But right that moment.

"Aoi-san is way too good!" I heard a voice from the direction of the TV.

When I turned around, Hinami had already casually whipped out Found and was playing at her full ability like it was nothing. *Wait, she's already letting her identity slip?* Or maybe she just didn't care anymore. Or was it that since this was her third time at these events, she'd figured her secret was safe no matter how much her playstyle resembled NO NAME's?

"I saw you evade like that before," she said.

"No way! You're charging the Attack there?!"

Hinami accurately read Max-san's spot dodge, and then by charging the KO Attack, she slammed him with it the instant after he dodged. Punishing a habit once the opponent has shown it once is my specialty, and after all her practice imitating me, her precision is impeccable. Or maybe it's better to say that she's well aware of the points I often read, and she's reading them in the same way.

"Ugh, she's still so good...," Rena-chan said as she watched the TV screen. She must have followed my gaze. She wasn't at all hiding her disgust. Well, I can get that's frustrating—she's probably been about the only girl at these meetups before, so when another girl suddenly showed up who was super pretty, great with people, and abnormally good at *Atafami*, jealousy wasn't a surprising outcome.

"Mm, yeah...she's super good," I agreed with Rena-chan.

Hinami's play was machinelike as always—she just makes no mistakes at all.

Even I'd get into matches, go from a combo into a rock-paper-scissors match between attack, shield, and grab to try doubling up the damage, and then screw up in the end. So if you were just talking about her technique, where she could reliably win against people of a lower level than her, then maybe she was better than me. Rather than technique, it might be more accurate to call that self-control.

As I was watching from a distance, Ashigaru-san, who was also expressionlessly watching the TV screen, said, "...Wait, Aoi-chan, have you gotten way better at this? Were you this good with Found?"

"Ahh..." *She's been hiding her real ability all this time...*, I thought, but in another sense, my feelings were similar. "It's true... She has gotten better."

And I don't mean in terms of the skills she'd shown at these meetups. Even considering the skills I was aware of before, I felt like she'd improved a lot.

"Good game!" And the match ended like that, and Hinami cheerily gg'd Harry-san. He said the same back with some frustration, then both of them put down their controllers and walked up to me.

Harry-san scratched his neck and looked at me. "Aoi-san really kicks ass with Found, huh?! Did you teach her, nanashi-kun?" he asked in his resonant commentator voice.

I hesitated as to whether I should answer that question honestly. "Ahh, um, well, kind of." If he was going to ask me like that, then I had to agree—we'd actually had a number of mirror matches with Found online after meeting, and even before that, she'd gotten good from imitating my playstyle. If you thought of it that way, it kinda counted.

"I owe nanashi-kun a lot," Hinami joked. So she was joining me on this.

"I knew it! Aw man, must be nice having the greatest coach right there…," Harry-san said, exuding a frustration that only made me like him more. Harry-san wasn't really a pro gamer who relied on his skills, but a streamer whose business came from making his stream entertaining. Still, he was a competitive gamer who took it seriously.

Anyway, now there was an open space in front of the TV, which was currently the match station. This was supposed to be a game night, and we were here to play, so I pulled my controller out of my backpack and got myself psyched up for a game. "Okay then, guess I'll go next… Do you mind, Ashigaru-san?"

"Ha-ha, guess I've been summoned," he said.

"Oh, no go?" I asked good-naturedly.

In his usual tone, like he was letting me hear him talking to himself, Ashigaru-san said, "…I actually welcome it. Let's do this."

"All right!"

I started moving my fingers casually, squeezing and opening up my hands, while he and I sat down on the sofa.

"Let's have a good match!"

"Yeah. Let's."

And so the game between me and Ashigaru-san began.

* * *

Half an hour or so later.

I ended my run against Ashigaru-san after seven matches and put down the controller for the moment.

Ashigaru-san, sitting beside me, was lost in thought for a while. "...It's odd."

"What do you mean, 'odd'?" I asked back.

Ashigaru-san set down his controller and said, "You're playing different from usual, aren't you, nanashi-kun?"

"Ah, you can tell?" I answered, smiling brightly at his discerning eye. *Pros really can tell, huh.*

"More like...your winrate's totally changed."

"Ah-ha-ha...yeah, true," I said, smiling wryly.

"But it doesn't feel like you were trying to specifically counter Lizard... Are you reconsidering your whole neutral game?" Ashigaru-san asked.

"Umm, yeah. I've been prioritizing different skills and stuff."

"I see...so is that why it wound up like this?"

Indeed. The outcome of our set was completely different from the last time.

My results were, in fact—*two wins and five losses.*
My winrate had clearly decreased compared with the last time.

Feeling eyes on me, I glanced behind me to see Hinami and Rena-chan were giving me awkward looks. Rena-chan was probably seeing that I'd lost and simply wasn't sure what to say, while Hinami had to be shocked at my abilities declining this much.

"Unusual...or maybe not. Online, you're always grinding to raise your winrate, aren't you?"

"Yeah, I guess I am."

Ashigaru-san gave me a cool, measuring look. "Are you busy with school? Or is there something else...some reason your practice time has gone down?"

Hearing that, my heart momentarily leaped. "Umm...actually, there's one really major reason," I said while recalling my recent games.

I actually hadn't told Hinami about it, either—I'd been looking at *Atafami* just a little differently lately. The weakening of my skills was definitely because of that.

Ashigaru-san considered a while, expression unchanging, until he eventually appeared to have figured it out. "...Could it be you got a girlfriend?"

I was surprised to hear him ask that so directly. I never thought that would be his first question. "Ohh, well...I actually did, but..."

"Huh? I was half joking, though," Ashigaru-san said with a level tone but a smile. Now I felt like I'd given a serious answer to a joke.

A little embarrassed, I continued, "And it was recently..."

"Uh-huhhh? So that's why your practice time has gone down?" he said a little teasingly, but he was still getting to the root of it.

I shook my head at him. "No, that's not why," I said with a wave of my controller.

"It's not?"

"The reason's in this."

Yes. That really did have nothing to do with it.

"Um, could I go another few rounds?" I asked.

"Sure, but...what's the answer?"

"Just a sec...," I said vaguely as I tapped the stick.

The character select screen. I moved the glove-like icon on the screen, which had remembered my cursor that was left on Found. And then... "I think this will probably answer your question."

The moment I pressed the button—

—a low voice called out "Jack!" from the cheap speakers connected to the monitor. In the column for my fighter was a human whose face was covered with a kind of mask, along with the name "Jack."

"No way...you changed your main."

"That's right." I nodded with full confidence.

Ashigaru-san smiled in surprise. "As your secondary?"

"Well, I'm still in the trial stage, but I'm thinking of using him as my main in the future."

"..."

That moment, I could tell Hinami's breath quietly caught.

Curious, I glanced behind to see her staring at me, shocked in a way she rarely was. Well, of course. Hinami and I had always been using the same character before, so she would know best my proficiency and the time I'd put into him.

Changing my main right now would normally be out of the question.

On the other hand, Rena-chan was watching me expressionlessly, and I couldn't read what she was thinking. Or maybe I was reading too deeply into everything, and her mind was elsewhere.

"Hmm, you really do have a few screws loose, nanashi-kun," said Ashigaru-san. When I returned my attention to him, he was looking at me and slowly shaking his head.

"Maybe. But...I do have my own plan," I replied.

He smiled. "All right. I don't know what your logic is, but I do understand your end goal."

"...You do?"

He nodded with a smirk before saying with a serious expression,

"You just thought you could be a better player that way, right?"

It was a straightforward remark, and I nodded aggressively. "Yes. I'm still not used to playing him yet, so please go easy on me."

"Well, I'd be glad to help out."

And so I used my new character, Jack, to begin a game with Ashigaru-san—

* * *

—A few hours later.

The sun had sunk in the sky, and even though it was still around six o'clock, it was completely dark outside.

I was done playing against Ashigaru-san. I'd gone up against the other members a bunch of times, and the game night had come to a close.

Hinami and I were sitting side by side at the dining table with our backs to the TV, taking a break together.

She was silent, a small plastic bottle of lemon tea in one hand. From behind her rang out the sound of Ashigaru-san's Lizard KOing Victoria, the character Rena-chan was playing.

Hinami took a gulp of the lemon tea and put the lid on, staring at the packaging without really seeing it. "...So you dropped Found." She wasn't talking like Aoi the lower-level player who came to meetups, but like Aoi Hinami—or maybe NO NAME. The emotion was smothered out of her voice, which sounded weaker than usual, but maybe she was just trying to keep the four people in front of the TV from hearing our conversation.

"Yeah."

"Right when I thought I could just about catch up to you... You really are a pain, nanashi," she said, her voice somehow more delicate than usual. It was like she didn't know how to respond. I'd just changed my character, but it was as if she'd lost something more important than that.

And I wanted to know the reason for that.

"Is it worth being that dramatic about?" I asked.

"...Why now?" Even more unusually for her, she was asking me a reason for my behavior. She still wasn't looking at me.

"Well, there's lots of reasons. One is that with Found, you wind up getting into a rock-paper-scissors match between attack, shield, and grab, which makes my position unstable when I'm playing against someone of a similar skill level. I'm good at reading you, so I didn't notice before, but I figured that with my current playstyle, it would probably lose me some games at important tournaments."

"Important tournaments...huh," Hinami muttered and set the plastic bottle on top of the table. Her gaze remained focused on it the whole time. "So then you're serious...about becoming a pro gamer."

"Of course I'm serious," I replied without missing a beat. Once I've made up my mind on something, I won't change it so easily. "So I figured I have to be able to make solid wins not just against you, but against other people."

"I see... It's aggravating to hear you say it like I'm easy to beat."

"You make choices that are a lot like mine, so they're easy to understand," I teased.

Hinami pulled her gaze away from the plastic bottle to glare at me. "That was uncalled for." Her gaze immediately slid away again, toward the TV. "So nanashi plans to get even better, huh."

"Well, my skills have been down for a while, though." The fact was that in my games against Ashigaru-san just now, my results had been zero wins and seven losses.

To be blunt, I'd been utterly owned.

"True…but your neutral game *was* more stable than when you were fighting with Found."

"Right? I lost every match, but each time, it was by just about one stock… I think if I keep polishing my neutral game, then my results will improve," I said, feeling the benefits of my hard work. Even if I had completely lost, it wasn't like I'd gotten worse. It's a common thing in the world of competition to temporarily have to lose something in order to get better.

"…Or, like, if we play now, you might beat me, too."

"There's no point to me beating nanashi if you're in the middle of changing your main."

"Ha-ha-ha. Well, I suppose that's true," I said, and I meant it. "So that's why you didn't play a game with me today." That was her competitive pride—or maybe it was her respect as NO NAME for nanashi.

"Like…why are you so fixated on me…on nanashi?" I asked, making sure to keep my tone of voice as unchanged as possible. I really wanted to know.

Hinami opened her mouth—but she didn't say anything for a while, then closed it again.

Eventually, she let out a sigh before giving it another try. "It's got nothing to do with you."

"Uh, yeah it does. I am nanashi."

"Even then," she replied, and I could hear the quiet *no* in her tone. Then she flicked her gaze away from me once more. "How I feel about it has nothing to do with you."

"…Is that right?"

It was a very Hinami rejection, and I felt hurt. I had intended to ask more. But I still wanted to be involved with her anyway.

"Agh," she sighed. "I get it, so get your skills back ASAP."

"Hmm, regain my skills? I can't do that."

"…What do you mean?" Hinami said, looking sulky.

So I decided to tell her what I really was going for, as nanashi.

"I'm not *regaining* my skills. I'm going to *exceed* my original skills as soon as possible," I said with full confidence.

Hinami finally smiled with some relief—and anticipation. "Then good... At least try to keep me from going past you," she said, and there was something genuinely hopeful in her goading.

It was like a hint of an expression she never showed. The only time I felt like I could touch her genuine feelings was when she was talking about this stuff. I had the sense that was probably the part that I wanted to hear from her.

I wanted to keep inviting Hinami to these game nights and discover her real self, mask off. This had to be a shortcut to my "goal."

As I was thinking about this, I remembered Hinami's games that day. "But it's true... You have gotten better."

She chuckled in smug pride. "Heh. Right?"

"Have you, like, changed how you practice or something?"

And then just like a child bragging about staying up late, she said, "Since our morning meetings are on pause, I'm putting them to use practicing *Atafami*."

"Ha-ha-ha!" I burst out laughing. There was a little extra morning time that we'd been taking up before, but I didn't think she'd be using it like that.

"...I didn't say anything funny, though."

"Heh-heh... Yeah, I know it's not funny, but...ha-ha-ha." I ignored her telling me off and laughed, and a sudden impact hit my shoulder. "Ow?!"

It really hurt—that was a legit shoulder punch. She'd actually used a closed fist. And she hit the place where I'd gotten chopped by Mimimi before, accumulating the damage for even more pain.

Hinami didn't seem to feel bad at all, her fist still touching my shoulder as she primly faced forward. "I didn't say anything funny, though," she repeated.

"Y-yeah, sorry." Now that my laughter had been interrupted by pain, I had no choice but to obediently accept her statement.

"...You really do love *Atafami*, huh," I said.

She was into it to a degree that was kind of suspicious. But it was the suspension bridge stronger than anything else that connected us.

Her fingers on my shoulder relaxed from a fist and dropped down on her knee. "...I was improving my skills by imitating your play." Her expression was complicated, her lips slightly parted. "Analyzing every little thing, practicing it just like you to be able to do more."

"I know that best. Better than anyone else."

Hinami gave a smile that was just a little lonely, and in a tone more childish than usual, she said, "...Changing your character really leaves me stuck." She was being surprisingly contrarian; she normally didn't even complain.

"...Well, deal with it," I said, not knowing how to respond.

It's true that Hinami got to her level by imitating my Found. So if I was to stop with Found, then her skills would stop where mine had been. To be more accurate, I suppose she would be at a level that shaved off any unnecessary movements and bumped up the precision a bit.

But...but even saying that, would that mess up her usual pace this much?

"And hey," I said, "then you should just start using Jack, too. Jack's good, you know."

Hinami blatantly sighed at my suggestion. "...Listen, unfortunately, I don't have the time to build up a character from square one again and perfect it, so there's no way... And you just got a girlfriend, and you have entrance exams—do *you* have the time to be doing that?"

"Who knows? Even if I don't have the time, I have the confidence."

"Huh." Hinami let out a whiff of a sigh, and I grinned proudly at her. She's normally always the one taking the lead, but when it's about *Atafami*, then I could always counter back, no matter what angle she came from.

Eventually, Hinami sighed again for some reason, like she'd resigned herself to something. "Putting our strategy meetings on pause and changing your main... Soon enough, maybe there'll be no point in having me around at all."

"What's that supposed to mean?" It wasn't like Hinami to be getting down on herself. "I still have things to learn from you in life, and I still have my important mission of teaching you how to have fun. It's ridiculous to say there's no point," I told her flat out.

But Hinami's visible doubts didn't budge. "How to have fun in life...huh."

"Yeah."

"...Do you think that will save me or something?" The word she used there sounded meaningful.

But I responded to her question with an affirmative. "Yeah. That's what I want to do," I declared.

"Agh," Hinami sighed. "Then do whatever you want."

"Fine, I will." I gave her another proud smile. Hinami was, unsurprisingly, exasperated as she smiled tiredly back at me.

* * *

A few minutes after that.

"...So wait, nanashi-kun, you said you got a girlfriend?"

"Urk...so we're going there, after all?"

The topic had slipped before due to Ashigaru-san's remark, and now the conversation was shifting to my private life.

"I'm sooo curious." Rena-chan came over from the sofa to slide into the seat opposite from Hinami and me. I dunno, it's like when she gets close, her smell keeps wafting into my brain and bringing up the memory of that photo. I really wish she would not with this. What was the deal with that photo—was it like a spell that binds my brain or something?

"How long have you been dating?" she asked like she was also highly entertained by this.

"Um, I guess it's been about two months."

"The first two months, huh. That's a fun period."

"Ah-ha-ha, I guess...," I replied a little vaguely as I considered. I mean, how I'd handled the Kikuchi-san situation was just something close to first aid. Not just that—it seemed like we were starting to lose a special something. I was still searching for a way to resolve that.

I did think for an instant that maybe I shouldn't really talk about this with other people, but hearing opinions from adults would probably be more helpful in the future than trying to hide the details. Ashigaru-san was an adult and an intellectual with a highly analytical perspective, and though Rena-chan was generally a whole lot of trouble, she was undeniably an adult woman with an abundant wealth of experience.

Thinking about it that way, even all the normies who had given me advice before were still just high schoolers, huh.

"Well, the truth is," I began, "we had a bit of a falling-out, I guess…"

"Huhhh," Rena-chan said in a relaxed, grown-up tone. There was an implicit temptation there, like, *So then why not go with me?* But I was just thinking too hard. Her spell was manipulating my thoughts.

Ashigaru-san looked surprisingly cheerful as he said, "Aww, nice. Okay, then let's go buy some booze."

"Hey, why are you trying to enjoy this?" I protested.

"You really need drinks with this sort of talk. Oh, of course, with soft drinks for Aoi-san and nanashi-kun."

"Everyone else is drinking, huh…"

"Of course. ♡" Rena-chan was grinning like, *I wuuuub drinking.* ♡

"Oh, sorry, we have a stream after this, so…" Harry-san raised his voice, and Max-san nodded at that.

"Oh, that's totally fine," said Ashigaru-san. "Make work your first priority here. It'll just be the rest of us with alcohol."

"Thank you very much!"

Listening to this conversation, I couldn't help but admire the guys who did streaming for a living.

Ashigaru-san stood up and called out to say, "All right, so then time for a drinking party, with nanashi-kun's romantic drama as entertainment."

"Whooo! ♡" Rena-chan whooped in response to Ashigaru-san's announcement.

This was followed by Harry-san and Max-san brightly remarking as they got ready to go, "We'll be sure to come next time!"

"Let's party another day! Oh, I don't want to make girls go, so I'll help go buy drinks!"

I did have kind of mixed feelings about being the entertainment here, but Hinami was also silent for some reason, with a distant sort of expression. *Hinami, could it be that you're on my side?*

Eventually, she lifted her head with a serious look and smiled at Ashigaru-san. "…Ashigaru-san, will his romantic woes alone be enough entertainment? If you want embarrassing stories about nanashi-kun, I have lots."

"I knew it, of course you wouldn't be on my side!" I groaned.

Even after that conversation we'd had, Hinami was still a level or two above me.

* * *

A few minutes after that.

I went out the living room window to the veranda, drinking water from a plastic bottle that had already gone lukewarm as I gazed at the cityscape of Itabashi. There was plenty of cloth-covered basic seating out on the veranda, so I sat down on a nearby rectangular bench and stared into the sky.

It was completely dark, and there weren't many neon lights in the residential area, perhaps because this was looking out to the opposite side from the station. Ashigaru-san had gone out along with the two who were heading home, so it was just me, Hinami, and Rena-chan in the apartment. The situation was kinda awkward, so I'd come out to the veranda.

I pulled my cell phone out of my pocket and opened up LINE. When I got to the chat screen with Kikuchi-san, the last messages were what I'd sent before coming to this meetup: [*I'll call you once it's over!*] and her reply, [*I'll be waiting.*]

When I went back from Kikuchi-san's chat screen to the messages column, suddenly Rena-chan's icon caught my eye. Just like the photo she'd sent me that morning, the one in her icon really emphasized the lines of her body.

The veranda was dim. The atmosphere was kind of covert, and there was nobody around.

That moment—a voice like caramel reached my ears once again. "Oh, Fumiya-kuuun."

The window opened with a rattling sound as Rena-chan came onto the veranda. I hurriedly closed LINE, trying to cover my agitation as I looked over at her.

But it was the worst timing. Even if it was just an icon, I had been look-ing at a photo of Rena-chan right before she called out to me—and now she was right there walking toward me, and I was looking at her whether I liked it or not.

The voluptuous white of her long and slender legs and the emphasized curves of her body struck a part of me that was far away from reason. My eyes were pulled toward her despite the fear in my mind. Having been touched by her many times, my body was getting hopeful for that ticklish sensation. With each and every step she drew closer, her inner thighs flashed alternately, stealing my powers of judgment from me like a hypnotist's pendulum.

"Umm, what about Hi…Aoi?" I said.

"Oh, she invited me to play *Atafami*, but when I refused 'cause I'm not in the mood right now, she went online."

"Geez…"

When I peered through the window to look inside, Aoi's back and the match start screen caught my eye. When she's gaming, her love for *Ata-fami* meant she had no considerations for anything else. So then for the next few minutes at least, she wouldn't be coming over here.

I felt my thoughts slowing down. Though I'd managed to stand up before Rena-chan's approach, my gaze was being sucked in, and by the time I had just barely squeezed out a reply, she was right beside me.

Unlike before, we were alone on the dark veranda.

"Here we go." Rena-chan sat down right beside me. Instantly, a sweet and lascivious scent wafted past my sense of reason to churn away directly at my instincts. My thoughts had been coming on a delay, and now they were just scrambled.

Rena-chan turned at the waist to lean close to me, her right knee bump-ing into my left, and the heat of her body seeped in to capture something inside me. *Stop, please.*

"Today was fun, huh," she said sweetly, flirtatiously.

Her voice, scent, frame, heat—her mere presence alone gradually encroached on all my senses but taste, making a shiver tremble down my spine. Was it the fear of being preyed upon, or was it something else?

"Y-yeah," I said. I was unable to look at her face, and my eyes dropped to where her knee was resting against mine. And then Rena-chan's captivating skin entered my view. Her curves aroused my instincts. "...Ngk." Out of the corner of my eye, I could see two striking thighs only partially covered by a tightly fitted black-and-purple sweater. At this distance, my brain started imagining how soft her skin had to be.

My head and my body were going to heat up past the point of no return. So I hurriedly looked away, then back at Rena-chan again. I had to say something.

And then there she was, watching my face intently the whole time. The moment our eyes met, Rena-chan gave me a salaciously domineering grin. Then as if she saw right through me to the fire she'd lit in me, she said, "Hey, Fumiya-kun. You were looking just now, weren't you?"

Her tone was accepting of my reaction—enjoying it, even. The guilt being exposed, and the sweet air that seemed to approve, tickled my sense of ethics.

"N-no..." I attempted to resist, but my mind was dominated by panic and heat; I couldn't produce any excuses.

"You *were* looking, weren't you?" And then Rena-chan's slim white fingers slowly, as if guiding my eyes, moved from her knee to her white thigh— "Right here."

She flipped up the bottom of her sweater.

It was such an outrageous thing to do. Now there was more of her skin exposed from between her spread fingers. The tempting curves of her thighs continued past them into darkness.

Before I could wrench my gaze away, Rena-chan dropped her sweater back. I was completely frozen, body and soul. "You're so dirty, Fumiya," she said comfortably.

I gave up trying to reply—all I could do was face forward.

Rena-chan giggled bewitchingly. "Hey. Listen?" She gave me a lidded, seductive look. "I sent you a photo, didn't I?" She pointed to her chest, emphasized by her sweater.

"—I'm wearing that right now."

*   *   *

"!" Just that one remark put the image into my head. And now what I'd seen in the photo was overlapping with the real-life Rena-chan, who was smiling enchantingly in front of me. Her body heat and a smell like honey were enveloping me.

"Urk…" My heartbeat quickened abnormally, and my blood was rushing in my veins. The way my heartbeat washed away my sense of reason was completely extraordinary.

Leaning toward me, Rena-chan brought her lips close to my ear, and then with a tickle that seemed to melt my brain, she said, "Why not come to my place after this? I live around here, you know."

The specificity, the clear invitation—I'm sure my flustered reaction was just what she wanted.

"—!"

Which is why I shook it off and glared right at her.

"Sorry. I have a girlfriend."

At that direct rejection, Rena-chan gave me a challenging smile and wet her lips with her tongue. "Hmm…" She laid a hand gently on my knee. "Oh, really…?"

"—Hey!"

Her fingers slid upward and sent me into an extraordinary experience. An electricity ran through me that couldn't be compared to the times she had touched me before. From knee to thigh, from thigh to the inner thigh—

The impending sense of danger was intense; I stood up right there and made to get away from her, but right before I did, her fingers suddenly and easily pulled back. I was so surprised, my legs wouldn't move.

Rena-chan giggled as if she was making a pet wait for a treat, then leaned even closer until her lips were nearly touching my ear again. "Hey. Were you getting hopeful?" Her caramel voice was coquettish, body heat emanating from her shoulder as that honeyed scent wafted around her. Her smooth hair stroked my neck, sending a shiver of electricity up my body.

"I—I wasn't…"

"But…you haven't gone that far with your girlfriend yet, have you?" Her words scrambled my thoughts, and her breath tickling my ear made my whole body tremble. "Then it's fine, right? Let's have some fun," she said as she slid her fingers from my knee to thigh once more to melt away my reason. That barest hint of contact made the current running through my body grow stronger and stronger.

Not good, I can't let this go any further. Before I could be swept away, I restrained my whole being with my reason, grasping Rena-chan's wrist firmly to bring it away from my body. "I said no," I told her.

Rena-chan raised her eyebrows like she was bored. "…Oh."

I stood up and put some healthy distance between us again, like before. She'd be right there in a flash if I let my guard down, so I had to keep my cool.

But Rena-chan looked utterly composed as she eyed me with flirtatious allure. "Then you don't get any more, hmm?" And then she walked off to the living room as if she'd suddenly lost interest.

Despite me being the one to reject her, for some reason, I felt like the one who'd been rejected. It was confusing. "Wh-what the hell…?" *Are all adults like that? No way, that can't be. And hey, what do I do about this dizziness whirling around inside me?*

"Agh! Come on!"

These days, people often tell me things like, *Hey, has something changed about you?* But no matter how you think about it, I'm a normal boy. Aren't I?

* * *

About half an hour later.

Ashigaru-san and the guys had finished their shopping at a nearby supermarket, and we were a few minutes into a party with the four of us, minus Harry-san and Max-san.

We were sitting directly on the floor around the low table in front of the sofa, drinking and sharing alcohol and soft drinks as we chatted. The only topic of the day was my romantic situation.

"—And then I got that message from Rena-chan on LINE." I talked about what had happened between Kikuchi-san and me—basically, our schedules not matching and our falling-out, her finding out about Rena-chan, and my causing her to feel lonely and anxious.

"So then she saw it?" Ashigaru-san prompted.

I nodded. "Yeah… My girlfriend saw that message."

When I finished telling them everything, the room burst out laughing. *What the hell? They're acting like I told them a funny story. Hold on here, I just want to ask them for advice.*

"This isn't a joke, okay!" I insisted.

"Ah-ha-ha! You're so funny, Fumiya-kun."

"If anyone is not allowed to laugh about this, it's you, Rena-chan," I complained.

But she just giggled with even more pleasure. "So meeean."

Uh, no, it's not. At all.

And then she kept acting all familiar, touching her palm to my shoulder and then moving her fingers just a little, until I swept her off.

"But yeah, that was one of the things that caused it," I said. "There was also me going to hang out with friends and walking home with a female friend who gets off at the same station as me—all that made her feel anxious, too, and that wound up causing our falling-out…"

"Ahh, I see," Ashigaru-san quietly remarked, while Rena-chan seemed impressed by something else.

"Huh, so Fumiya-kun gets girls," she said, sounding pleased for some reason.

I felt like they were misunderstanding me a little, but it's true that I had a girlfriend, hung out with other friends, and had been walking home from the station with a female friend… Objectively speaking, I guess that comes off normie-like. My gameplay in life was pretty smooth, if we were just talking form. Though, I don't think that fact in and of itself has much value.

"Even kids in our class have been talking about how it looks like things aren't going well with them," Hinami informed them.

"Wait, really?" I said.

Well, I had asked a number of people for advice, and Kikuchi-san was also asking Izumi-san for advice—it wasn't much of a leap. After all, we were an official class couple, having gotten together through the cultural festival play.

"Huh, so you're making her feel anxious," Rena-chan said enchantingly while touching her index finger to her lips.

"Yeah. And that's not good...," I said.

"Hmm, I don't agree," Rena-chan suddenly commented, leaning aggressively toward me as she did.

"Hmm?"

"What's wrong with keeping her in a little suspense? That's what's fun about relationships," she said with a devilish smile and a spellbound gaze.

"Suspense is fun? How...?" How did we get from that to this? It's too masochistic for me. Well, I really could imagine Rena-chan enjoying anxiety and turning it into pleasure or something—that suited her.

"I *meaaan* like...that anxiety makes your chest so tight, but all you can think about is that person..." Her eyes were glossy from drinking, but deep inside was pitch-black. It was so black that if you touched it, then you would fall right in—maybe forever. "But then when you see them, you're so happy. Just a little contact makes you lose your mind, you know?"

"I-is that how it is...?"

Her expression was one of blissful enchantment, as if she was getting turned on remembering something. "Mm-hmm. Maybe a normal, fun, and stable relationship also works, but...I don't know if that's enough to make it last."

This relationship talk was way over my head, and I couldn't keep up. I was already lost and confused over my very first girlfriend. "But isn't that just you, Rena-chan...?" I said.

"I think all girls are like that," she replied to me with a serious look.

Hinami reacted swiftly to that remark. "Hmm, I don't think I am..."

"Oh, really? It was just me?"

Seeing Rena-chan's response, Hinami teased her in a familiar manner, "So you're a masochist, Rena-san?"

"Hmm, I can go for either. ♡"

"Ha-ha-ha, you're funny."

The two of them were smiling at each other.

But I dunno—those smiles were kinda scary. I don't think they were really being sincere. They were emitting a constant aura of negativity toward the other person at just 10 percent, just at the edges of their words. I didn't think Hinami actually found one single iota of this to be funny.

Rena-chan was smiling as she drank a chuuhai through a straw. Her expression and voice were both utterly syrupy as she said, "Don't you know, Aoi-chan? When you mix anxiety with love, that person becomes all you can think about. Until you lose your mind."

"Hmm...maybe I've never experienced something like that before," Hinami replied.

"Your feelings will destroy your reason, common sense, everything... but that's how you get transformed into the shape of the other person. *That's* the real thrill of love, you know?"

It was hard to describe, but it was like every single one of the words that came out of her were so advanced, I couldn't quite digest them. What she was saying felt extreme, which made me think it might be a bad idea to just accept it unexamined.

It was like Rena-chan was immersed in her own world, can of booze in both hands, as she said:

"That's why I love losing my mind like that—and leaving someone else's head a mess, too."

She spoke in a sweet voice like dribbling honey, and then she smiled. That smile was both intoxicated and cruel.

But Hinami shot back with zero hesitation. "Just so you know, I'm an expert in making messes."

"Ah-ha-ha, that's very you." Rena-chan chuckled. "You act like you'll get close to people, but you won't let them get close to you."

"You might be right about that." Hinami raised one eyebrow.

But Rena-chan studied her for a long moment. "You don't want some-one else to change you, do you?"

Hinami's eyelids twitched. "...I don't. I ultimately want to be the one deciding what I do."

"I figured."

Then reaching slowly into Hinami's softest spots—discovering what she really meant, Rena-chan said, "—So you're a coward?"

That was a somewhat unusual thing to say to Aoi Hinami, top-tier character.

"A coward...?" Though Hinami seemed uncomfortable, her reply was devoid of malice. "More like if I left it to someone else, then they might get it wrong."

"Fair enough. I'm the type who wants to enjoy all of it, that part included."

"I don't want to head in the wrong direction...so maybe we just think differently about those things?"

"Yeah." Rena-chan nodded amicably, sending back an enchanting smile. She quirked her lips up, as if she saw right through Hinami. "I think I've come to understand you a little, Aoi-chan."

"Ah-ha-ha, I hope so." Hinami laughed gently.

But Rena-chan was still staring at her. "Mm. I think you might be a little like me."

"Huh? You think you and I are alike?" Hinami asked brightly.

The corners of Rena-chan's lips raised up. "You know, I want to be acknowledged. I want someone to acknowledge that I have value; I want to be desired."

"Ahh...I can see that."

"Right?"

The way Rena-chan so casually acknowledged something so delicate and personal amid this conflict was scaring me, but maybe that style of talk was easier for those two. Ashigaru-san and I were both watching like referees.

"I think you're more realistic and greedier than me, Aoi-chan, so—,"

Rena-chan said as she suddenly reached out to touch Hinami's cheek with slender fingers.

"—that wouldn't be enough to satisfy you."

Her tone was somehow sensual, but what she was saying was deeply interesting to me.

"...That's right. If I value someone telling me I'm good, then that's just dependence," said Hinami.

Rena-chan smiled like that made sense to her. "I knew it." Then she withdrew her fingers with trancelike slowness and dropped them to Hinami's shoulder. "I love empty girls like me."

Her gaze was calm, a dangerous air still wafting around her despite the smile.

Hinami responded with a smile that was just as composed, perhaps even more so. "Thank you very much. I'm rather fond of myself, too," she said evenly. She was playing the mask, putting on her armor.

That was when the main referee, Ashigaru-san, put a hand to his chin with a *hmm* as he intruded on the discussion. "Aoi-san, it is true that you... How do I want to say this? You have an incredibly unique degree of precision."

"Huh?" Hinami tilted her head.

"Er, I was talking about your playstyle."

"Umm, oh, in *Atafami*? ...I'm told that a lot, but why are you bringing that up now?" Hinami asked, confused.

"I mean," Ashigaru-san said like it was obvious, "your playstyle in *Atafami* reflects your life to some extent."

"Ahh...well, that's true, but..." Hinami trailed off.

"I completely understand that feeling, Ashigaru-san," I said.

"I knew you would, nanashi-kun."

Ashigaru-san and I exchanged a glance full of emotion.

"Aoi-chan...what's up with them?"

"Dunno..."

Huh? I thought Hinami and Rena-chan were glaring daggers at each other just a moment ago, but now they're totally acting like it's girls against boys. But I was also listening with deep interest to Ashigaru-san. I wanted to know how he saw Aoi—and how he saw Aoi Hinami's playstyle.

"Aoi-san," Ashigaru-san continued, "everyone says that you're incredibly precise in all your movements, right?"

"Ah, yeah. They do say that a lot," Hinami agreed.

"I know," Ashigaru-san said so bluntly that Hinami giggled.

"Harry-san told me just today, and nanashi-kun is always saying it," Hinami said.

"Well, you're just so accurate, even though you've referenced my play...," I cut in.

"But I don't think that's quite it," Ashigaru-san commented with a pensive *hmm.*

That surprised me. "Huh? You think?"

If there was any point that was most characteristic of Hinami's playstyle, I figured that was it. Normally, what with the habits of your fingers, the general flow, or just excitement, you would move with some imprecision, but Hinami hardly did that at all. This seemed so much like her "form" that you could say the same about how she conducted herself in life.

"Well, it's not like it's wrong, but I'm not sure it's right," Ashigaru-san said.

"Hmm." I fell into thought. I did want to come up with the answer on my own, based on that earlier talk with Rena-chan, but knowing Hinami for over half a year now, that answer hadn't come to me. It seemed rather unlikely. After racking my brain for about ten seconds, I surrendered. "What do you mean by that?" I asked.

Ashigaru-san looked at me for a while, and then he eventually turned his gaze to Hinami.

The glint of his eyes was neither sharp nor relaxed—just an ordinary temperature, levelly dealing with the information.

"It's not that her movements are precise—it's that there's always a reason for every single one of them."

*   *   *

Maybe what he said wasn't all that different from what had been said before.

But there was something about that subtle disparity that really made sense to me. "...Ashigaru-san. You might have something there."

"Ah-ha-ha. Right."

Ashigaru-san and I once again shared an understanding.

It wasn't that she was precise, but that there was always a reason. I had the feeling that this wasn't just in *Atafami*, but in her whole approach to life as well.

"Hmm...?" But Hinami didn't seem quite convinced.

"Huh? Doesn't look like you're following. Maybe you actually weren't thinking about it that much?" Ashigaru-san asked her smoothly.

Hinami seemed to be having trouble with the question, blinking a bunch at Ashigaru-san. What did this mean?

I was kind of confused by her reaction—I mean, Ashigaru-san's question had been really normal, and I couldn't see anything especially difficult to answer about it. Why would she be this bewildered by it?

"Oh, it's not that...it doesn't make sense, it's just...," she trailed off.

"Mm."

Tilting her head, Hinami said:

"...Why would anyone make a move for no reason in the first place?"

Time stopped momentarily for Ashigaru-san and me.

What we sensed there was nothing other than madness.

"—Ah-ha-ha-ha-ha-ha!" Ashigaru-san burst out laughing in a way I'd never heard before.

"Wh-what...?" Hinami's eyebrows came together like she was embarrassed. She was in heroine mode, so of course part of that was acting, but the fact that she wasn't aware she'd said something strange was probably genuine.

"Ha-ha-ha, I never thought you'd be that far out in the stratosphere," I said in a deliberate attempt to leave Hinami behind.

"…Hmph." She wordlessly prodded at the shoulder she'd punched earlier with her thumb.

"Ow, ow!" *Stop it! That's the third time my shoulder's taken a hit recently. Don't press it if you know it's gonna hurt.*

"What are both of you laughing for? What do you mean?" Hinami said sulkily. Since she was in heroine mode, the gesture was cute and manipulative, but her confusion seemed to be for real. *Ha! Take that for a change!*

"Ah-ha-ha. Umm, look, Aoi-san," said Ashigaru-san, "for most players, the majority of their actions, or almost all their actions, are muscle memory habits, set play, or unconscious behaviors. They're just playing without really thinking about it."

"Huh…?" Hinami still kind of seemed like she was trying to play cute, but I could see past that to recognize NO NAME's genuine shock.

"Of course, the closer you get to the top, the more players will have reasons for their actions…but someone who says they can't even make a move without a reason… Frankly, I don't think I've ever seen that before."

"Umm…are you and nanashi-kun like that, too?" Hinami asked.

Ashigaru-san and I both looked at each other and nodded.

"There's a lot I do based on feel, too," I said. "Of course, when I'm trying to figure out my opponent's next move, I do think about it in a concrete way, but I generally play on a lot of hunches, like *This distance from the opponent feels bad* or *I feel like they're gonna jump right now.*"

"Yeah, me too," Ashigaru-san agreed. "Well, I play Lizard, so it's a little different, but I guess I do have a lot of set plays and habits."

"Really…?"

At first, Hinami had looked like she couldn't believe it, but it seemed she was gradually accepting reality. If anything, I was the one who couldn't accept reality. Just how good at rapid concrete thinking do you have to be to put reasons to every single action at that game speed?

But it was true: Nothing seemed to more accurately describe Aoi Hinami as a person than the idea that she had a reason for all her actions.

I mean—yeah.

Her smiles, voice, and gestures, from the smallest movements to the subjects she talks about—

—there's a reason for all of it. To a frightening degree.

This was the playstyle of Aoi Hinami the player, who controlled the character Aoi Hinami.

"So…I figure that even in a relationship, you wouldn't want someone to get too close and ruin all the reasons you've built up for yourself," Ashigaru-san finished.

"And now we've come full circle." Hinami smiled like that made sense to her.

Though the atmosphere was relaxed, I was surprised. That was just the inner facet of Aoi Hinami that I wanted to know.

"That's probably why you're such a good player. There's a reason for every move you make, and when you can't find a reason, you step back and watch. Then once you're in a situation you recognize, you do what you know is correct for the circumstances." Ashigaru-san fluently verbalized the principles behind her moves, and I was impressed. As the one being described, Hinami probably felt even more so.

"I think," Ashigaru-san continued, "you probably don't like the idea of doing something for no reason or making the wrong move. As Rena-chan just said."

"Well, it's not like I don't get what you mean…," Hinami said, although I could sense some displeasure with the analysis.

Meanwhile, I was surprised by his statement.

Ashigaru-san should largely only know about Hinami's playstyle in *Atafami*.

But he'd just described what sounded like the secret side of the perfect heroine—like he was talking about who Aoi Hinami really was as a person.

But Ashigaru-san wouldn't have ever seen the hidden side of the perfectionist Aoi Hinami. He wouldn't even know that she was NO NAME, with the number two online winrate in Japan.

"But hey, why are we talking about me?" Eventually, Hinami took charge of the situation and changed the subject. Her gaze shifted back and forth between me and Ashigaru-san. "What do you think, Ashigaru-san? About nanashi-kun's relationship!" Taking the lead, she brought us back to something that was easy to talk about.

And with that, she ended the discussion about her, but I suspected the various things that had been voiced there would be clues to uncovering her true nature.

The hidden side that I knew, and her unique traits as seen from others— wherever those intersected, that was where I would find what I wanted to know.

* * *

Some time after that.

Ashigaru-san, now rather drunk, was speaking with just a little more intensity than usual. "...Nanashi-kun, what do you think it means for two people to date?"

Rena-chan burst into giggles. "Ashigaru-san, it's funny when you say it that seriously."

"There's nothing funny about it, though," he said, but he seemed a little shy. He comes off like an adult who has it all together; if Rena-chan could toy with a guy like him, she was downright terrifying.

What it means to date, huh. I mulled over the question he'd thrown at me. "I've thought about the reason for choosing someone to date...but if you're asking what dating itself means, that's a hard one." What had changed between Kikuchi-san and me in going from friends to dating? I tried to think of the specifics as I offered what seemed like an answer for now. "...Like hanging out regularly together or helping each other with your goals and stuff, I guess."

"Come oooon, that's so booooring," Rena-chan said with utter relaxation. She was even more drunk than before.

"B-boring?"

"I mean, Fumiya-kun, a friend could do all that stuff, too," she said.

"Urk...that's true." Yeah. You could also hang out with a friend or help them with their goals; so long as your interests were aligned, you could even do it with a stranger. Those weren't really great reasons to be dating.

Ashigaru-san agreed with Rena-chan. "Yeah. Well, being in a relationship does make those things easier, but it's not like that's *why* you date."

"H-hmm…" *So then, as for something you can only do if you're dating…I can only think of one answer…* "Then…um, it's okay to, uh, cross the line?"

"You mean kissing and sex?" said Rena-chan.

"D-don't be so blunt about it."

But Rena-chan shook her head. "You can do that with friends, too."

"You can…?"

Rena-chan smiled seductively. "The option is right there."

Hey, are you for real? I mean, it is physically possible, but that's just such an adult opinion, even within the world of adults. That world was so far removed from mine that it had to be too early for me to consider that as reference.

"Well," Ashigaru-san said, "that's an extreme argument, but maybe you're right."

"You too, Ashigaru-san?" Now I was in a solo battle. *Hey, Hinami, you're a high schooler, too; you've got to be on my side.* "But…so then is there any other meaning to being in a relationship?" I asked.

Then Rena-chan smiled as if she'd been waiting to pounce. "Umm, well, in my opinion…," she said in her syrupy way, "it's permission to put constraints on each other."

"Constraints…?" This was kind of grown-up in a different sense from before. *This is starting to get a little sordid.* "You mean like…not meeting with others of the opposite sex or stuff like that?" I said.

Rena-chan nodded. "Yeah, yeah. You can't restrict normal friends or *those* kinds of friends, right?"

"Th-those kinds of friends…?"

"Yeah. So your lover is probably the only person who can complain about your behavior." Rena-chan readily expressed her adult opinion.

I was feeling overwhelmed, not even sure if I got it or not.

Meanwhile, Hinami agreed with her. "Yeah, that's what happens when you get a boyfriend. Like, you can't do things you want to do, and you have to do things you don't want to do."

"Ahh! Yeah, yeah, I get that! That's why I don't really want a boyfriend right now."

"Ah-ha-ha, me neither."

And now finally, the dangerous-looking pair of girls had found their common ground. It was great that they'd avoided clashing, but this was the first I'd ever seen Hinami say what a boyfriend was to her.

Then Ashigaru-san jumped in. "Hmm, I know what this is like."

"You mean being tied down?" Rena-chan asked.

Ashigaru-san nodded. "I mean, if you define it as a relationship that's neither friends nor allies…then it's something like what we call doubles in *Atafami.*"

"Ohh, I get it!"

"Uh, no, I don't."

"Those two are weirdos, aren't they, Aoi-chan?"

That made sense to me, but Hinami and Rena-chan took jabs at us. Ashigaru-san and I were on the same wavelength, but those two just didn't understand.

Then after a little hesitation, Ashigaru-san said, "Umm, then to translate it into Japanese…I think it means that you stop being two separate people."

"That's not Japanese, either…and, like, how is that similar?" Rena-chan didn't quite comprehend.

"In doubles, you're part of the same team. In other words, no longer being a separate person means that you gain the right to interfere with their actions. Isn't that kind of like a constraint?"

I nodded at that, like *I get you.*

Hinami and Rena-chan seemed to clue in then, too. "Oh…I see, that's true!" said Hinami.

"Hey, Aoi-chan, don't you think he should have led with that?" Rena-chan complained.

But Ashigaru-san was animatedly talking now. Normally, he's so intellectual, but he's so childlike when he talks about *Atafami.*

"You can interfere with your partner's actions. Since you're in the same unit, you can complain about their friendships, future, or family problems, things that you wouldn't be able to touch if they were just friends—you can even interfere in areas that you might not be able to take responsibility for."

Ashigaru-san was almost thinking aloud at this point, so I took over. "You mean it's possible that they could interfere with your actions, too."

"Uh-huh. That's how it works in doubles."

"Fumiya-kun and Ashigaru-san are sure having a good time," Rena-chan quipped, but what Ashigaru-san was saying made sense to me.

Kikuchi-san wasn't happy about me going to this meetup.

So then if, as Ashigaru-san and the others said, dating meant gaining the right to interfere with your partner's choices—to interfere in the play content of the game that was their life—

—that would mean Kikuchi-san had the right to say she didn't want me coming.

"You're crossing boundaries that you wouldn't be able to if you were two fully separate people, and by doing that, you entrust each other just a little responsibility in life... If there's a reason to become a lover and not a friend, I think that might be it," Ashigaru-san finished.

"Responsibility in life," I repeated, though I wasn't certain about it. I couldn't exactly say he was wrong. But it also didn't seem like those words were correct for me. "Is that what dating is for you, too, Ashigaru-san?"

"Yeah... Am I wrong?" he asked, and I organized my thoughts.

The *Atafami* doubles metaphor did appear to be apt.

But in my mind, dating was a little different. "I dunno, it's like...I think I believe that even if we're dating, if there are things each of us want to do, I'd like to respect those as a higher priority."

Ashigaru-san nodded, folding his arms with a thoughtful *hmm*.

And then to supplement those thoughts, I spoke again. "I think... even dating wouldn't be doubles... Maybe more like someone playing one-v-one with me."

"I get that." Ashigaru-san grasped that right away as his eyes locked on mine, while Rena-chan and Hinami seemed skeptical. "In other words, even if you're a couple, the individual is ultimately the individual, and each person should carry responsibility for their own actions."

"Yes. That's exactly it."

The individual is the individual.

That kind of felt like the basis of the values that I'd always lived by. Even now that I'd opened up my life, that was the one thing that hadn't changed.

"I mean, I think that's the principle of a gamer who fights in an individual competition," I said.

Ashigaru-san nodded like that made sense to him. "I see. So that's what you mean."

Yeah.

In a game, there are rules for everything, and results to everything—and a cause connects those two elements.

The cause is created purely through your own actions.

Winning and losing are your own responsibility. Whether that's due to character compatibility or the character being weaker in the first place, that character choice is still your responsibility. That's the basic principle of the game, and the moment a gamer loses sight of that, you start trying to place the responsibility for the cause of your results elsewhere, hindering your growth.

Having held that position at the top of the leaderboards, I have never once lost sight of my understanding of the individual responsibility one has for their own results, not for even a moment. I'd managed to tell off Nakamura when he blamed the game for his loss even before I started training in the game of life, because that value was so fundamental to me.

"I believe that so strongly that at New Year's every year, I've prayed to get results commensurate to my effort," I said.

"Ha-ha-ha! I see!"

"You really are weird, Fumiya-kun!"

Ashigaru-san and Rena-chan both laughed with real amusement.

But I was serious—this wasn't fishing for laughs. Hinami stayed silent the whole time, taking a bird's-eye view of the scene.

"But I kind of get that," Ashigaru-san said. "I don't think I'd take it to such an extreme, but I figure people who are serious about gaming will be at least somewhat similar in that regard."

Hinami's breath caught for just an instant. I nodded in reply. "Yes, I agree."

I looked back on my life thus far.

I've lived on my own for seventeen years, and it's been just a little over six months since I've started to broaden my view.

Still, the individualistic impulse to take responsibility for my own actions has seeped deep into my heart.

"Nanashi-kun, even if you've felt respect, affection, or gratitude for someone, maybe you've never let anyone get too deeply close to you."

"...Maybe." His words cut close to my darkest areas, but I nodded.

He really was right.

And I'm sure—Kikuchi-san, who was now my girlfriend, was no exception.

"I don't think I've ever entrusted responsibility to anyone, including my girlfriend right now," I mused, and Ashigaru-san nodded with genuine sympathy.

And then with his expression still unchanged, at a level temperature like he was dispassionately writing out proofs with a pencil, he said:

"You might not be cut out for relationships in the first place, nanashi-kun."

It was a harsh opinion, but I couldn't really disagree.

"If you don't intend to play doubles, even though you're dating—if the individual is the individual and you don't entrust any responsibility to each other, then there's no point in being partners, right?" I said.

"Yeah." Ashigaru-san gave a short affirmative. I felt like I'd been checking off his answer sheet.

Rena-chan looked at me with concern. "But doesn't that sting, Fumiya-kun?"

"...I dunno." Ultimately, I wanted the individual to live as an individual. So then being alone is taken for granted in a sense, and I've never thought of that as a negative thing.

Those were the beliefs I'd held when I really fell for Kikuchi-san through the play, found a reason to make that special, and chose to confess to her. None of that meant I was joined with her by fate; if I had to say, it was a manifestation of my own feelings.

And that individualism was the catalyst that turned our opposite and unbalanced "special reason" into a contradiction, undermining our relationship.

Hanging out with each other, sending her home, and coming to school together.

Those were things to do when you're dating, but we could have done them as friends.

Mizusawa had called those things formalities.

"So if everything I'm doing for my girlfriend is just for the sake of form—do you think that's because my stance toward a relationship was that it was a 'formality' to begin with?" I asked with trepidation.

"Formality, huh." Ashigaru-san nodded. "If there's no reason that she has to be your girlfriend, I suppose it would mean that," he said frankly. He wasn't pulling punches, but that was why I was able to understand myself now.

Accepting what he said, I remembered that thing again.

"It's true. If she were to tell me that she didn't want me coming to this meetup—"

That feeling that had overflowed in me then—that emotion—

When I'd told her that I was going to this meetup, that Rena-chan would be there, and that I was going with Hinami, Kikuchi-san had been uneasy about it.

To respect her feelings, I had checked with her first and asked if maybe I shouldn't go.

At that time, she'd said she wanted me to go to the meetup, and that she wanted to support my future—

—but what if she'd said no?

"If that happened, I—I think those feelings would be too much of a burden for me."

*   *   *

I just said it honestly.

I was even surprised at myself—I hadn't realized I felt this way before we'd had this discussion.

But now that we were talking, it made sense to me. Something like the aesthetic that I've always had, playing as nanashi, was alive in it.

"That's because you're a gamer, right?" Ashigaru-san saw through me, drawing a nod from me.

It wasn't just because my future was at a higher priority than my relationship with Kikuchi-san. "As a gamer, I trust my intuition, and I'm proud of it... My own decisions are more important to me than anything else."

My decision to make *Atafami* my life was my own, taken with my own responsibility.

So whether it was a girlfriend, a friend, or even family—I would never allow anyone to stop me but myself.

Now that I was aware of those feelings lurking inside me, I thought of Kikuchi-san.

The two of us were walking toward the doors to the future, and maybe we could become partners walking side by side. Maybe we could become comrades who worked together in the same direction. But the paths we were walking were ultimately in parallel. We could wave at each other across the way, but no matter how much we might say or feel—in my heart, those separate paths would never intersect.

I'm sure we each had separate doors at the end of those paths, too.

This conclusion would never change in my heart.

"Is this weird? ...Do I not care about people or something...?" As I was saying that, I got scared.

I mean, I've never been in a relationship like that with anyone in my life before. Not in the sense of a friend and of course not in the sense of a girlfriend—I've never let someone get close enough that I would be offering up myself.

But if that's something that everyone else takes for granted—if these ten-odd years that I've spent alone have caused me to be missing something inside—if I can't do that anymore—

What if, even after facing life seriously these past six months and transforming my world, this couldn't be taken back? What if it was irreversible?

"...!" My hands and my lips began trembling.

I mean, maybe the values that had been enabling me to believe in myself and continuously put in effort—maybe they had cost something unthinkable.

"Would someone like me not be able to have an actual relationship with anyone?" I asked listlessly.

"Fumiya-kun...," Rena-chan murmured.

Hinami pierced Ashigaru-san with a long, hard look.

Ashigaru-san just watched me with a calm, straightforward expression. There was no hint of pity in his eyes, and I was glad of that.

And then as if he was chiding me—

"If something that's in the minority and generally not well understood is *weird*—then I think that would mean you, nanashi-kun."

"!" I felt something cold stabbing into my chest.

But Ashigaru-san kept going. "On the other hand, speaking personally—" His expression didn't change, but his tone was somehow courteous. "That's not a bad thing, or even a weird thing."

"...Why not?" My mouth opened on its own as I grasped at this thread.

"It's true sometimes people will feel distant from you. They might get hurt in some situations." Finally, Ashigaru-san looked to Hinami and Rena-chan. "The person who likes you might not want to be an individual. They'd want to get closer, to become the same."

"...Yes."

That did ring some bells for me.

You may not mean to hurt someone, but your actions wind up hurting them—I'm sure that's just like how I've tried to get to know Hinami, and how I've been rejected and hurt.

That's born of the difference between the boundary that keeps them detached and the will to push that boundary.

Many people rose in my mind as I slowly nodded.

"And I'm sure you can't accept that," Ashigaru-san continued. "But that isn't necessarily because you've been alone all your life."

"So then why…?" I asked, looking for a light in the darkness.

He remained silent, eyes pointed toward the TV.

Jack, the new character I'd chosen, was standing alone and facing forward, gently touching the mask on his face with one hand.

"I guess you could call it the karma of a gamer, from really only believing in yourself and always putting in the effort."

"…Karma."

That single word lingered deeply and powerfully in my mind.

* * *

The Saikyo Line was running along the Omiya-bound route with me and Hinami aboard.

The earlier discussion must have been lingering in our minds, as we didn't talk much, and all we did was wait for the train to gradually approach the prefectural boundary.

Each *click-clack* of the train wheels rattled the anxiety that had built up in my chest; it was bouncing around wildly, looking for a way out in an answer or excuse.

"…"

"…"

The air between us was cold, unlike the usual relatively comfortable silence. But maybe I was only feeling that because of my own mood.

Unsurprisingly, I was the one who gave in to the silence. "…Hey, Hinami."

"I figured you'd say something soon."

"Hey." Her typical joking got me back to normal just a little. She was wearing her usual confident smile.

"What do you think of that conversation before?" I asked vaguely.

But Hinami seemed to pick up on the implications, as she answered readily, "Nothing much. It's true of any game—others are others, and you are you. You don't have to feel shocked about the way you are."

I couldn't help feeling comforted by the disregard in her answer.

"Plus," she continued, "I hated having to listen to that discussion about whether or not it was laudable. Not that I could say as much back there— but the individual lives as the individual. You don't shift responsibility to anyone else. You make sure to carry yourself and move forward. Is there anything more beautiful? ...There's no reason to deny that."

Her tone was emotional but filled with the strength that enabled her to declare that without hesitation—I felt like if I wasn't careful, I might lean on that strength.

"Ha-ha...you really are a top-tier character," I said.

Hinami's brow furrowed for just an instant, and then eventually, she said like it was obvious, "No, you're just a bottom-tier character. If you can't live your life alone, that's because of a lack of effort and analysis."

Those words once again drew relief and a smile out of me. "...You never change," I said.

Hinami's eyes widened for just a second. And then she shifted her gaze out the window, plucking at the ends of the silky hair that hung to her shoulders.

It was a rare gesture for her. I felt like I'd been seeing a lot of rare things from Hinami lately.

"Yeah...I don't," she said.

Now that her hair was a little away from her face, I caught a tinge of determination in her expression. The hair ends fluttered down again from her fingers, mingling with the rest of the strands until they couldn't be found again—not even by Hinami herself.

"But...isn't that a lonely way of life?" I said, letting my anxieties about the future run free for the moment.

But Hinami moved and just glanced back at me again. "I dunno. But at the very least..."

"What?" I asked back.

She gave me a look of determination—strong, artificial, and yet for some reason, it seemed like an expression of what was inside her.

"...I'm fine with being lonely."

The train arrived at Kitayono.

Before I could reply, Hinami pushed at my back. "Come on, don't zone out."

"O-oh yeah."

"See you at school."

"S-see you."

After she basically chased me out of the train, the doors shut with Hinami aboard to depart for Omiya. Left all alone, I stood there in the middle of the platform and watched the train go.

The passengers who had gotten off the train with me cut by me, ignoring my presence. I stared down the tracks in a daze, where there was no longer any sign of the train to be seen.

I couldn't bring myself to move from that spot.

The night sky was the only one watching me, but hardly any stars could be seen at Kitayono Station.

My fingers should have been warmed by the aggressive heating inside the train, but they were chilled in just a few minutes by the temperature of the nighttime. It was as if there was no blood going through them.

Eventually, remembering what Hinami had said, I almost spat out my reply here, where nothing but the concrete could hear.

"There's no way you're not lonely."

I slowly turned around, and by the time I started walking, there were no longer any passengers on the platform but me.

4

An elven bow pierces weaknesses with high accuracy

It was less than an hour after I parted ways with Hinami.

I was walking the streets of Kitayono alone, staring at the screen of my phone. I was engrossed in the story there—letting it permeate my heart, which had chilled from the amorphous loneliness. Or maybe I was just letting it distract me.

The name of the story was *Pureblood Hybrid and Ice Cream*.
The author's name was Fuka Kikuchi.

It was the new novel she'd talked about that morning in the library a few days ago. I'd found it from a tweet on her writing account a few minutes earlier.

Whether it was from learning about my karma or out of sympathy for Hinami's loneliness, I wasn't in the mood to be absorbing someone else's story, but Kikuchi-san's writing was different. I wasn't ready to be in any relationship with someone who didn't leave us as two individuals. But as Kikuchi-san's boyfriend, and as a fan of her stories, I wanted to read it.

And while I was reading, I recalled what she had said.

"…This story…"

Just like she'd told me, I felt the essence of both *Poppol* and *On the Wings of the Unknown* in this story.

—But it was a little different from what I'd imagined.

It was set in a fantasy world where elves, orcs, werewolves, *yukionna*, and all sorts of races coexisted—thirty-two in total. The main character was named Alucia, a girl who lived in a castle, and she was one of the "bloodless," those who had no blood in their bodies.

"...Alucia."

The name surprised me. She had also been a major character in *On the Wings of the Unknown,* also as a girl who lived in a castle—and that character had also been based on Hinami. In this story, a character of the same name appeared again with completely different characteristics.

And this time, she was the protagonist.

That play had only ever been shown at the Sekitomo High School cultural festival, and there was nothing wrong with using the name again. But if she'd expressly chosen the same name, it had to mean something.

Was it supposed to be like a cameo, or was it a totally different character who just had the same name? Whichever it was, I was sure the story was important to Kikuchi-san, and the themes would be related to her own life.

The sight of Hinami's profile as we'd parted ways less than an hour ago stayed in my mind as I read more of the story.

In this world, members of different species could marry and have children. If an elf and a dragon had a child, they'd give birth to a flying dragon with magical wind-controlling wings, and if a werewolf and a *yukionna* had a child, they would give birth to a snow werewolf covered in white fur and resistant to the cold.

In this world with few barriers and restrictions, Alucia was a "bloodless" girl who had no blood at all.

This meant she couldn't survive on her own. With nothing in her veins, she was unable to create the five elements that were the energy necessary to live in that world, and she would eventually weaken and die.

But that very trait meant she could take the blood of any other species into her body. If she absorbed just one drop of blood using her magical needle, which was thinner than a hair, she could put it in her body, increase her volume of blood, and become any species.

*　　*　　*

The part where Alucia was a girl from a castle was the same as in *Wings*, but I could also sense inspiration from *Poppol* in some of her background.

The part about being able to crossbreed between species was different from *Poppol*, but this gentle world full of different species had to be influenced by *Poppol*. Or maybe that was the kind of world Kikuchi-san wished for... But.

"She takes it into herself and copies it...huh."

That part of Alucia's background was what drew my interest.

Alucia had to take in someone else's blood, or she couldn't wield her power. If you had to nail down what her power was, it was that she was sensitive to the scent and flows of blood; just by being near someone, she could tell what bloodline they had, and with just one drop of blood, she could dramatically increase its volume inside her. Those two powers over blood were what made Alucia unique.

But her powers were ultimately borrowed.

She would temporarily increase the volume of blood from another to gain their power, but once her time was up, it was gone, and she would never get the real thing. She could memorize the powers she'd used more than once during that time, intellectually and reflexively, enough that she would be able to use them somewhat. But they would never be carved into the core of her body as a sense that surpassed knowledge. She would never reach the power of the purebloods, who were said to be the strongest.

But if she wanted to rise up in life, she had no choice but to copy those talented purebloods, gaining their powers as knowledge and reflexes to cultivate herself.

In other words, Alucia was an extreme master of none.

"This...really is..."

The name was part of it, but I would have come to the same conclusion even without it.

In order to produce results in every field, she would meticulously imitate the methods of the top player in that field, and then she continued to prove she was right by virtue of exceptional effort alone.

Just as she had imitated nanashi in *Atafami*, Aoi Hinami had most likely used other examples in her studies, clubs, and personal relationships, imitating them until they became her flesh and blood. She practiced over and over and over until the knowledge became memory, and her brain acquired those movements as reflex.

That was just how Alucia was in the story.

Then Alucia stopped by a town for a board-game event and ran into a mixed-blood boy called Libra.

Having grown up in a small town, Libra didn't even know what his past or his bloodline was—he was a mutt among mutts. As one who didn't know his own species, he was similar to Poppol.

But then Alucia sniffed out the truth.

Being born of such mixed blood meant that Libra had no characteristics of any one species. He was thought to simply be a crossbreed.

But he was not just a mutt—his blood was a special type that had *every single one of all the bloodlines in equal measure.*

Two purebloods gave birth to a half-blood, and that child got together with a half-blood from two completely different species, giving birth to one with an equal mix of four types of blood. And then that person got together with another person of four different bloodlines, giving birth to someone with eight equal parts of different species.

That person had a child with someone else who had eight completely different bloodlines mixed in them—incredible coincidences occurred again and again.

After five generations, a child was born who had a mixture of thirty-two equal parts of the thirty-two races that coexisted in the world—he was not a mutt, but a special bloodline that since ancient times had been called the "Pureblood Hybrid."

Essentially—Libra was the Pureblood Hybrid, born by chance in that little village.

With the authority of the royal family, Alucia scooped up Libra from the village and invited him to the Royal Academy she attended, and so their relationship began—

And the first chapter of *Pureblood Hybrid and Ice Cream* ended.

It felt like the portrayal of Hinami under the name Alucia had been deepened even further than in *Wings*.

I suddenly realized that I'd been standing there in a daze.

I hadn't told Kikuchi-san about Hinami's secrets yet. She shouldn't know the specifics.

But in spite of that.

This story seemed to depict Hinami at her core, her values and the ideology behind her behavior portrayed about as well as my understanding. No, Kikuchi-san was reaching even more deeply in some parts.

* * *

Once I arrived home, I stood at the sink.

I gazed into the mirror, making a smile and then relaxing it, over and over.

This was a weapon I'd been given from Hinami. She must have borrowed blood from a "pureblood" normie and imitated it, and then she had taught me the skill she'd gained as a result. For me, it was one of my skills as "Poppol" for expanding my world, and a mask that gave me the chance to build relationships with people.

I'd never mistaken it for my true nature, but it was a first necessary step to confirming whether the grapes on this vine were sweet or sour. Ever since Kikuchi-san had validated this "skill" during summer vacation, I'd kept this mask on as a means to an end and never forgotten that it was a mask.

Using that skill, I pursued what I wanted to do—creating many goals and relationships.

Some of those had become really important to me and had fit into where I wanted to carry them in my arms.

I couldn't see anything wrong with this, so long as the blood of "what I wanted to do" was flowing in my veins.

But Alucia's "bloodlessness" rose in my mind.

She could become any species—but that was why she couldn't really *become* any species.

Just like Alucia in *Wings*.

Unlike Libra, who had a little bit of every bloodline, she had no blood at all, so the skills she'd obtained would never match with who she really was.

She could only accumulate "correct" knowledge: *If I do this, then things will go well.*

Being first place in everything, but none of those things being what she *wanted* to do—that was Aoi Hinami.

Just what was her ultimate objective?

I lay down in the bed in my room, gathering my thoughts and reflecting on Kikuchi-san's new story, *Pureblood Hybrid and Ice Cream.*

I sent Kikuchi-san a message saying that the game night had ended and that I wanted to talk to her. As soon as I turned off my phone screen, it shone and vibrated.

"Ahhhh!" The sudden flash and buzz made me yelp. *Hey, I was just trying to psyche myself up there.*

It was indeed Kikuchi-san—she'd replied immediately to the message I'd just sent. Had she been waiting the whole time to hear from me?

I opened up the chat screen and checked the message from her.

[*Hope you had fun at the meetup! I can talk any time from now until I go to bed, so please give me a call once you're ready!*]

Her calming holiness was nothing like Rena-chan's ensnaring devilishness. It was like a gentle aura purifying the naughty feelings inside me, and it made me really want to hear her voice.

"O-okay." I stared at my phone screen.

And then with a *here we go!* I called Kikuchi-san.

"…"

The *doo-da-da, doo-da-da* dial sound played over and over, and each time the loop ended abruptly, it made me think that she'd picked up. And then it rang again. I was getting teased by my phone.

Finally, around the seventh ring, Kikuchi-san answered the call. "H-hello!" she said in a slightly shrill voice. Her nervousness came across right with her first word—I could tell that it wasn't just me, and that she was nervous, too.

When I heard her voice, my apprehension suddenly eased. "Hello."

"Oh…that sounds like Tomozaki-kun," she said, sounding kind of soft.

"Ah-ha-ha, what's that supposed to mean? Of course it's me."

"Tee-hee. I got kind of nervous, but hearing your voice makes me feel better," she said. What a kind way to put it.

But I understood the feeling. "…I think I feel that, too."

"Y-you too, Tomozaki-kun?" she asked back.

Oh crap, I thought. *I might have to say something embarrassing again.* "U-um…hearing your voice was kind of a relief."

"—!" An anxiety-inducing silence followed that for a while.

What are we doing, starting off this conversation like this?

"U-um! …I hope you had fun at the meetup."

"I did… Thank you for waiting, too."

"…Oh, it's nothing." I could tell how hard she was trying to respect me.

With just those couple remarks from her, my tiredness from the day began to fade.

And then as if she was steeling herself to suggest something, she suddenly said, "A-ah…um!"

"Yeah?"

"…Are you at home right now?"

I tilted my head at the sudden question. "Uh, umm? Yeah, I'm at home…"

"…R-really?!"

"Uh-huh. What is it?" I asked.

Kikuchi-san was silent for a while, and then as if she was somehow embarrassed— "…I was thinking…I'd like to see your face…"

"My face?"

"I was feeling just a little anxious, so I'm glad I could hear your voice… Um, it made me want to see you."

I was shaken by her honest answer and the word *anxious*, but another part of me was thinking calmly. "…Right now?"

Yeah. Right then, I was at my house. It had to be pretty far from there to where Kikuchi-san lived.

"U-um...LINE has video calls..."

"Oh, really? You know a lot about it," I said, surprised. Well, it's probably common knowledge out in the world, but it was unusual for Kikuchi-san to know. She had to be about as uninformed on normie common knowledge as me.

"Y-yes...I often use it for talking with my little brother..."

"Ohh, I see." Now it was starting to come together. "Huh, wait, Kikuchi-san, you have a brother?"

"I do..."

The image of a little cherub like out of a Western painting rose in my mind, but Kikuchi-san was a normal girl, so that would never happen. He'd just be a boy who kinda looks like her.

"Huh...so I guess that means he's got to be cute." As I was saying that, I realized what I was implying about her, and I choked.

"Yes, he's very cute... Ah."

Kikuchi-san also seemed to notice a second later. "U-um, Tomozaki-kun, why would you say...'that means'...?"

I was totally at a loss, but I had no choice but to answer. "Uhhh, umm, ah." Actually, this sort of thing had been happening a lot lately. I was even developing the theory that Kikuchi-san could be trying to make me say that stuff. Maybe she was the type to make you want to. *Nghh.*

I braced myself and opened my mouth. "U-um...because you're cute, too..."

"...!"

Now the both of us were left speechless. *What the heck are we doing?*

"A-agh, geez! Th-then let's have that video call!" I said.

And so in order to make up for the time I'd made her anxious, we deepened our relationship through the connections of phones and stories.

A few minutes later.

"O-okay."

"Y-yes... Then I've pressed it," she said. When I looked at my phone screen, it displayed a message saying *You've received an invitation to a video call.* A big window with Kikuchi-san's face was showing.

Hold on here.

"?!" One look at that was like getting punched in the stomach.

Kikuchi-san was on my screen. It was indeed, without a question, Kikuchi-san, but—she was wearing her pajamas, which were a little looser than her normal attire.

"Wh-what's wrong?" she asked.

"N-no, it's nothing."

There was no way I could say what was on my mind.

Indeed. That whole day, no matter how I'd tried to sweep it from my head, that immodest photo Rena-chan had sent me that morning and the white, supple skin I'd seen in person when she'd flipped up her sweater had never left my mind. Nor could I forget the ticklish, teasing sensation when she had traced up my thigh with her fingers.

That impact had been carved someplace deeper than reason; even if I tried to think with my head to erase it, the other parts held on to that heat as if they still wanted to see what happened next.

And now Kikuchi-san on my phone was in button-down pajamas with the top two buttons undone. Her chest was more exposed and sensual than usual, and the background behind her was a normal house instead the library where I usually talked with her. Everything about it was so direct and real that it made my heart jump.

I was already sensitive from the continuous assault of those seductive techniques at the meetup, and this was too much stimulation for my brain. "U-um."

"Tee-hee. Hey, Tomozaki-kun."

"U-uh-huh."

With my heart thrown into chaos from impure thoughts, we talked to each other through the screen. I should have been so relaxed right then, but my hands were totally full distracting myself from the stimulation. *Am I spending all my time fighting this stuff lately?*

As I was resisting, the subject of the meetup that day came up.

"So that's why I decided to change my character…," I explained.

"Ohh, the character you use?"

I'd been telling her honestly about how the others at the meetup had been really shocked by the change, and about how Hinami's playstyle in life had been exposed.

The stuff about karma that Ashigaru-san had brought up—I hadn't yet been able to mention.

"...I see. It really does sound right to say there's a reason for everything she does." Having a curiosity in Hinami in particular, Kikuchi-san nodded with deep interest. It seemed less like she was finding out about something new and more like she was confirming something she was already aware of. "Um...Tomozaki-kun."

"Yeah?"

Hugging a mint-colored cushion with a white border, Kikuchi-san lowered her eyes hesitantly as she said, "Do you remember that party after the cultural festival?"

"Hmm? Oh yeah, I remember that."

"...Back then, I spoke with Hinami-san...alone."

"...Ah."

I remembered that moment.

On Christmas Eve. It had been at the cultural festival after-party we'd held at an *okonomiyaki* place in Omiya.

Izumi had made a long-winded address, Takei had been Takei, and I'd talked with Mizusawa about the play and stuff—a lot of things had happened that night.

That was the one thing that still hadn't been resolved in my mind.

"It was in the hallway in front of the washroom, right?" I said.

"Huh? Yes, it was." Kikuchi-san was surprised by my question.

"I saw it from a distance... It stuck with me. Like, *Oh, it's unusual to see you two together.*" And then after that, Izumi had walked by and told me that Kikuchi-san was apologizing to Aoi.

In the end, I hadn't managed to ask either of them about that—why was it coming up now?

Kikuchi-san continued, "That time, I told Hinami-san something similar to what you just said."

"...You mean about there being a reason behind everything she does?"

"Yes," she agreed, and this time, she fixed a serious look on me through the screen. "Um, do you remember this line of Alucia's from the play? There's a part that goes *I have everything. But—that's exactly why...I have nothing.*"

That line had left an impression on me, too. Kikuchi-san must have written that line with firm intent; when Hinami had said that line in the performance, you'd think she wasn't even acting.

"Actually, during the after-party, Hinami-san came to ask me more about what that line meant."

"Huh? She did?" I was surprised to hear that.

As part of her mask of the perfect heroine, she does often start up casual chats with different people. But that's exactly why I assumed she would never choose to touch on any topics that seemed dangerous, in particular those areas that could threaten her mask.

And the content of that play was exactly that sort of delicate subject.

"Yes. It really is a little surprising, isn't it?" Kikuchi-san said.

"...Yeah."

Kikuchi-san shared my surprise, but I didn't think she was as surprised as me. I mean, for Hinami to step into that dangerous position herself— that meant that she was really curious about the truth of the matter.

"So then what did you tell her, Kikuchi-san?" I asked eagerly, and she squeezed her cushion tight.

"That there's nothing that Alucia really loves...and her own validation of herself isn't enough."

I had nothing but astonishment for what Kikuchi-san was saying at this point.

"And that's why I think she wants proof that it's okay for her to be like this."

I immediately realized what Kikuchi-san was trying to say.

"Proof that it's okay for her to be like this? That means—"

"Yes, um—I think it might be something like a reason for her actions," Kikuchi-san explained, as if she was talking about a character she had written—or telling a story. "That's why she pursues standard values, like winning a prize or first place—"

I was more than just a little surprised.

It was as if she was giving concrete motives to the themes and actions of Alucia, as represented in *Pureblood Hybrid and Ice Cream*.

"I think she finds the correct 'reason' in her value being acknowledged by society."

Over the past six months, I'd had an ongoing view of the secret side that Hinami hardly ever showed to anyone—and this was the inner world that I'd only just grasped an abstract outline of.

Kikuchi-san had interviewed some people, observed her, and heard some things from me for the play.

But from just that alone—would she get so incredibly close to my own evaluation of her?

The bloodless girl Alucia, who tried to learn every pureblood skill in order to survive, rose in my mind. She needed another's power because she had no blood flowing in her own body. She was empty.

"...I can't believe...you figured all that out," I said.

"Yes. From interviewing her, and thinking, and then..." With clear eyes, as if she was bringing everything in her field of view into focus, Kikuchi-san said:

"I tried making Alucia move through her world."

I started thinking.

That time, reading the playscript—and maybe that day, reading her new novel.

I really did believe Kikuchi-san had talent as a writer. And maybe I also thought that for the sake of her stories, she could even break into Hinami's dark inner world. That sort of nerve she had to expose people's true nature through observation would be an asset for creating.

But I'm sure that wasn't all.

I mean, there was still one more thing inside me that felt off.

"And you told that…to Hinami?" I asked.

What Kikuchi-san had said just now was a relentlessly probing hypothesis. Nobody would ever have said that to Hinami, not even me.

Worst case, she might have been overstepping, and she'd said all that to Hinami's face. It was baffling that the gentle and reserved Kikuchi-san would do such a thing.

I mean, even if Hinami had been the one to ask her, the more correct Kikuchi-san's deduction was, the greater the violation it would be of Hinami's privacy. Kikuchi-san had to know that.

"I wasn't sure whether I should tell her, but…" Kikuchi-san's gaze wandered around uncomfortably, and then she looked at me as if she'd made up her mind.

The next words that came out of her mouth—completely changed my personal image of Kikuchi-san.

"I thought if I talked about it—maybe I could dig up the other side of her that she hides."

While her tone was reserved, there was a quiet pressure in it.

A normal person would probably think her priorities were crazy.

Exposing the soft inner spots that someone had been hiding—digging into them to try to drag out what was there—

—it was starting to feel extreme.

"Kikuchi-san…do you want to keep learning more about Hinami?" I asked.

She reached a hand off-screen to pick up a big stack of A4 papers—they had to be a manuscript she'd written. Then she looked at me, and after a moment's hesitation, she spoke.

It didn't seem like she was hesitating about what the answer was—just about whether she should tell me. That was the feeling I got.

"Yes. I'm sure that what I want to write is there."

*   *   *

Kikuchi-san answered clearly, and I felt like her writer's eyes were looking through the screen at my eyes—and into their depths, where Hinami lay.

Eventually, she seemed to snap out of it with a start, then returned the stack of paper to her desk and tossed the cushion onto the bed.

I'm surprised she does things like that at home.

"...! I'm sorry, I keep talking about myself...," Kikuchi-san said.

"Ah, no, that's totally okay..."

She was so different when she was showing consideration compared with when she was trying to expose Hinami's true nature. I still didn't know how I should respond.

As we were talking, Kikuchi-san finally said with some level of impatience, "U-um, Tomozaki-kun...I really can't..."

"...Can't what?" The sudden remark left me confused, and I couldn't help reading something seductive into the heat of her voice. With the coals smoldering all this time, the fire got lit again so easily.

"Um, couldn't I see you tomorrow...?"

"Huh?" The invitation had come out of nowhere. "Where's this coming from?" I asked.

Kikuchi-san blushed bright enough that I could tell even through the screen. "Umm...I thought if we had a video call, I'd be able to resist the urge to meet up with you..."

"U-uh-huh."

"But seeing your face...made me want to see you even more."

"..."

Her directness made me heat up even hotter. Just seeing her face made me want to meet up, too, but some of my reasons for that were a little difficult to tell her. My face and body were hot enough that I could feel it.

"But I told you before, tomorrow's...," I began.

"Ah...oh, yes, of course."

I'd made plans way back to go to Spo-Cha with a bunch of people from class. I'd refused an invitation from Kikuchi-san for it, too.

"But...what should I do?" I wasn't sure.

I'd never ranked out my priorities before—I'd always just put whatever appointment was made earlier first. It was the simplest rule to decide my plans. I think you could call this sincere in a sense, but right then, I was remembering what Mizusawa had said.

He'd said I was just taking all comers and watching when they slipped from my grasp, and that I wasn't choosing what to drop.

What I could hold in my hands was limited, and if I tried to pick everything, then eventually, something would spill out on its own. But I'd only ever chosen to take things on; I'd never been prepared to set aside those things I couldn't carry.

…So then.

"Maybe I'll make some time for you tomorrow, after all," I said.

"Huh…? Um, but…" Kikuchi-san hesitated as she spoke, but she couldn't hide the gladness in her tone. With her values, she normally wouldn't want me to turn down other promises I'd made for her sake. But she was showing me what she wanted now. That had to be because I'd hurt her, even if I hadn't meant to—because it had become harder to believe we had a relationship special enough to inherit the badges.

Right now, I should gradually be putting an order ranking on those burdens I couldn't carry.

When Kikuchi-san gave me a questioning look, I declared with confidence, "It'll be fine. I think if I tell everyone, they'll understand. Besides… the couple who are going to receive the old school badges of destiny can't be having a fight before the big event, right?" I went ahead and used the chance we'd gotten from Izumi.

Kikuchi-san giggled. "Tee-hee, that's true." There was heat in her voice again. "I'm glad…you'd choose me."

After we told each other our plans, we decided on a time. I wasn't sure how I should explain things to everyone, but honesty and directness would probably be best.

"S-so then, tomorrow…," she said.

"Yeah."

"G-good night!"

"Yeah, night."

And then I hung up the phone, and we both went back to our days. When our connection was severed, maybe we really did live as different species. But the distance between us was connected by a world called fiction.

"...All right."

I still didn't know if just talking like this would be enough, and I was sure I hadn't found that special reason in a real sense, either. Maybe what we were doing was really just treating the symptoms of the problem. But despite the awkwardness, filling up the rift between us seemed necessary for our relationship.

But as a separate issue...

"～～～～!"

...my body was already in the danger zone.

The heat in Kikuchi-san's voice when she said things like *"I really can't"* and *"I want to see you,"* her face through the screen, with a childlike air lingering in it, and her more careless and open dress than usual—

That had been enough to once again set fire to this impulse that had been smoldering right on the verge since that morning—to put it simply, it was getting pretty dicey for me, as a guy.

I buried my face in the bed and flailed around, but I was also kind of relieved. Until now, I'd only ever gotten this kind of feeling about Rena-chan, who would hit on me directly...but now I was feeling it for Kikuchi-san, who was actually my girlfriend. That had to be a healthy thing, right?

...But be that as it may.

"～～～～!"

I was still suffering.

* * *

The next day.

"Tomozaki-kun!"

I was meeting up with Kikuchi-san at Kitayono Station.

"...Hello."

"Mm, hello."

We exchanged our usual conscientious greetings, then came up side by side in front of the station.

Kikuchi-san was wearing a long brown coat with a beige scarf wrapped around her neck, and the skirt peeking out from the bottom of the coat as well as the socks coming up from her black leather shoes were also browns of slightly different hues. Her color-coordinated outfit was beautiful, reflecting her otherworldly character in reality.

By the way, I was just about out of clothing that Kikuchi-san hadn't already seen, so I was wearing the Chesterfield coat I'd bought when I was out shopping with Hinami. My socks and scarf matched like before. *Thank you, Hinami-sensei.*

We were headed to an Italian restaurant that had good salad. I'd visited a bunch of times, since Hinami had brought me there.

"Okay, then let's go," I said.

"Right."

"This way!" I escorted Kikuchi-san in as bold, bright, and manly a way as I could. At first, when Kikuchi-san and I had gone to see a movie together, I hadn't been able to manage this kind of thing at all, but now I could do it somewhat naturally.

After a few minutes' walk, we came to the restaurant. I opened the front door, received a greeting from the staff, and told them, "Reservation for Tomozaki." With that, Kikuchi-san and I went on in. By the way, I hadn't said that line very much, so I recorded it beforehand to practice and cover all my bases.

"Wow, the atmosphere here is so nice and calming," Kikuchi-san said.

"Right? I like the salad here..."

We were going to a restaurant on Kikuchi-san's request, but she hadn't specifically picked this place out.

When I'd asked her where she wanted to go for the date that day, she'd asked to visit the place I liked best, so here we were. I had some attachment to this restaurant, and it was just legit really good. Hinami was fond of it for a reason, and she's fussy about food.

"So this is your favorite place...," said Kikuchi-san.

"Yeah," I said, pretending I was used to it as I opened up the menu.

Even if I had actually come to this restaurant a number of times, I couldn't help but get fidgety amid all the chicness. Still, I was trying not to show that. "There's a pasta lunch and a salad lunch... If you can't eat that much, then I recommend the salad. It's really good..."

"Ohh!"

And so in that vein, I told Kikuchi-san what I knew. But I didn't babble on too much, just bringing up what I could talk about enjoyably. I'd spoken too much on prepared topics during summer vacation, and it had made conversation harder.

Once we ordered the pasta lunch and the salad lunch, we chatted as we waited for their arrival.

* * *

"I never thought salad could be this delicious...!"

"Right? It's so good... It's been a while, but it's just how I remember...!"

We were enjoying our time together and some really great food. It makes me really happy to be able to share something I like with someone I like.

"I'm glad I got the chance to eat this with you," I said. Telling her my honest feelings made me feel a little warm.

"Th-thank you very much..."

And then suddenly, the subject of the meetup the day before came up. "U-um...about yesterday...," Kikuchi-san began. "Was that girl there yesterday, too...?"

"Ahh..." She was definitely talking about Rena-chan. I hadn't been sure what to do about that the day before, so I'd chosen not to bring it up.

But if Kikuchi-san was going to ask, then I couldn't lie. "Yeah. She was there."

"O-oh, I see...," Kikuchi-san said, smiling to hide her discomfort. I could see she wasn't sure if she should ask any further.

"Umm..." I hesitated. How much should I tell her about what had happened with Rena-chan?

It would be easy to just tell her everything, but I wasn't really certain if that would be good for either of us. Still, conveniently hiding it wouldn't be very sincere.

I decided to try asking her. "Do you want to hear the details about what happened? ...I don't think I've done anything I shouldn't, but I don't think all of it would be pleasant to hear about."

Kikuchi-san's lips trembled a little in fear before she took the bull by the horns. "Umm...I want to hear as best I can."

"...Okay." I nodded and decided to tell her all about how Rena-chan had acted at the meetup.

I told her that Rena-chan was a twenty-year-old woman and aggressive enough to nonchalantly talk about friends with benefits. That at the meetups, she would come close to me and stuff, and that she was probably pursuing me. That she had directly propositioned me and kind of...used her body as part of her strategy.

"S-so that's the sort of person she is..." Kikuchi-san was clearly shocked.

I mean, yeah—you don't really see that type of person among high schoolers, and since Rena-chan had once called when Kikuchi-san was there, Kikuchi-san had even seen her face. Rena-chan was very conventionally attractive, so it would be no wonder if Kikuchi-san saw her as kind of a threat.

So I honestly told her how I felt, to put her at ease. "But I did tell her that I have a girlfriend, so I'm not doing that stuff with anyone but y..." I started to say *you*, then noticed what I'd said.

It seemed Kikuchi-san noticed that at the same time. "W-with me...!"

Yep. It had been indirect, but I'd wound up saying basically that I planned to do that stuff with Kikuchi-san. *Hold on, is this okay? Saying something like that to the pure Kikuchi-san—I'm not going to get arrested, am I?*

"U-um... You mean..."

"Ahh! Um! Err! I-it's nothing!" I covered for myself incredibly badly, panicking all the while.

Kikuchi-san seemed to wilt. "I-is it nothing...?"

"Huh?"

"Am I really not…?" Then she lifted her head, and for some reason, there were tears in her eyes. "Do boys prefer sexy girls like that…?"

"H-huh?!" That wasn't like Kikuchi-san at all.

"N-no, you're actually…," I started to say.

But she must have been remembering the icon of Rena-chan's she'd seen that time, as her head was hanging as if she was looking down at herself. "But…I don't have…" Her voice sank, as if she was feeling down. She looked up again, eyes dewy. "Um…that sort of…charm…"

"!" Those tears were ready to spill over now. I had to do something before they did—or I wouldn't be able to wipe them away.

I had to make sure they wouldn't fall.

What rose in my mind then was, as always, my real feelings.

Before I knew it, I was yelling, "Th-that's not true!"

It was too strong to resist.

"I—I *do* see you that way! Okay?!"

The moment that was out of my mouth, the world stopped.

My thoughts stopped; Kikuchi-san stopped; everything stopped.

Only one thing was changing—the color of our faces was rapidly reddening with unprecedented speed.

Eventually, once Kikuchi-san's face had become as red as it could possibly be, her mouth opened with a *pop*, like she was going to explode. "Wh-when you say it right to my face like that…!" Shrinking in on herself, she looked up at me; there were still tears in her eyes, but they were filled with much more heat than before.

And then she asked for details. "Um…like when…?"

You know, it had crossed my mind before, but I think she wants to hear this stuff after all.

But I had to tell her so she could stop worrying, my own embarrassment be damned. "U-um…like yesterday when we were doing a video call…your outfit was different from usual."

"~~!" Kikuchi-san turned sideways and covered herself with her arms.

She glared at me huffily, though I could see she was a little glad.

"…You're dirty."

With that one remark, I came to see Kikuchi-san—uh, well—even more that way. W-well, that's healthy, so it's fine, right?!

* * *

And so we finished eating our desserts, and we were drinking tea after the meal.

"That was really good," Kikuchi-san said.

"Right? I like this place," I replied. It was nice sharing our honest and open opinions as we digested a moment of happiness.

"The tea is also really good. This has been a wonderful time."

"I'm glad I got to eat with you, too."

"M-me too."

I'd had this food a number of times, but it's always a little different depending on who you're with. Of course, it was fun coming with Hinami, too, but with Kikuchi-san, it was kind of like, I dunno—like being rocked in the gentle flow of time, sharing its warmth. When I was with Hinami, it felt like both parties bringing sharp weapons to have a duel.

"Okay, then shall we get going?" I suggested.

"Yes, let's go."

Right when we were about to get up out of our seats…

"—Huh? Fuka-chan and Tomozaki-kun?"

…a familiar voice, made to sound bright and cheery, reached my ears.

"Huh?"

When I turned around, I was surprised to see Hinami. Her appearance was so unexpected, my shoulders wound up jolting a lot. *Huh? Hold on, is she some kind of mythic beast that gets summoned whenever you think of her?*

"Oh, Aoi, are these two of your classmates?" A woman in her thirties or forties was standing behind Hinami and speaking in a classy, friendly tone of voice. Beside her was a girl with a youthful face who resembled Hinami a lot...which meant—

"Um...are you Aoi-san's mother and little sister?" I asked. Since I was talking to her mother, I managed to remember to say *Aoi-san* without too much awkwardness, which felt like progress.

The women smiled like a child and nodded. "Yes. Thank you for always being a good friend to Aoi."

"O-oh, no, she's the one always helping me out."

"M-me too... Um, I'm Fuka Kikuchi."

"Ah, and I'm Fumiya Tomozaki," I introduced myself like Kikuchi-san did, and Hinami's mother smiled back with crinkles around her eyes.

She was wearing a long black coat with a classy texture over a white turtleneck, and a necklace with white, fancy pearl-like decorations. Her comportment and expression were very warm overall, and she seemed more youthful than her age and general appearance suggested.

"Thank you for introducing yourselves so nicely. I hope you'll continue to be kind to Aoi." Her tone was genuinely friendly as she smiled again. That smile wasn't like the one Hinami gave in Sewing Room #2, but closer to the perfect heroine she was in class. But at least to my eyes, it didn't seem artificial.

"Go on, Haruka," she prompted, and the girl beside her turned to us.

"Um, I'm Haruka Hinami! Thank you for being a good friend to my sister!" she said in a slightly formal tone, then bobbed a bow. Guessing from her appearance, I figured she was in middle school. Her tone struck me as quite childish for that age, but maybe middle schoolers just seem childish to high schoolers in general.

"And that's the younger sister, Haruka. I'm glad you could meet," her mother said in a mischievous tone. She really was friendly, and I already liked her, even though we hadn't spent long talking.

"What a coincidence! You just leaving?" Hinami addressed me in perfect heroine mode, perhaps because Kikuchi-san was also there.

"Yeah, we are," I replied, but my gaze was flicking over to Hinami's mother and little sister. *So this is Hinami's family.*

They were— Hmm. They looked like a warm family; that stuff

Kikuchi-san and I had heard from Hinami's elementary school classmate, that her parents were attention-getting, made sense now.

"Okay, then see you at school tomorrow!" Hinami said.

But her mother opened her mouth with a giggle. "Aw, we could talk more."

"It's *fine!*"

It was basically a very natural exchange between a parent and child, and it was normal to not want your classmates to see you with your parents—if you ignored the fact that we were talking about Aoi Hinami.

...But.

"Yeah, okay," I said. "Let's get going, then."

"Y-yes!" Kikuchi-san followed.

"Bye, see you tomorrow."

"See you another time, Hinami-san."

And so the two of us paid and left the restaurant.

"What a cute couple."

"Ah-ha-ha, right? I heard they started dating just recently—"

I caught the voices of the Hinami family coming from behind us. Even as I faintly overheard them, I was just thinking one thing.

So Hinami puts that face *on with her family, too.*

* * *

We wandered the winter streets of Kitayono for a while.

It was the station closest to my house, so you'd think I would be used to walking around this area, but as soon as I left my usual route, it was like venturing somewhere new. Well, it is the closest station to home, so I actually don't spend much time here, aside from the road to the station.

Kikuchi-san was walking slowly at my side; her feet were clapping on the pavement as if she was kicking out her toes for every step. She was humming so quietly that even I could barely hear, and her cheerful gait made me think of a little girl. Her round-toed leather shoes gleamed under the winter sunlight, and the hem of her long skirt swayed gently in the wind.

Watching my girlfriend out the corner of my eye, I was fulfilled. Ashigaru-san was probably right that I couldn't let people aside from myself—like Kikuchi-san—deep into my life. But even if we did have conflicts sometimes, just chatting like this and walking side by side—this relationship made me happy.

So isn't that enough? Or was thinking that the exact karma we'd been talking about?

"You know lots of wonderful restaurants, Tomozaki-kun."

"Hmm? I do?"

Kikuchi-san spun around, and then she said with a mixture of cheer and respect, "Yes! There was that café in Omiya, and that restaurant today was also wonderful!"

"Ah…"

"I can always get to know something new and wonderful, and I have a really fun time when I'm with you," she said, smiling.

I was happy to see her happy, but my feelings were just a bit complicated. Since…

And just as I was thinking about it, I was hit with a question about that very reason. "How do you find these places?" she asked.

The answer to that was— Well, it wasn't really a terrible thing, but it was a little hard to say to her. "Um…I've been to the restaurant today a few times with Hinami, so that's how."

"…Hinami-san." Kikuchi-san's steps came slightly closer together. The cheer slowly left her stride, and she blinked a few times at me with unease.

Urk, knew it.

"I—I see. That's why earlier…"

"Um…yeah."

Yeah. I'd almost thought it was an incredible coincidence to run into Hinami there, but Hinami had been the one to tell me about that restaurant. And if it was her favorite as well, then of course it wouldn't be strange for her to come with other people. In fact, maybe it was her mother who had told her about the place to begin with.

"Umm, so then the restaurant in Omiya…" Kikuchi-san trailed off.

"Ahh..." I realized again.

Now that she mentioned it, that café was the same. "Umm...I've never actually gone there with her, but the one to tell me about it...was Hinami."

"O-oh, really...?" Kikuchi-san's feet stopped flat. "Before...you two came to my workplace together, too."

"Ah..."

At around the very beginning of all this life-gaming business, Hinami and I had visited a café where Kikuchi-san had coincidentally been working... Thinking about it now, Kikuchi-san was the only classmate who had actually witnessed Hinami and me hanging out one-on-one.

"Back then...you weren't yet friends with everyone, were you...?" Kikuchi-san realized.

Yes, that was back before I'd become friends with my classmates, so it would have seemed especially strange.

But there was a reason for that.

"Um, Kikuchi-san." That's why I wanted to invite Kikuchi-san to *that place* where it all was. "There's a place I want you to come tomorrow morning."

"In the morning... Not the library?"

I nodded. "There's a classroom...and I want to tell you something there. That's the place where I want to tell you, if possible."

Then after considering a while, Kikuchi-san seemed to figure it out. "Is this about...Hinami-san?"

I was surprised, but I looked straight at her and nodded. "You know how we talked about Hinami and my relationship recently? I asked her, and now it's okay to tell you."

"...!" Kikuchi-san's expression carried mixed expectation and apprehension.

"So tomorrow—I want to tell you everything there," I declared clearly.

"I understand...!"

I'd been unable to talk about the reason things were special between Hinami and me. Being able to tell Kikuchi-san about it would be important for our relationship. "And then finally...you can know, too."

But then.

Perhaps reacting to my words, suddenly Kikuchi-san seemed to be bracing herself. "I...want to know more about you..."

"...About me?"

She nodded. "It's sort of like—even though I'm dating you, I feel like I don't know anything about you..."

"Th-that's not true..."

She shook her head, head tilted downward. "You've talked to me about so much, but it's all just things you've heard...and I think, um, we've spent less time together compared with when we first met." She seemed to be struggling to say it, gazing into my eyes awkwardly. "I want to be the person who knows you the best..."

Those sweet words were like a numbness concussing my brain, melting me from the eardrums in.

"Since...I'm your girlfriend...," she added softly.

"...!"

Her charming eyes and the way her fingers fidgeted with uncontrollable anxiety drew me in. She had such a strong gravitational pull, it made even a bottom-tier character like me feel compelled to protect her.

"S-so, um..." Still looking downward as she stood by my side, she looked up at me—

—and with her slim, white fingers, that girl who was so dear to me plucked the cuff of my coat.

"Can I...go to your house now?"

The pink that tinged those round and soft-looking cheeks was infecting me again.

* * *

And so that brought us to my house.

Yes. Not me—it was *us*.

"...P-pardon me!" Voice squeaking, Kikuchi-san came into my room behind me, posture timid as her eyes darted around. My parents and little sister were out, so it was just me and Kikuchi-san there.

"Ahh...umm..." Never mind my voice squeaking; I couldn't even get full words out. My heart was going exactly five hundred million times normal speed, and even in my own room, I didn't even know where to sit anymore.

I figured I'd sit on the bed for now, but that might lead to Kikuchi-san sitting down beside me or something, which made me feel like *whoa*. So I avoided that and sat on the floor, leaning back against the bed but keeping my back ramrod straight while I tried to organize my thoughts. Hinami-sensei said that changing your posture will change your mindset, after all.

Kikuchi-san imitated me and sat down a little ways away from me, timidly facing forward. She was completely frozen stiff, but of course I couldn't look her in the eye, either.

I couldn't really think of anything to say, so I tried just making sounds for starters. "Uhh...um."

"Y-yes...?"

But nothing would come out with my mind this scrambled, and the pressure created by the weird beginning to this made me go entirely blank, body and mind.

"Uhh...umm," I tried again.

"...Yes?"

"Uhh...so basically..."

"M-mm-hmm...?"

When I was totally unable to proceed—

Suddenly, the door to my room opened. "Fumiya, I'm home. Is there any laundry...? Huh?"

Standing in front of my room was my mother, who was supposed to be out, carrying the laundry basket. Her gaze was shifting back and forth between me and Kikuchi-san beside me.

Eventually, she put on a smile. "Oh, you had a friend over. Well, take it easy." Still with that smile pasted on her face, my mother closed the door. A few seconds after, I could hear the thudding of her going down the stairs. "F-Fumiya with a girl... Wait, nobody's home!" It seemed my sister and father hadn't come home yet, so my mom had wound up bouncing around on her own.

What the heck is she doing?

"U-um..." Kikuchi-san seemed completely embarrassed, and I was, too.

But I was less nervous compared with before. We even had something to talk about now. "Ah-ha-ha...sorry, my mom is always like that," I said in a joking tone.

Kikuchi-san's eyes widened for a second, and then she giggled. "She's funny."

We looked at each other and giggled together this time. *All right, we're relaxed now.* So the mom helping out when you bring the girlfriend home is a thing that happens IRL, huh? I've only ever seen that in manga, so it was very new to me.

But...

"Umm, wh-what should we do...?" I stuttered.

"R-right!"

The two of us had come here because Kikuchi-san had said she wanted to know about me. But now that we were here, what should I talk about? I'd already shared my secret with Hinami, which was the biggest thing, and I couldn't think of anything else I hadn't told her about.

"Umm...ah." And then she glanced over to the monitor on top of my desk. "Your favorite thing is that game, right...?"

"Yeah, that's right." That question came from an unexpected angle, but I was really confident in that area. I gave a sharp nod.

"So...I'd like to know about *Attack Families*."

"Huh?"

"I'd like to...play with you."

"Huh?!" I yelped. But my surprise wasn't at all negative—it was a shout of total glee.

Now I could play a game I liked with someone I liked. What could be better?

While I was frozen in bliss, Kikuchi-san tried to fill the silence "Um... since you..."

"Mm?"

And then as if recalling a happy time of her own—

* * *

"Since you learned about Andi's books, too."

"Ah…"

That was when I realized.

Our relationship had begun from a misunderstanding that I also read Andi's books, but then I had actually read them and learned about how good they were. I'd gone to the movie with Kikuchi-san, bought the new book and everything—and then before I knew it, it had become a very important thing that connected the two of us.

"So I'd like to know, too. About…the things you like." She was a little shy, but her smile was warm as an embrace. She was so incredibly precious.

"All right!" I pulled the controllers, which were still plugged in, off the shelf and switched on the game console. "Then let's play together. I'll teach you anything."

"Tee-hee… You are number one in Japan, after all."

"Ah-ha-ha. That's right!"

Watching the screen excitedly, I eventually realized.

I wasn't quite sure, but…

Maybe Kikuchi-san was trying to get closer because of our falling-out.

Before long, the familiar opening theme played on the monitor, and a video played on screen of the many characters who appeared in *Atafami* showing off their special moves as they ran all over the place.

"Umm, this is an action fighting game starring a lot of popular characters from different franchises—," I explained as I moved on through the appropriate screens. Kikuchi-san was listening and hmming like she was very interested in what I had to say. I kept talking and talking, having a great time.

I gave her the whole rundown, beginning with the history of the initial creation of the game, and then how it became popular in the fighting-game scene, to its popularity as a simple party game. The words just kept coming and coming, even stuff that I maybe didn't need to explain.

"—and that depth and broad appeal is what makes it one of the greatest games of all time… Ah!"

Eventually, I realized.

Kikuchi-san was listening with such a bright smile on her face, so my otaku blood was all heated now. I'd been gesturing wildly, like I was making a speech. *Calm down, man. We haven't even started; what am I doing here?*

"...Oh, s-sorry, I talked too much," I said.

Her eyes went wide for a moment, and she stared blankly before smiling as if granting me a pardon from heaven. "Not at all. Please...tell me more." She was even accepting my uncontrolled infodumping.

"She's an angel..."

"Huh?"

I'd said it in my head a bunch before, but the word had probably never come out of my mouth. Now it had. I mean, I can't help it. It was like being embraced by the light.

My remark surprised her, and she turned away and fiddled with the end of her hair shyly, then looked up at me with a slightly huffy expression. And then in a quiet and sweet voice: "Please...that's too much."

Her manner stirred up so much protective instinct, I was just about ready to drop my controller. But this tool would eventually be needed for my career, so I firmly readjusted my grip, took some deep breaths, and looked at her one more time.

Kikuchi-san blushed even harder than before, and her holy aura kicked up a level. "...Please don't look at me so much. I'm getting shy."

"She's a fairy..."

"P-please, come on!"

And then I lost my mind again.

* * *

A few minutes after that.

"H-hya! ...Huh?"

"Ah-ha-ha, you probably got the wrong button."

Kikuchi-san and I were holding controllers in front of the monitor, trying out characters in training mode.

When you think about it, this situation—a girl coming to your room to be alone with you—is a pretty drool-worthy situation for a high school boy. But once we started *Atafami*, I became a gamer and nearly forgot about all that, just enjoying gaming together with Kikuchi-san.

When she made that enthusiastic *hya!* Victoria on the screen didn't do anything in particular. Kikuchi-san was probably pushing the wrong button. Actually, there shouldn't be any buttons in *Atafami* that don't do anything, so maybe she didn't even press anything to begin with. Also, Victoria is the character Rena-chan uses, so I was kinda wishing she'd choose someone else.

"Not like that; here," I said.

"Here...hya." Then Victoria made her magic wand shine, shooting an attack ahead of her. "I—I did it!"

"Great!"

"W-was it?!" Kikuchi-san was glad, eyes sparkling.

If we're talking about mechanics, all she did was press the A button, but she was glad, so I decided to give her lots of praise. I'd keep on spoiling her. The Tomozaki-style *Atafami* school encourages positive reinforcement.

"Umm, so then next..." As I was thinking, I was randomly tapping away to move my character around, and I noticed Kikuchi-san watching it with surprise.

"Wh-what's that way you're moving...?"

"Oh, it's nothing, just a habit..."

On the screen, Jack was doing short hops and wavedashing to jump and slide around over and over. I was doing it completely unconsciously. But even an amateur would see that these were very subtle movements, so it was no surprise she'd be weirded out. Way back, I think Izumi was weirded out by these movements, too. Though these days, she's a student of mine.

Eventually, Kikuchi-san's gaze dropped to my controller. Given the relationship between the number of button inputs corresponding to a single movement, my fingers were probably moving with such precision that it was a little freaky. *My fingers are moving even more weirdly than the character on screen, huh.*

"...How much did you practice to be able to do that?" she asked.

"Huh? I'm not sure... But if we're talking just about getting the movements down, then I think it was about a week… If you mean until I could do it unconsciously in a match, I guess about a month."

"Ohh…" Kikuchi-san nodded like she was impressed. "How much have you practiced the game overall?"

"Uhh, I dunno… I guess about ten thousand hours?" I said casually.

"T-ten thousand…" Kikuchi-san was speechless.

But it's true, from the perspective of someone who just enjoys a game normally, it's kind of crazy to play one game for over ten thousand hours, huh. Even for entrance exams, they say a total of three thousand hours of study can get you into the toughest universities. This is actually over triple that. How 'bout that? Amazing, right?

I'd started *Atafami* about three years earlier, and if we were to assume that was a thousand days ago, then that would mean I'm practicing an average of ten hours a day—I've sacrificed the majority of my youth to *Atafami*. Wait, I've sacrificed the majority of my youth to *Atafami*?

"Well, I don't think it's that rare for a gamer, but I think I've done about that much."

Kikuchi-san considered just a little and said cautiously, "But…you changed your character, right?"

"Ah…"

Yeah, that was the question. Even Ashigaru-san and Hinami had told me I was crazy for doing that, so to Kikuchi-san, who didn't know all that much about gaming, it had to seem even crazier.

"Yeah. 'Cause I wanted to be a better player," I answered with confidence. The reason for that confidence was largely because I'd sorted it out in my head after Ashigaru-san had asked me.

But that surprised her even more. "…Wow. Um…you're the number one in Japan in this game, right?"

"Yeah. In terms of online winrate anyway."

Timidly examining my face, eventually Kikuchi-san ventured, "I see… So you're a gamer right to the core."

"!" My heart leaped at that small remark.

I was reminded of what Ashigaru-san had said the day before—*my karma as a gamer*. Those words seemed to express my true nature.

That must have come out in my expression, as Kikuchi-san questioned me. "…What's wrong?"

I wasn't sure how to reply. It was like a darkness within myself that I was only just becoming aware of, and I hadn't yet sorted it out. It was probably fine to avoid it and say it was nothing, then change the subject.

But.

"Hey…," I began, "actually, someone said something to me at the meetup yesterday."

"…They did?" The sudden change of subject made Kikuchi-san tilt her head at me.

Well, yeah.

The same thing had happened over that time with Rena-chan. The reason I'd had that falling-out with Kikuchi-san was because I'd hardly told her about the stuff that had happened at the meetups and what I'd been thinking; we hadn't actually been able to talk.

In that case, I should tell her about these things that were difficult to talk about, too.

"That I might not be cut out for relationships," I said.

Kikuchi-san was watching with some apprehension, as if she was trying to see what I really meant. "Wh-why not…?"

I explained so that she'd understand. "It's like…I really believe in my own decisions and judgments and stuff, so I think that the individual is the individual…"

"…Mm-hmm."

"But that's because…well, like you just said. Because I'm a gamer."

"…You mean your thing about putting efforts toward a goal and producing results yourself, don't you?"

"Huh?" She'd come up with an answer so quickly. It was such a direct thrust at the truth of the matter that I made a noise of surprise.

I mean, she was completely right. Gaming in the world of 1v1 is really about repeated effort toward a goal.

"Yeah. That's right… I'm impressed you just got it."

Kikuchi-san flicked her eyes away and said something different from what I'd imagined. "…I think about you a lot when I'm alone, too."

That lovely remark made my heart leap in a different sense from before. "Th-thank you."

But for some reason, she seemed sad, and then she tried to dig deeper. "Wanting to be an individual...won't change even when you get into a relationship, will it?"

"...!"

Kikuchi-san quietly spoke from the heart, a precise thrust at the weakness I had difficulty talking about.

That's why I was forced to acknowledge it. "...For now, that is true."

"I see... Are you like that...with anyone?" she asked.

I nodded again. "I think...I've felt affection or gratitude toward people, but I don't know if I've ever let anyone get really close..." I quoted what Ashigaru-san had said to me as I shared my fears with Kikuchi-san. That was one of the things I was concerned about most right now. "That's why I'm kind of worried. It's like...I can only live as an individual...and when I think about how maybe I can't connect with someone else in a real way, I get scared."

She nodded with sad eyes, squeezing her hand on the table into a fist. "That's...very lonely, isn't it?" she said, dropping the remark right there.

"I guess...it really is. If I don't figure this out, I'll be lonely forever...," I started to say in a self-deprecating way.

Kikuchi-san bit her lip slightly. "That's...true, but..." And then with tears faintly rising in her eyes, she gave a sad smile.

"...I'll be...lonely, too."

Regret surged to my heart. I had my hands full with myself; I hadn't even considered how it would make Kikuchi-san feel to hear that. I opened my mouth, hoping to smooth things over somehow, but no words came out. It was probably better that way than to say something thoughtless.

So I just apologized. "You're right, sorry."

"Oh, no." Sill smiling sadly, Kikuchi-san shook her head. "Here I am going on about myself when you're struggling with things..."

"N-no, I'm the one going on about myself..."

Here we were yet again, trying to yield to each other.

But the words that popped out of her next left me a little taken aback.

"—I'm sure Hinami-san is the same way."

"Huh...?"

A tense moment of doubt crossed between us.

"Hinami-san also puts in effort toward a goal to produce her own results, doesn't she?" Sharpness and anxiety coexisted in her gaze.

I felt like that was striking at the real essence of Hinami—maybe both of us.

"...Yeah. I agree, but..." I couldn't manage to finish with *Why are you bringing that up again?*

Kikuchi-san lowered her eyes at a diagonal. Gazing at her fingers, her eyes were still somehow sad.

* * *

"Thank you very much for today. I had a lot of fun," Kikuchi-san said.

We were in front of Kikuchi-san's house. She and I were facing each other under the darkened sky.

"No, thank you," I replied. "I had fun, getting the chance to play games together."

"Yes, and...thank you very much for taking me all this way again."

"Don't worry about it. We decided we'd try to spend as much time together as possible, right?"

"...Mm." Bashful, slightly guilty, and a little happy, Kikuchi-san looked down. "I'm glad I got to hear a lot about you today... Now I feel like I can do my best, too."

"Oh...I'm glad."

She raised her head with a smile. I couldn't say for sure that there was no hint of anxiety there, but her general vibe was positive.

"Then see you tomorrow at school," I said.

"Yes, see you. Then good night."

"Ah-ha-ha. It's a little early, but night."

And after we parted ways, my feelings were not at all cold.

* * *

That day, at one AM.

"…Huh?"

I was surprised to find something on Twitter.

I've posted the latest chapter of my novel on CanRead.
Pureblood Hybrid and Ice Cream 002—School

I found a tweet that had been posted two minutes ago, indicating an update to Kikuchi-san's novel. It was a little unexpected.

From our usual exchanges on LINE and our conversation before we'd said good night, I'd thought she always went to bed pretty early. And it had been a pretty full day to begin with, after running into Hinami at lunch in Kitayono and then playing *Atafami* at my house, so I'd assumed she would go home and have a bath or something before going straight to bed.

But this update had come a little past twelve. I doubt she would have bothered uploading something that she'd written before right now, so that meant she'd been working on her novel until this moment.

"…Hmm."

Had she been feeling inspired from the excitement of an active day, or had she been very close to done and happened to finish it now? Whatever the case, I'd been curious what would happen next, so I was glad despite my surprise.

But the update of chapter two of *Pureblood Hybrid and Ice Cream* was unexpected for me in a different sense.

The bloodless girl Alucia had discovered that the mutt Libra was actually a "pureblood hybrid," and so she had invited him to the academy at the royal castle. Alucia's home in the castle was the same as in *On the Wings of the Unknown*, but the main setting was different.

The academy was a school where the wealthiest strata of the world gathered, and a lot of them were from families who thought about bloodlines before any marriages occurred. Most of the students were either pure-blood or half blood, and those with blood any thinner were treated like failures. It was that kind of school.

Though Libra was a special "pureblood hybrid," it wasn't good for that fact to be widely known. He was a transfer student and a mixed blood, who weren't cut out for the academy, which made him exceptional on two counts. The story started with Libra getting the usual treatment as one at the bottom of the pecking order, and with advice from Alucia, he made his way through life on his skills. That was the plotline of the story.

But more to the point, this story…

A shiver ran across my skin.

This was basically a direct depiction of the path Hinami and I had gone down.

It felt like I was reading a true story with Hinami and me as the protagonists.

The story was made up of alternating training sections, where Alucia taught him the ropes and how to live at the academy, and school sections, where Libra put those things into practice. While Libra failed many times, he got back up again each time to gradually come closer to success. It was kind of a classic underdog story.

His effort was sometimes met with failure, but then one thing would lead to another and another until he eventually succeeded. If someone was to read about the path I'd taken, maybe they'd think of it like this.

But even though I couldn't call it perfect, the story made extremely accurate guesses about details that I hadn't even shared.

Libra's special characteristic was his adaptability. At this stage, I was unsure if I had that, too, but as I read onward, I was starting to see it.

Libra was from a particularly remote town, and being an introvert, he didn't have any friends in his life—kind of like my own situation. Libra had played a board game that was the most popular one in that world—a sort of single-player shogi—and through playing it over and over again, he had mastered it completely. Though this depiction wasn't as extreme as with me and *Atafami*, it made me think that maybe I would have been the same if I'd been in Libra's world. Perhaps due to his experience analyzing that game, even living a life that would normally be pitiable, he was able to survive and thrive by thinking about things from a different angle and fighting in his own arena. I know I'm the same—and as I kept reading on, I felt like my own life and Libra's were getting all mixed up. Like I was becoming Libra.

Thanks to his experience with that game, Libra was more open to putting in effort, he was quick to pick up on things, and he was competitive like me. It's true that I've personally experienced that mastering a game does produce that effect, so maybe other people would think I'm a fast learner like Libra.

Though Libra had the special bloodline of the pureblood hybrid, he only had a little of each bloodline without much ability in any. Though at a glance, you could say this made him a "bottom-tier character" like me, Libra's hybrid pure blood also meant that he could use just some characteristics of any race; as someone who wouldn't mind putting in effort, I envied that. That was compatible with Libra's character as well. Maybe everyone should take a page from Libra's book.

Libra, me, Libra, me. I don't know if I should call it a whirlpool of themes or the power of the storytelling, but I was interpreting Libra through the lens of my life and reinterpreting my own life from the depiction of Libra. Something I'd never experienced before was churning up in my heart.

It was true that in that play, *On the Wings of the Unknown*, Libra had also been modeled after me. But that was mostly superficial, like how he was also good at being direct about how he felt, and how he could forge ahead despite being awkward.

But this time was different.

It depicted the truth of me through the stories I'd told Kikuchi-san, exposed by her interpretation.

*   *   *

And then with a certain line at the end of chapter two, I was sure of it.

Since Libra had every type of blood and could become anything, he had no fixation on any one thing, no resistance to change.

So even if he mastered the skill of one race, he would abandon it without hesitation. Even in his decision to follow Alucia out of his small town and survive as a mixed-blood transfer student, he treated survival itself as a game, enjoying it regardless of how dramatically it would change his fate.

And then one day, Libra gave a long speech to Alucia.

Libra, the only pureblood hybrid, the boy different from everyone, said:

"I can only ever live as an individual, so maybe I can never connect with anyone in the true sense."

Instantly, all the confusion and surprise inside me transformed into surety and chills.

I mean, that line.
That struggle.

That was my karma as a person that I'd confessed to her then.

"…!"
And then I understood everything.
That day in Kitayono.
How Kikuchi-san had told me that she wanted to know what I like and said she wanted to come all the way up to my room, and there, I had told her about my life and the way I thought.

Or in the library in the morning, when she'd said she wanted me to tell her in order from the beginning about where my thoughts had come from—and where they were headed now.

My past, and present, and future.

That time in the library, at Kitayono, what she'd asked me in my room—of course, she had to have asked partly just because she wanted to know.

But at the same time—

—the writer Fuka Kikuchi had been interviewing me.

The chills that ran down my back eventually transformed into something close to fear.

I'd thought Kikuchi-san had listened to me because she was trying to patch things up after our falling-out or simply because she had an interest in me. That hadn't been a conversation with my girlfriend Kikuchi-san, but…observation by the writer Fuka Kikuchi.

I recalled what she'd said back then.

"I think about you a lot when I'm alone, too."

That remark was hitting me differently now.

I hadn't been using my phone for a while, so the screen suddenly went black. The unexpected darkness reflected my own face.

A serene presence watching the world from above had seen into things I hadn't even noticed, to be reflected in themes and made into a story. It was like the murk at the bottom of my heart was slowly being churned up. I was getting scared to read what came next in this story.

And—

"…Hinami."

—now that it was me, it was giving me chills and almost dread.

For the first time, I understood.

Yeah—

This was the same thing that we did to Hinami that time.

*   *   *

In the play, *On the Wings of the Unknown*, Alucia had clearly been modeled on Hinami. Not only had we interviewed Hinami, but the character had also been molded to expose an essence that she had never revealed before. The story had actually been constructed to actively dig deep into that.

Thinking of it that way…just reading a story like this felt like having my layers peeled back. It gave me an indescribable fear.

But Hinami hadn't just read that as a script.

She hadn't just watched it from the audience.

She had played her own darkness as an actor.

The line that had become the key—

"I have everything. But—that's exactly why…I have nothing."

For Hinami, that was probably the darkness that lurked close to the core of her heart, the kind that I couldn't even be sure if she was aware of herself.

To have it shoved in her face so specifically—to be forced to say it in a line like a confession in front of an audience—how much would that have shaken Aoi Hinami's heart?

"…!"

Why hadn't I realized?

Making her say herself that she was empty, knowing that might be how she really was—

What a cruel thing that was to do.

That was when I understood.

The "desire to be a writer" that Kikuchi-san had settled on through the play.

She was probably just as strong and determined in this as I was to make *Atafami* my life.

She prioritized what she wanted to do over the possibility of hurting someone.

She was probably more aware than anyone how she could hurt someone, thinking about it more than anyone, but regardless, she had to do it—

I'm sure she was the same as me.

She had the karma of a writer.

5

There's always a price to pay for a secret ability

The next morning, I came to Sewing Room #2 for the first time in a while.

Hinami and I had crammed ourselves in here for half a year—it was the place only she and I knew.

And now—I'd brought another girl to check out the room.

Eventually, she sat down in front of me and greeted me in the usual manner. "…Good morning."

"Yeah. Morning."

Yes—it was not Hinami there, but Kikuchi-san, and this was probably the first time I'd come to this place at this time with anyone else.

In this place that held everything, I put a hand on the usual chair as I stood facing Kikuchi-san.

"…So look. It's about Hinami," I said to change the mood.

Kikuchi-san's eyes widened with a start, and she straightened her back to sit properly. And then she drew in a big breath as if she was steeling herself and looked at me with strong eyes. "Yes. Please tell me…!" Her expression was filled with expectation—this issue of Hinami's secret did involve both Kikuchi-san's jealousy and her curiosity as a creator, after all.

"You might have sort of picked up on it already, but…," I began slowly, and Kikuchi-san held her breath and gazed into my eyes.

I revealed something I had never told to anyone.

"…the *certain individual* I told you about before, the one who gave my life color—that was Hinami."

I put it briefly and simply, but I was sure that was enough for Kikuchi-san to understand.

"...So it really is her," she said. She sounded surprised, but not enough to challenge the notion. She also seemed a little upset, but I didn't know if I was right to assume that.

"Yeah. Um...to start from the beginning..."

And so I told her honestly about the most important time of my life, a time that had been so impossibly full, when everything had changed so much that I could hardly believe it.

"We didn't meet at school... We didn't even meet IRL. It began with *Atafami*..."

I told her there was a number two ranked player in the world of *Atafami*, that the player had a similar playstyle as me, and had probably referenced my own play. I told her about how accurate their imitation was and the degree of effort they'd put in—that they were sincere enough that you didn't have to ask and could just tell from fighting them. That I'd respected and acknowledged NO NAME before even meeting them.

"So you mean...," Kikuchi-san said.

"Mm-hmm. I went to meet NO NAME offline, and—it was Hinami."

"Th-that's a crazy coincidence..."

"Ah-ha-ha, right? But after that first incredible coincidence...what came after that was pretty much inevitable."

I told her about how after that, Hinami had told me that life was a god-tier game, and that I'd decided to try following her purely to see if that was true.

Then when I started taking life seriously, I'd quickly come to enjoy the game. As I started to get into it, I also started to like myself.

Thanks to Hinami—I started to like my own life and Kikuchi-san.

That was why I was able to see a colorful world together with Kikuchi-san now—that's exactly why I was trying to show Hinami how life could be fun. I slowly told Kikuchi-san the whole story up to that point.

What came after that, I still didn't know.

I mean, even after all she'd done for me, I didn't really understand her.

"Oh…yes, I see." I'm not sure why, but Kikuchi-san had tears in her eyes as she listened. "She's…so incredibly important to you."

"…Yeah."

"So she really is special…more than me."

"Th-that's not…" But nothing came out after that.

When we started dating, I'd told Kikuchi-san that our differences were the reason our relationship was special, but it also meant our natures contradicted each other.

And it had even created conflict between us—and I had hurt Kikuchi-san several times.

"So Hinami-san has been meeting with you every day in this room."

"…Yeah." I nodded, and Kikuchi-san's lips twitched.

I don't know if it was the strength to be herself or something else, but—

—Kikuchi-san finally spoke.

"But…don't you think that's a truly incredible story?"

The expression on her face was also Kikuchi-san, the writer.

"Hinami-san has not only used magic to change the color of your world—but I think she also must have to work hard at her studies and at her club to produce results."

There was something warped in how she put a lid on her jealousy, and a stubbornness in her pursuit of the truth.

"I think she would only use her time on things that seem like they have clear value."

That was the question that Mizusawa wouldn't understand and that I wouldn't dare to ask. The only one allowed was Kikuchi-san.

"But then why would she want to use her magic to change someone?"

*   *   *

What Kikuchi-san had brought to the foreground here was the great black box of Aoi Hinami that was only known to me.

When I'd met NO NAME back then, I'd said that life was a garbage game with no rules or concept; that if you're born bottom-tier, then you couldn't change characters; and that it's unfair. Then she had dragged me to her room, told me she would disprove that, and started teaching me her strategy guide for life.

Until now, I'd sort of figured that her desire to disprove my assertions was competitiveness, but that reason didn't seem to be enough.

That time she'd taken me to her room, she'd said, *"If the person I respected is worthless, then doesn't that make me worthless, too?"* But again, that alone was a weak reason for supporting me to such a practically self-sacrificing degree.

"Hinami-san should have a reason for everything she does, right?"

So then why?

Kikuchi-san's words really had broached a territory that I couldn't.

Kikuchi-san and I were on two parallel paths. There were two doors beyond that, but I felt like right now, we were aiming for the same place.

"Actually—that's always bothered me, too," I said, asking for her help. Because maybe, with what I knew and Kikuchi-san's keen insights— —maybe we would reach that place.

I had the feeling I could accomplish my mid-term goal.

"I'd like you to think together with me…about Hinami's real reason," I said, and Kikuchi-san's eyes shone as if they'd struck down to the truth. Those were her writer eyes.

"All right… But." She was looking right at me. "You think of the individual as the individual, don't you?"

"Yeah, I do." I'd told her about that before, but why was that coming up now?

"So then…"

I immediately learned the answer.

* * *

"…why go this far to try to know Hinami-san?"

She confronted me with that.

"…!"

It deeply questioned my motives.

It was the same sharpness that had searched for the reason for Hinami's actions—it was Kikuchi-san's karma as a novelist.

Right now, it was directed at me, too.

"I want to know Aoi Hinami."

I'd been thinking about this ever since the Tama-chan incident, with what Hinami did to Konno. But this was an emotional urge, and I had no clear reason for it. "Umm…"

But Kikuchi-san was still talking, telling a story and crystallizing my feelings. "Isn't it…because Hinami-san is special to you?" Her clear gaze seemed to know me better than myself.

"Special…" Her question illuminated the thing I'd pretended not to see, stabbing someplace deep.

"This is what I think," Kikuchi-san said. "*Alucia* doesn't have her own blood, doesn't have something that she wants to do. So the world she sees is just like yours and mine before: gray. She only looks for the right answers, and there's nothing she wants to do for herself, based on her own feelings."

"…Yeah."

As if she was using a story to dig deep—as if she was guiding me—

"What do you feel, looking at a girl like that?" she asked me. It was a vague question.

But her eyes held a tinge of anxiety and jealousy.

I could tell my feelings were being drawn out by her contradictory speech.

"I…probably don't want *Hinami's* world to be gray," I said, replacing that world with the real one.

"Mm…" Kikuchi-san smiled with an adult expression, but faint tears were rising in her eyes.

"…I think because she's important to me. Because she's given me more important things than I can count—I don't want her to feel sad." I put my feelings into words and followed Kikuchi-san's guidance.

"Yes…of course."

But…

…the more she listened to me, the bigger the tears in her eyes became. "Is that because…Hinami-san is the one who brought color to your world?" Her voice was unsteady and a little choked.

But Kikuchi-san's question made me notice another feeling that overflowed as words, as an emotion. "Just like you said back then, Hinami… is a magician to me. That's why…!"

The more Kikuchi-san stirred up my heart, the more my feelings for Hinami spilled out of my mouth. And the more Kikuchi-san heard, the more her eyes welled with tears, but she never stopped trying to dig at how I really felt from my heart.

I think—that was karma.

"She's the one who…made you Poppol, even in this world, isn't she?" With some trepidation, Kikuchi-san said, "She's the one who made your world colorful?"

She asked question after question, diving down to my motivation. I don't think she had a choice.

"Without even knowing it or trying, she was using the most amazing magic in the world… She has no idea what she gave me… She doesn't understand just how much I value what I got from her, and just how thankful I am to her."

Once the truth started spilling out—I couldn't stop it anymore.

That was the greatest evidence of how special Hinami was to me.

"…Yes. I…think that's true…," Kikuchi-san said in a quivery voice as a fat tear dropped from her eye.

But even then—

"Since…you two are the same…both of you live as individuals…!"

Kikuchi-san never stopped exposing my heart, my feelings for Hinami, my important reasons. Diving as deep as she could go, her words led me to summon up the feelings that slept at the bottom of my heart.

"Yeah...that's why even if I thanked her, she'd say she didn't do anything. She'd say she's just doing it because she wants to. She'd say she just chose it of her own will...but I understand those feelings better than anyone! ...I'm a hopeless gamer, and an individualist... I've always played *Atafami* like that." My heart was all mixed up now, flowing out of control into a continuous whirlpool that wouldn't stop.

With Kikuchi-san pushing into the depths of my heart, feelings I'd never seen before were spilling out endlessly. "Even if I thanked her, she wouldn't get it. She wouldn't accept it... That's why I..."

The world was beginning to blur with tears.

"I want to make Hinami's world colorful, of my own will. I want to bring color to her world. I want her to enjoy the game of life."

I let my feelings take me.

"That's what I want to do."

And I said what I was thinking, along with my karma.

I'd never before been aware of these feelings that Kikuchi-san had led me to.

But once I tried putting them into words, they were so substantial that I was certain they were not wrong.

And they were just slightly crossing the boundary of the individualism that I'd had all this time.

"...I thought so," Kikuchi-san said. When I lifted my chin, I saw tears on her cheeks. "That's why...Hinami-san is...special to you...," she said like an admonition.

Kikuchi-san had pressed into my heart more and more, and she had drawn out words from the bottom of it.

But she was also the one crying.

Those tears had to come from the contradiction between feelings and ideals—between herself and her karma.

Wiping her tears, she put on a smile, but her voice was trembling as she said, "I'm sorry... Hearing you say that was so overwhelming. It's such a wonderful and beautiful relationship, I cried tears of happiness."

Like a storyteller, but also expressing her emotions honestly, she continued, "...But along with that...I'm realizing I really can never beat Hinami-san... And I felt sad." She was kind of getting down on herself but also celebrating this special relationship. "You love the same game and respect each other, but by doing something for herself, she gives something important to you, and then you want to do your best to repay her... That's just such an ideal relationship. It's so wonderful..."

Kikuchi-san smiled brightly, but when she spoke again, I could hear jealousy in her voice.

"That's why—there's not any room for me...!"

She was tearing herself open, baring her heart and soul. This was her cry of pain from the wounds my karma had inflicted. It hurt how much I understood.

But now that she had revealed her feelings to me, I couldn't look away from them.

Deep, deep down, I knew what she meant. For me, it was an important goal that I had to make my number one priority.

"I...do like you, Kikuchi-san," I said in a serious tone.

"...!" But her breath caught as if she already knew what I would say next.

"Those feelings aren't a lie... Even now that I'm aware how important my feelings for Hinami are, I still feel that you're the one I like. That's even a relief, in a sense."

"...Mm." Kikuchi-san's expression was serious, tears in her eyes as she listened.

"But...my desire to teach her how to enjoy life, to make her world colorful—"

And then I told her the answer that had been illuminated by our conversation.

Maybe Kikuchi-san had known it before I did.

"—that might be more important than love, or those sorts of feelings, to me."

That was the moment I clearly selected one item from those important things I held.

"Yes…I agree." You would think that would be cruel, but Kikuchi-san quietly accepted it.

"I don't mean that I want her as my girlfriend or in that sense. I think I care for her as, like, a benefactor, a friend, or comrade…more in that direction." *So even though it might make you feel anxious, I want you to stay with me*—I couldn't say it. That was just my own selfishness.

"I want you to let me think about it a bit. I want to keep being involved with Hinami, and I like you, and I want to keep dating. But I know I'm also telling you to put up with the loneliness of dating me."

I remembered the day we'd gotten together. "After the play… After you came up with your answer, I'm the one who used the magic of words to choose you. So I will think over it as much as it deserves, and I'll come up with an answer."

Back then, she'd been abstractly thinking about the reason Libra and Alucia were special, and the reason that Libra and Kris were special. She had been caught between ideals and feelings.

When Kikuchi-san had explained why she thought Libra and Alucia should be together, I had given her a reason after the fact for the sake of validating her feelings. Though she'd sought an ideal relationship, I'd convinced her with the argument that Libra should choose Kris and convinced her to prioritize feelings—as Fumiya Tomozaki, I had chosen Fuka Kikuchi.

That's why that was my choice. If I wanted to be sincere, then I should take responsibility for that.

At the very least, if I was going to continue to try to be a gamer—

"...I understand. I'll be waiting," she said.

While it was also special, the relationship between the fireling and Poppol was also unbalanced.

At some point, *special* had become a contradiction between two species, then eventually changed form to human karma.

Did our relationship not have enough magic to validate its specialness?

"Tomozaki-kun, you're the one who said that I should pursue both ideals and feelings."

This really was the same as before.

"Feelings aren't the only thing that matter to me. Both are important. That's why...I don't want just one... To me, your and Hinami-san's relationship is also important, not only my own feelings." Kikuchi-san smiled again, but she was putting on a strong front.

She put her hand on the back of the sewing-room chair.

Now that I thought about it, that was the place Hinami was always sitting.

"So, Tomozaki-kun. If you have too many burdens to carry, and you have to drop something—"

And her eyes slowly crinkled up in a smile, leaving crooked trails on her cheeks to wet the floor of Sewing Room #2.

"—it's all right if you let go of me."

* * *

Kikuchi-san and I didn't talk any more that day.

We weren't the type of couple to go around flirting at school anyway, so nobody really thought it was weird— Well, maybe some people did, but they didn't feel so strongly that they would bother to talk to me about it.

When Mizusawa came to ask me about Kikuchi-san during lunch break, it didn't seem like he really sensed anything was off.

We were in the cafeteria. Nakamura's whims had led Takei, Mimimi, and the other jocks outside for a game of catch, while Izumi, Mizusawa, and I remained indoors. To be more precise, Mizusawa felt bad for me because I wasn't in the mood to keep up with their energy, so he had stayed behind for me. Izumi had done so as well, playing the grown-up of the group in an *Oh, they're such children* kind of way.

"So then what happened, Fumiya?" Mizusawa's vibe was purely chatty.

Having just had a fight that morning, I couldn't help but get a little gloomy. "...You mean with Kikuchi-san?"

Izumi seemed worried. "Ah! I was curious about that! Do you think you can accept the school badges?!"

"Umm, sorry... Actually, we kind of fought this morning, too...," I said vaguely.

"Huhhh?!" Izumi cried out in shock. "Should we start looking for someone else now?!"

"Ha-ha-ha, you're fighting a lot lately. Are you okay?" Mizusawa asked.

But I couldn't be as casual as him. "Oh, this time, I think maybe..."

"Hmm?"

"Resolving it...might be difficult," I said meaningfully.

Izumi tilted her head with a serious look. "...What do you mean by that?"

Remembering my exchange with Kikuchi-san, I said, "Those school badges... They say you'll have a special relationship, right?"

"Uh-huh."

"Well...I think Kikuchi-san and I were a contradiction from the start...so maybe it would be difficult for us to have a special relationship...," I said, though I left it vague.

"What do you mean?"

"In contradiction how?"

I reflected on how our relationship had been in our last conversation. "It's kinda like...I had something I absolutely wanted to do, and there's someone important enough to me that I just couldn't cut them off..."

Mizusawa twitched a bit but didn't say anything.

"That person being there makes Kikuchi-san feel lonely and jealous... but she wants to respect what I want to do, and my other relationships..."

"Hmm...," said Izumi, "like a 'Which to choose, your female friend or your girlfriend?' sort of thing?"

"That's similar, but I think this friend is probably a little more special, I guess...," I explained with some difficulty.

But Mizusawa accepted that in an easygoing and subdued manner. "Yeah, I get that." Maybe he knew who that "other person" was.

"I had no idea... Your relationship is complicated, huh?!" It seemed like Izumi was over capacity, and her brain was about to pop. But her honesty was reassuring.

Mizusawa lifted one eyebrow, rubbing his chin with a finger. "Well, frankly, this is your problem, so there's nothing I can say..."

"O-oh, I guess so, huh...," I said, overwhelmed.

"But," he continued calmly and lightly, "I can tell you there's one thing you have the wrong idea about."

"What do I have wrong...?" I asked. He gave me a confident grin, while Izumi stared blankly.

"So part of this is on me for bringing it up, but...right now, you're getting yourself all worked up thinking about your responsibility in choosing her, what's special, and who deserves the school badges and stuff, right?"

"...Yeah." I nodded.

Mizusawa smiled knowingly. "But, like...well, maybe I shouldn't say this in front of Yuzu, but—"

"Wh-what?! Me?!" Suddenly being named, Izumi's back snapped straight, and she tensed up like she was bracing for a shock.

Mizusawa continued without pausing.

"—first of all, the badges of destiny are just a couple pieces of scrap metal that some people wore once, you know? You don't need to deserve crap like that."

"I can't believe you just said that!" Izumi cried. As the committee member responsible, she was unable to take the shock.

"But you know what I'm saying, right, Fumiya?" Mizusawa said to me.

And I was following more or less. "You mean that it's fundamentally just scrap metal...but it has the formality of a romantic story attached?"

Mizusawa smiled. "Yeah. That's why girls love it so much."

"There you go talking like a pickup artist again..."

"H-hmm...?"

Mizusawa was referencing an earlier discussion of ours, leaving Izumi with nothing but question marks. Still, she was doing her very best to keep up.

"So, like," Mizusawa continued, "I get that you're worried about it, but don't let yourself be controlled by those kinda formalities. You should just fight with the things you're good at."

"...Sure, but still..." The difficulty of that issue had me at my wits' end. "We made that script together, shared important personal things with each other, and reconciled our views... We talked from the heart. That wasn't formality." That talk we'd had after the play had been neither casual nor superficial. "So I thought that we'd solved all the problems we had there before we got together..."

I thought we'd been carefully making our way through each thing one by one, but problems were still surfacing anyway.

"...Are relationships this hard?" I said.

With that smug look on his face again, Mizusawa furrowed his eyebrows. "You've got some weird ideas about this, Fumiya. You started dating after solving all your problems? You think dating is that easy?"

Then he stuck a finger at my chest and said quietly:

"Obviously, you're only able to talk to each other about what's really important *after* you start dating."

* * *

After school, I was thinking.

I want to be involved with Hinami.

But I also wanted to be with Kikuchi-san, and I didn't want to make any insincere decisions that she'd have to put up with.

Was there really no option of keeping things as they were and staying involved with both Hinami and Kikuchi-san? Did I just have to give up on one of them?

Kikuchi-san wanted to know Hinami as a writer, and that was why she had noticed that "specialness."

But while Kikuchi-san had the karma of a writer, she was also a normal girl. The more she learned, the more anxious it made her, which lead to further jealousy and anxiety. So long as Kikuchi-san was that way, she would want to know about Hinami and end up in contradiction with her personal desires. That would eventually bring about the destruction of our relationship.

Couldn't I do something about that?

I'd been gathering opinions from different kinds of people, hoping to figure out how to walk on the unfamiliar path that was love. I'd been putting together those different ways of thinking about love, exploring what to do, and searching for the light. But in this case...

"...Ah."

...what came to my mind then was that unexpected remark from an unexpected someone.

It hadn't come from Mizusawa, the veteran of a hundred battles of love, or Izumi and Nakamura, who were currently deployed, and of course, it hadn't come from my teacher in life, Hinami.

"What's wrong with keeping her in a little suspense? That's what's fun about relationships."

Rena-chan had said that at the meetup.

Though that view had felt kind of extreme to me, the framework of her ideas acknowledged the anxieties of love, which nobody else had offered.

Of course, it wasn't like I wanted to force that idea on Kikuchi-san. But I figured some of Rena-chan's ideas held a viewpoint I lacked. I'd basically wandered into the dead end of a contradiction; maybe I could find something new there.

"...Okay."

Well, I really didn't want to see Rena-chan now of all times, but she was the only one I could ask in detail about that perspective.

So I opened up LINE and sent a message to Rena-chan.

* * *

[Hey, there's some things I want to ask about. Do you mind?]

* * *

The place was a dark bar in an alley a short walk from Ikebukuro Station.

Rena-chan and I were sitting next to each other at the counter, in a corner a little ways from the entrance.

"Tee-hee. I'm glad that you'd be the one to invite me, Fumiya-kun."

"U-uh, thanks," I replied vaguely.

Rena-chan, sitting on my left, leaned over to peer at my face and into my eyes. "But, like, can I ask just one thing?" She scooched just a little closer than before. A sweet scent enveloped me, and that along with the vibe of this location was getting my heart all messed up.

Her gaze went straight to the seat to my right side. "...Why are you here, Ashigaru-san?"

"Ha-ha-ha, don't ask me." The man at my right gave an easygoing laugh.

Yep. I wanted to ask Rena-chan about relationships, but I'd obviously figured one-on-one would be dangerous, so I'd also called up Ashigaru-san. He was unexpectedly amused by the whole situation, and he said he'd come if he was free.

"W-well, it kinda seemed like a bad idea to be alone with you...," I said.

Rena-chan smiled devilishly. "Ohh. It's true. If we're all alone together, we might give in to desire, huh?"

"Hey..."

That seductive smile was scrambling my emotions again, and I almost regretted inviting her. But I told myself that it was for the future of my relationship. With video games, you always need to take a risk to gain something.

"So what was it you wanted to ask?" she asked.

"Um..." I mixed the nonalcoholic cassis syrup into the orange juice in front of me and looked at the purple cherry on top. "The other day, you said that the anxiety in relationships is fun, but I wanted to ask what you meant..."

"Hmm? Why are you asking about that?"

"The truth is…things have happened with my girlfriend."

I briefly explained about how there was someone else besides my girlfriend who was special to me and was the opposite sex, that my girlfriend had felt upset when she'd found out, and that she was anxious about it.

To me, this was an issue that couldn't be any more dire, but Rena-chan seemed kind of bored. "…That's it?"

"Y-yeah…"

Then she picked up her long, slim glass containing a translucent-pink bubbly drink and twirled it back and forth, gazing vaguely at the light coming through it. "Hmm. Okay, Fumiya-kun. You're putting love on such a pedestal."

"Y-you think…?" Though she wasn't getting too specific, I kind of got what she was saying.

"She's your first girlfriend, right, Fumiya-kun?"

"Yeah."

"If you start suddenly saying things like *Nobody ever feels anxious in an ideal relationship* or *It's insincere to make her feel lonely*, you won't be able to date anyone."

"Urk…" I was ruthlessly cut down.

"Everybody's different, but at the end of the day, relationships are just about common interest."

That opinion was adult in a completely different way from the other day; I was taken aback.

"So if she's anxious but still keeps chasing after you anyway, then that's fine. Love isn't something where you resolve everything and make it perfect."

"But that's so self-centered. I mean…shouldn't you try to make it so neither party is anxious…?" I said, without much confidence.

"Hmm." Rena-chan made a sound like there was room for disagreement. "Maybe some people could have a relationship with no anxiety, but that really is just a few people. If you're talking about it in *Atafami* terms, it's something like the top players, you know?"

"B-but if there only few, then shouldn't you try to be one of them…?"

Rena-chan sighed. "Fumiya-kun, you can think about *Atafami* and your life realistically, but you suddenly become a dreamer when it comes to dating," she said as she touched one of her dangly golden earrings. "So I'll listen, but..." She gave me a testing look. "Imagine you bring in someone who's a total beginner at *Atafami* and you have that person... You've been dating for...what, about a month now? You train that person hard for one month in *Atafami*. Do you think that can make them one of the top players in Japan?"

"Ah..." That was a lot like something Hinami had asked me at some point, with one major difference. "...No."

"Right?" In a lighthearted but flowing tone, Rena-chan voiced her thoughts. "So it's impossible to have that kind of ideal relationship immediately after you start dating. You haven't even had sex, have you?"

"I—I said we haven't, okay!" I shot back, flustered, and Rena-chan giggled.

"Tee-hee, I'm not even teasing you right now? But you're blushing so hard. It's cute."

"L-like I said..."

Rena-chan brought her lips to my ear like she was enjoying herself, and with a sigh, she added, "Hey...how about I teach you some things?"

"No! Thank! You!" I shoved her head away.

Is she drunk, or is her body heat just really high? This was pointless; I'm really weak when it comes to this subject. Somehow, I managed to get this discussion back on track. "I'm not talking about that! I just want to resolve this normally!"

"But sex is a normal thing, too," Rena-chan said, though the corners of her lips were upturned in good humor. "If you're making her feel anxious, then there's a cause for that? Nothing will make it all go away like magic, so you've got no choice but to resolve each thing one by one. It's the same as a video game, you know?"

You could see Rena-chan's gamer side in that remark. And she was completely right— Wait.

"I—I forgot...," I muttered.

"Hmm?"

"About cause and effect. And then resolving that. I knew that was the basics of the basics in *Atafami* or anything...," I said.

Rena-chan gave me a syrupy smile. "The basics of *Atafami* are the basics of life, after all?"

"Y-you're completely right..."

She'd wound up teaching me something super elementary. It was fair to say that this sense of values was the foundation of the way I thought—had I lost sight of that? In other words, I was seeing love as something so special that I'd even lost my understanding of that and forgotten my good judgment.

Rena-chan seemed to sense that I'd gotten what she was saying, as she nodded and took two big gulps of the drink in front of her. Then letting out a heated "Ahh...," she looked back at me again with flushed cheeks. "...If you can create an ideal relationship, that's fine...and if you wind up with an unbalanced relationship, then you should just enjoy it all—anxiety, excitement, pleasure, everything."

"I see..." I hmmed and batted away the hand that came sneaking up my thigh when she said *excitement* and *pleasure*. For some reason, Rena-chan smiled happily. She enjoys both acceptance and rejection, huh.

"Someone who gets anxious will get despondent and insecure...so you've got to take good care of her, okay?" she said. Her words seemed to validate everything about love, and that was reassuring to me right now.

"Insecure, huh..." I was remembering my conversation with Mimimi and Tama-chan—about someone who stood on their own, and someone who leaned on them.

Then Ashigaru-san suddenly decided to join the conversation. "You probably don't understand how weak people feel, nanashi-kun."

I was surprised to hear that. "Th-that's not true..."

I mean, no one has prided themselves in being weak as much as me.

"Well, it's true I'm the type to believe in their own ideas...but that's not what I mean. I was kinda different until a little while ago."

"Different?"

I nodded. "I can kind of talk with people like this now, but I didn't used to have friends. I was a really hardcore bottom-tier character."

Ashigaru-san gave me an examining look with a *hmm*. "What do you think confidence is, nanashi-kun?"

"Confidence?" I hesitated just a little, imagining someone confident as I searched for the answer. And then I found what seemed like the answer surprisingly fast. "I guess it's having a clear basis to say, like, 'this is why I'm so great.'"

The one who came to mind was Aoi Hinami herself. She's always full of confidence, and she actually gets results. But behind that was the unshakable foundation of overwhelming effort and analysis.

Ashigaru-san shook his head with an intellectual smile. "Nanashi-kun. You've got that backward."

"...Backward?" I couldn't get what he meant. Rena-chan was tilting her head, too—but maybe that was just because she was drunk.

"Yeah...," Ashigaru-san said, taking a drink from his cocktail, which had some powdery stuff on the glass rim, and slowly began to expound. "Listen. Real confidence has no basis."

"Huh?" I blinked. That was the opposite of what I was thinking.

"Once someone like that has results, they can abandon those results very easily."

That was difficult to understand at first blush.

"If you're going to define change, it's shifting from one situation to another, and it doesn't matter what direction. Good or bad. Change is change. It becomes progression or regression."

"...Yeah, that's true," I agreed.

Ashigaru-san was laying this out like a mathematical proof. But as someone who was continuously going through changes that might pan out or might not, I could understand it well.

"You get it if you think about it in terms of *Atafami*, right? When you sensed the limits of your ability and you put in effort to change how you worked your neutral game. And there was changing your main in the first place. There's no guarantee that you'll progress. You won't necessarily get better than before."

"Yeah. I think that's true."

When you change yourself, there's no guarantee that the change will be for the better.

The fact was that since changing my character from Found to Jack, my winrate still hadn't gone back to my Found era. Maybe it never would.

"That's why for normal people, change comes with fear. If you put in effort to change yourself, but that change isn't for the better—that invalidates the time and effort you put in."

Being someone who could change easily, I didn't really feel this, but I could imagine this would generally be the case.

"But, nanashi-kun, though you should be satisfied with your current situation, you choose change anyway, without fear for it...and from what I've heard, that's not just limited to *Atafami*, either."

"...Maybe you're right," I agreed.

"Of course."

I mean, it was just like he said.

For example, my "character change" in the game of life—maybe the game of life wasn't a god-tier game to begin with, but what Hinami had said had sounded plausible to me. I'd done as she instructed and abandoned my old life as a loner who still decently enjoyed my lifestyle; I'd wanted to see if she was right, so I did a character change and took my life seriously.

"I think that in *Atafami* or in life...thinking that way is what enables me to change," I said.

And it goes without saying, but that was my selection as nanashi.

Ashigaru-san nodded with a smile, tapping on the surface of the counter for no particular reason as he gave me a look of confidence. "I think that's what makes you the number one player in Japan."

I stopped breathing for a second and looked at my fingers, which were always holding a controller. Right now, they were being chilled by my glass, but they held a great deal of confidence.

"For example," he continued, "when I first met you, you lost to me in a first-to-three, but your overall winrate was higher, right?"

"...Yes, I think that's true."

"In other words, you were plain superior in ability."

I hesitated a moment, but I decided to not be modest. Those are the results, so that's reality. That's how the world of competition works.

"After that, you didn't meet up with any other pro players but me, right?"

"No, I didn't."

Ashigaru-san nodded as if to say, *Thought so.* "And your online win-rate's still solidly at the top?"

"Of course. Head and shoulders above the rest," I answered instantly.

The corners of Ashigaru-san's lips lifted like he was amused. "So okay. Put it all together, and it means this—" Adding a little bit of heat to his words, he smirked.

"—you've never met a single person who's stronger than you in your whole life."

That sounded like an incredible boast, but now that he'd pointed it out, it was the reality.

"...Maybe...that's true." Unsurprisingly, I hesitated, but I still agreed with him.

The grin stayed on Ashigaru-san's face as he rubbed his chin. Rena-chan was watching our conversation intently, but she didn't say anything.

"There wouldn't have been any reason for you to change your character in the first place. But now you're not only trying to change your neutral game, you're also even changing your main... Frankly speaking, that's almost unheard-of." He studied his glass with cool eyes. "Weak people need a reason in order to believe in action or in change."

"...!" My breath caught.

Because I knew one person in my life who always needed a reason to change their behavior.

"But you can change as much as you like, just because you intend to," he said.

"Yes...I do agree with that."

"Even without any reason or basis to believe it's right, you can take it for granted that you'll move forward. That's... I don't know. It's like you have something that other people don't."

That reminded me of something. Or rather, I'd had a similar discussion many times before. This was different from how Mimimi and Hinami were. Conversely, it was the same as Tama-chan.

The only thing I need is the answers that are right to me.

"Maybe that comes completely naturally to you," Ashigaru-san continued. "But it's a very valuable, different, and special thing." Ashigaru-san's glass clinked as he drank down the cocktail in front of him. "And..." Setting down the glass, he turned toward me and fixed a level gaze on me. "I'm sure that means that nanashi-kun—you, Tomozaki-kun, as a human—"

The words that Ashigaru-san said next—

"—in life, you're *the* top-tier character."

—shook the biggest assumption that had been carved into me.

"You're probably not going to resolve your issue unless you accept that."

Those words were sharp as the fangs of a reptile, but I'm sure what they ripped open—

—was the mask that I'd been wearing unconsciously.

6

When you try to throw away something important, someone will always come stop you

I was on the way home. Even though I hadn't drunk any alcohol, I felt intoxicated, as if my field of vision was blurring and warping. It was like, I don't know. Like the biggest assumption in my life had been disproven.

"—I'm a top-tier character?" I muttered to myself as I looked at the shadow that stretched out of the streetlight at my back.

All this time, I'd placed myself at the bottom—I had started thinking of it as my identity. It was why I felt kind of proud about improving myself. Why I had been a little afraid of choosing someone.

Because I was a bottom-tier character, I could make excuses when I lost in life.

But the "top-tier character" argument Ashigaru-san had made was indeed consistent with everything I'd been cultivating thus far, and it had thoroughly convinced me. It felt like thin strips were being ruthlessly peeled off my heart, layer by layer.

My head was spinning, and my legs were wobbly.

"He's right that I'm not afraid of change, but..." I gazed at the fingers that had been holding a controller for so many years, these fingers that had enough confidence for me to be able to validate myself. "This change really is kinda freaking me out, though..."

This was flipping everything upside down. Like a mutt becoming a pureblood hybrid.

My character change was even bigger than the one Hinami had shown me before.

*   *   *

Walking the streets of Kitayono that I'd been down with Kikuchi-san, I thought about the problems I'd been running into.

When I'd been there before in the daytime, I'd been so happy. But once I tried it alone in the dark, it felt totally different. Just lonely. Kikuchi-san had even dyed this small little world different colors.

In the library after that play.

I'd chosen to take on a relationship with Kikuchi-san of my own will. I believed in my own choices. And I want to take that choice seriously.

I've lived as an individualist, avoiding involvement with others to the extreme, but it was my choice to choose Kikuchi-san.

But if my nature to be unafraid of change and to continue moving forward caused her anxiety and loneliness, while my desire to stay an individual was preventing resolution of that—then that conflict would never end unless I became someone else.

This conflict was created by my personality, values, and standard of judgment itself, so if I was to continue dating Kikuchi-san, I would have to change something more fundamental.

If Mimimi and Tama-chan were right about me, that I'm the one who will stand on his own, the one who gets leaned on—a top-tier character— then that's what I should choose.

What Rena-chan had told me was exactly how I thought. If there is a problem and a result, there's also a cause; if you want to resolve the problem, then you simply have to eliminate each individual cause. I'd just forgotten that because I'd been putting love on a pedestal, but those were the video game fundamentals that had been etched into my own flesh and bones.

And there were a number of causes for Kikuchi-san's anxiety.

Like Mizusawa said, I had to *make choices* for each individual thing.

So then first, I decided to make choices about the various burdens I carried.

* * *

I went back home, and in my room, I opened up LINE.

Displayed on screen was the group chat that had been made to plan for the trip to Spo-Cha.

I was thinking.

What was important to me, what I wanted to deal with sincerely, was making *Atafami* my life, showing Hinami how to make life fun—and my relationship with Kikuchi-san.

If anything else was causing Kikuchi-san anxiety—it would be best to set it down.

I could even change my main from Found if needed, so I should be able to do the same thing with my life.

Since the members aside from me had already gone once, the conversation in the chat was like [*That was fun, huh, thanks!*] and [*Let's go again!*] and then stopped after that. So if I were to nonchalantly slip out of it now, it wouldn't really bother anyone. Well, maybe it would be a bit weird, but apparently, I'm kind of a weird person to begin with. It wouldn't be bad enough to invite criticism.

"…Mm-hmm."

So I quietly left that LINE group.

The group disappeared from my chat column, and I couldn't see any of the conversations anymore. Though I felt a pang, I was personally satisfied that this was for the best.

If that group were to become active again and they went a second time, it was less likely that I would be invited.

With this, I have one burden less.

And similarly, I looked up the Searching for Ourselves Alliance group that I'd made.

There was some casual messaging back and forth about how we should hang out again, with an ease that was different from the other group.

This group hadn't been active for the past week, either, so leaving this one wouldn't cause any major issues. Frankly speaking, I was comfortable with this group. I'd felt like it would become important to me, so it would be a lie to say it wasn't hard to leave. But I was sure that I could find a different kind of enjoyment in the game of life, too. That was why I was able to accept this change.

I left that group in the same way, and the temperature in my heart went down again.

One less burden.

Leaving the Searching for Ourselves Alliance group wasn't just lightening my load—it was a rejection of something that had been given to me.

I opened up my chat with Hinami.

And then I typed in this message.

[*Sorry. It doesn't look like I'll be able to finish that assignment of being the center of a group. So please let me give up on this assignment.*]

I read over it once, then sent it.

That was what it meant.

In order to create a group where I was the central figure, a necessary step would be to expand my world and pull lots of people into it and form a community among them.

That group chat was one of the things I'd made for that, and if I wanted to carry out that assignment in the future, then I'd follow a similar process.

But that would create anxiety for Kikuchi-san and take up lots of time.

On the other hand, putting her in that community would contradict her nature as a fireling.

So I had no choice but to give up on making that group.

That's why I stopped putting effort into it.

I'd use the time for more important things.

That's what I decided.

*   *   *

This was a slightly heavier decision than not telling Kikuchi-san I liked her during the fireworks festival.

What I'd abandoned then had ultimately just been the assignment for that day. But what I was doing now was a step beyond that, the thing Hinami had said was the most important.

For the first time since beginning my sessions with her, I'd chosen to abandon the *mid-term goal.*

"...That's it."

Finishing up all the mental sorting-out I could do right now, I let out a lukewarm sigh that didn't come out quite right. Several feelings were swirling around inside me—a melancholy resignation, a sense that something was off, and a similar sort of muddy gravity. But even this choice still felt sincere toward the things that were important to me.

I still wasn't sure if this was the right answer or not. But even if it wasn't, I was confident that if I put in the time someday, I could create something for myself again.

This could be called a "character change."

Just as I'd changed from Found to Jack in anticipation of future trouble, I'd just made a big change in my fundamental stance toward the game of life in the hope of eliminating my contradictions.

When I happened to glance around the room, I found my school bag lying there. "...Ah."

Attached to it was the amulet that was a pair with Kikuchi-san's, which I'd bought when we'd visited the shrine at New Year's, and the uncute haniwa charm I'd gotten from Mimimi before summer vacation that everyone had one of.

Then I remembered.

When all our different color charms were on, when I was with everyone, my schoolbag became like a part of a colorful fireworks show.

Kikuchi-san's schoolbag only had her matching amulet with mine.

*   *   *

The contrast between the two was somehow an expression of the situation I was in now and the contradiction that had me stuck.

Maybe I even had to make a choice here if I wanted to resolve that contradiction.

If it was an either-or decision.

"..."

When it felt like the circulation to my arms was getting weaker, I stretched them out and picked up my bag.

And I chose to remove from my person a part of that colorful scenery I'd once acquired.

* * *

A few days after that, I was having a day that wasn't really any different from before.

Even after our last encounter, Kikuchi-san continued to come to school with me, and when I said that I wanted to have more time together, she agreed to that, too.

No one from class questioned me about the LINE group, either, and I engaged with everyone as much as I could without taking my time from important things. Fortunately, my face was accustomed enough to fake expressions that no one would notice something was off.

"Ooookay!" Takei cried. "Let's go to a family restaurant! You come, too, Farm Boy!"

"Of course!" I replied. "Today, I'm out!"

"That's not what 'of course' means?!"

My dry joke and empty laugh would help me leave that world. I would distance myself without causing trouble for anyone.

I had obtained this world by my own will, through the lessons Hinami taught me, but I was sure I could move on without all of it. I could find new scenery. I mean, the world is more than just this school.

So for the sake of what matters to me, I decided to quietly set down this burden, too.

The sand that I'd scooped up was spilling out from between my fingers, leaving behind just the largest pebbles. But I knew those large pebbles were what I wanted.

And it seemed to me that cherishing those large pebbles was my playstyle in life.

* * *

"Then see you tomorrow."

We were at Kitayono Station. When Mimimi got off the train with me and we went out the ticket gates as usual, I casually raised a hand to say good-bye. We'd been doing this for the past week; my custom with Mimimi had changed in consideration of Kikuchi-san.

But.

"...What's wrong?" I said.

That day, Mimimi wasn't waving back like usual. She was licking her lips hesitantly as her gaze wandered around. "Um...Brain."

"Um, what?"

Her gaze was wavering, as if she was struggling to find the words. Eventually, her eyes landed on my school bag—to the empty place where that charm used to be.

She bit her lip and didn't say anything.

"Oh...um." It was a pathetic response, like I was looking for an excuse. But my logical side forced my mouth closed and kept me from talking. At the end of the day, this was the decision I'd made, and Mimimi had to see it as a betrayal. Trying to find a reason for her to forgive me would just be selfish.

So I put on a smile again and waved to her. "...What's wrong? It's kinda scary to go home alone after dark, you know? ...C'mon, you need to get going."

I was sure I'd managed to deliver my joke well. But Mimimi was staring at me and wouldn't leave. Her expression lay somewhere between anger and sadness, but it had enough strength to pin me to the spot.

Eventually, with steely determination, she took a step forward.

*   *   *

"No. I'm walking home with you today."

She grabbed my arm and tugged me along.
"Huh? ...Hey."
Mimimi ignored me and pulled me the usual way home.
And so for the first time in a while, I started walking back from the station with Mimimi.

* * *

"And hey, sorry I suddenly couldn't go to the Spo-Cha the other day! How was it?"
I was unconsciously tossing out trivial topics in an attempt to hide my intentions. It was like, I dunno, using the mask for self-defense. The more I talked, the darker I could feel my heart becoming.
But I had to do it to protect myself. "Well, I did hear about what Takei pulled, though..."
"Brain, hey," Mimimi cut me off and took a step closer. She stared straight at me.
There was a strength in her eyes that made me think of Tama-chan.
There were no excuses there; her eyes were seeing through me right to the messed-up parts.
"You're acting like how I was back then," she said.
"..."
I immediately got what Mimimi was trying to say.
That's a memory I'll never forget.
Someone was trying to abandon something important for the sake of something else that was also important. And then someone else stopped them and walked home together with them. That situation had happened once before.
And that time, the one to step in and say *let's walk home together* hadn't been Mimimi; it had been me.
"You know," Mimimi said cheerfully, as if she was casually recalling

the memory, "if you hadn't invited me to walk home together back then…I bet I'd be living a totally different life right now."

"Mimimi…"

That was when Mimimi had been getting jealous, when she'd been about to start hating Hinami. But she loved her friend, and she wouldn't be able to forgive herself for that—so instead, she'd throw away something else that mattered to her: the track club.

It had been after school when Mimimi had made the decision that she would set down her burden, before the large pebble that was an important friend was crowded out of her palm.

"If things had stayed like that, you know—I don't think I would have been able to go back to the track club again. And probably…things with Aoi would have gotten a little messed up. Tama's nice, so I think she would've forgiven me, but she would have been frustrated."

That time, I'd dragged out Mimimi and taken Tama-chan with us to walk home together. And Tama-chan's words had broken the spell over Mimimi.

"After school that day, you mustered up your courage in front of everyone, embarrassing yourself to drag me away… I know that was a really important thing for my life." Letting out a white breath beside me, Mimimi smiled with nostalgia. "And on top of that." She wiped at the corners of her eyes with her fingers, and this time, her smile was sad.

"If that hadn't happened…I don't think I would've gotten the chance to fall for you."

Her words weighed on my heart. It was a far heavier and more painful feeling than what I'd thrown away.

"Like, it never went anywhere, and you didn't return my feelings…but I really do like you, Brain…and knowing I can feel that way helps me like myself, too. I'm grateful to you for that."

I could hear the sound of sniffles at my side. Even I could tell it wasn't from the cold.

"So...talk to me? ...Brain..."

Then she looked straight at me again with her piercing eyes.

"...do you not like us anymore?"

"...!"

Of course that wasn't it. But now that I'd chosen to abandon that, how should I explain? What kind of excuse could I make?

Mimimi's voice was getting tight with sadness. "You know. You're always on my mind, so I've noticed. You left all the LINE groups. And when you're with us, your jokes are more on the ball than normal, but you don't seem like you're enjoying yourself at all."

Then her hand gently stroked the part of that colorful world that was attached to her own school bag. "And a little while ago...you took the charm off your bag, too."

"..." My vision was gradually blurring. I don't know if it was because I felt guilty, pathetic, or helpless.

"I'm grateful to you, so I don't want to see you like that... If there's something I can do, then tell me?" Tears were beading in her eyes.

But I was still unsure. "...Sorry." Before my weakness could slip out, I clenched my fists and resisted again. "What I chose was already making you sad, and I'm making even more trouble for you... I..." My clenched fists tensed. But I needed to be sincere about my own choice and sincere to Mimimi. So I refused her.

Exposing my weakness here would make Mimimi shoulder part of the responsibility for my own choices.

Then she let out a sad sigh like, *Oh*. And then.

"Then I'm asking a different way, okay?"

Saying that, she came out one step ahead of me and turned back.

I'm not sure why, but her expression as she looked straight at me was full of something like fighting spirit.

*　　*　　*

"As my comrade in arms who fought with me to beat Aoi, I want you to tell me."

"…!"

I'd once said that very thing before.

That was what I'd said before, when Mimimi and I had been comrades with a shared goal.

I recalled just what a powerful thing had connected me with Mimimi.

Being competitive, focusing on the same goal, teasing each other, sometimes being serious—we'd spent an important time together.

"That's…cheating," I said brokenly, vision blurring as I looked back at Mimimi. "If you say something like that…then I can't lie…"

Mimimi wiped her eyes with her sleeve in a comical way and smiled proudly to encourage me. "Heh-heh-heh! That's just proof of how unfair you were back then!" Then she laughed. "Haah!"

She was unquestionably my comrade in arms, and I owed her for the times when I was feeling down and she took better care of me than I did myself.

"…I've always been alone before…" Suddenly, I was starting to talk to Mimimi about my greatest weaknesses. "…I managed by myself, so I don't know how to really connect with people."

"…Uh-huh."

I felt like exposing this was a form of running away, but I couldn't stop myself. "…I chose Kikuchi-san. When she said it shouldn't be her, I pushed my reasons on her. I said I don't care about ideals; I just want you…"

Once, she'd rejected me with the play, and Mimimi had given me courage then, too.

And then when I'd rushed to the library, I'd chosen Kikuchi-san one more time.

"So I have to take our relationship seriously…but all I've been doing is making her lonely."

That's why—

"—I decided to set aside things I couldn't keep a hold of. Which includes my time with you guys."

—I came to a conclusion in my heart.

"Because to me, that's what it means to take my relationship with her seriously."

"...I see." Beside me, Mimimi nodded twice slowly. "Hey, Brain." As if she'd remembered something, she gazed up at the orange sky. "I happened to run into Kikuchi-san recently, and we talked about stuff...and she and I were the same."

"The same?"

Mimimi nodded slowly and looked right at me with those big eyes of hers. "...I mean the reasons we like you."

"Huh...?" Her words, her eyes, drew me in.

"You do your best to change yourself and expand your world more and more... Both of us like how you're strong and straightforward. You shine bright."

"Expanding my world..." Kikuchi-san had basically said as much in different words.

And then in a voice like she was holding back emotion—but also unsteady as if she was smothering sadness—

—Mimimi said urgently:

"Tomozaki, what you're doing right now is like stopping. You're not expanding your world or heading to new places. You're shrinking your world to keep Kikuchi-san from being jealous..."

Voice trembling, Mimimi continued:

"You're trying to change the things me and Kikuchi-san like about you."

My breath caught.

"I said before, right? That I still like you," Mimimi said, shoulders trembling as she hung her head weakly. "Maybe it's selfish, but...I don't want to see you change so much." Still looking down, she wiped her cheeks, then came up to clunk her forehead against my shoulder.

Even I could tell what that was trying to hide, and that was exactly why I couldn't say a word.

"And plus...I know I'm the only one who can tell..."

She said that without looking at my face, wiping her face with her sleeve just once before lifting her chin to look at me with reddened eyes.

"...Kikuchi-san doesn't want to see you like that, either."

"...Mimimi."

After saying all that, Mimimi immediately buried her face deep in my shoulder again.

"...Headbutt," she said childishly, but even she couldn't make it sound like a joke.

She wasn't managing to hide her shyness, or the facts, or anything.

"O-oh..." This hit to the shoulder was not a Mimimi Slap or a Mimimi Chop, but a Mimimi Headbutt that caused no damage at all. I felt my vision clearing. "...Thanks. You...helped me again."

With her face still buried there, Mimimi gave a little nod. Her voice was still weak. "So just for now...can I stay like this for just a bit?"

"...Yeah."

My shoulder gradually got wetter then, but nothing hurt anymore.

* * *

After parting with Mimimi, I was in Kitayono.

I didn't go straight back home, walking and thinking.

No—to be honest, I didn't know what I should do.

Trying to drop my other burdens for Kikuchi-san would make Mimimi sad—and if I changed, it would hurt both of them.

But if I was to continue my relationships with Hinami and everyone the same as before, that really would make Kikuchi-san anxious. It might even end our relationship as boyfriend and girlfriend.

It was just like a badly made puzzle, with the various pieces in irregular shapes that I couldn't all fit in a frame. Even if I took out one of the particularly large and colorful pieces, something would still be sticking out.

Maybe if I'd been prepared to distance myself from Hinami, then I could have resolved it.

But staying involved with her was something I wanted to do from the bottom of my heart—I couldn't abandon it, not for anything.

So basically, yeah.

The time to choose that Mizusawa had told me about had come.

I had to take one of those things that was important out of my hand and set it aside.

* * *

Right after talking with Mimimi, I went back to the station, then visited Kita-Asaka Station, which was closest to Kikuchi-san's house.

After talking with Mimimi and desperately thinking to myself, a conclusion had come into form inside me.

If there weren't many things to me that were special in the real sense...

...and Kikuchi-san didn't want me shrinking my world...

...but two of the things that were really special to me were in contradiction...

...then now, I just had to make a choice.

A few minutes earlier, I'd sent a message on LINE to Kikuchi-san. I told her, [*I want to talk now, so once you see this message, come outside—in front of your house is fine*]. Now I was headed from the station to her house.

Even though we'd only walked this route together a few times, just seeing the scenery brought back so many memories—talking about the reason I'd come to like her, both of us blushing. The way I'd felt warm on the way back alone after walking her home. Those small, trivial memories really were irreplaceable to me.

But right now, knowing I was going to go see her, I was frozen from my fingertips to my heart. That had to be because of what I was about to tell her.

The bridge we'd crossed many times together came into view. Once I passed it, I'd be at her place in just about three houses. After that, I could just take my time waiting there.

As my feet approached the bridge, I spotted the shadow of a girl dashing out toward me from the wall a little ahead. She wasn't carrying a bag, and she was glancing all around like she was in a hurry for something. Then when she noticed me, she came trotting toward me.

Kikuchi-san and I faced each other in the middle of the bridge.

"…Good evening," she said.

"Yeah… Evening."

We exchanged our usual greeting, but we couldn't look each other in the eye. Maybe she'd also figured out what I was about to talk about and what I was about to choose.

"Umm…," I said, "It's cold, so we could go somewhere first…"

"…Here."

"Huh?"

Bracing herself, Kikuchi-san said, "Let's make it…here." She must have felt some attachment to this place, too. She turned to watch the river flowing by beyond the railing. "Let's make it here."

This wasn't a bridge many people used, and right now, it was just the two of us.

The water looked much the same as it had during that summer vacation, but without the light of the fireworks.

We were enveloped in cold and quiet.

"All right…so," I slowly began, "I've been thinking about lots of things—what I should do to keep you from feeling anxious. How I should change."

"…Mm-hmm," she answered quietly.

"I wanted to get rid of the conflict… I tried to set aside those burdens that weren't special to me, but it didn't work out." I'd been taught that

Kikuchi-san and Mimimi cared about me expanding my world, too. "But what's left is Hinami and *Atafami*...and no matter how anxious you feel about those, I can't change them."

Since those were choices from my heart.

Since even if I did choose Kikuchi-san, I still couldn't give up on those.

"So...I can only be who I am now. But if that's going to be hard on you...if it will hurt you..."

We had a special reason, but we were unbalanced.

We were bridging the difference between two species, but there was a contradiction there.

But if I tried to change the things that weren't as important to me, then I was no longer Poppol.

And for those important things that remained, I had realized I didn't want to change them.

If there was no way to change those from the fundamental rules—

—then there was nothing more I could do.

I got that far, but I didn't have the courage to say any more. I mean, Kikuchi-san was important to me, and I wanted to care for her along with everything else, if I could. But I couldn't choose everything. If I was going to choose the other thing I cared about—to continue being involved with Hinami—then my conclusion was foregone.

Kikuchi-san squeezed the skirt of her uniform, lowered her head, and bit her lip.

Eventually, she relaxed her clenched fists, and her skirt stayed where it was, slightly crumpled. "...Tomozaki-kun, our relationship started as feelings, and you used the magic of words to give it meaning as something special." Her hands wandered awkwardly in the air to eventually arrive near her chest. "As the protagonist of the story of life, you used that magic to choose me."

Then she squeezed her shirt in her hands.

"But I know you came up with that reason after the fact."

*   *   *

"…Yeah."

My breath caught. That was exactly what I'd been thinking.

I'd thought that our opposite worries, and our opposite logic to make up for it, was the proof that we were special. But now that had created conflict between us.

"I think there was just one thing missing in our relationship." Kikuchi-san looked up at the dark sky. There was nothing there but the barely visible stars, with no lingering smoke from the beautiful fireworks of that night.

"I was caught between ideals and emotions. When you reached out to me then, I accepted the reason that you'd made for me." She walked up to the railing to put both hands on it. "So I don't think…there is a reason, in the real sense, that it has to be the two of us. But I found myself being all right with that."

In other words, what was lacking between Kikuchi-san and me—

In order for an individual to connect with another in a real way, they need a special reason. At least, Kikuchi-san and I did.

But the reason I'd given Kikuchi-san was not special, in the real sense. So then.

That reason changed shape to become a contradiction, then eventually became karma, and our relationship was all—

Kikuchi-san turned around and slowly opened her mouth.

"—So this time, please let *me* choose."

I was surprised.

"I've been thinking ever since then."

One step at a time, of her own will, on her own feet, Kikuchi-san approached me. "We started from feelings, and you came up with a reason to make me special, even if it was forced. But though you chose me…"

Though I hadn't moved even a step from that place—though I thought what I'd chosen hadn't been Kikuchi-san—the distance between the two of us was slowly shrinking.

"…I haven't chosen anything at all myself yet," she continued.

I'm sure this time it was her spell—to change our reason.

"That's not an ideal relationship at all. So…"

Kikuchi-san was there, close enough to touch if I reached out.

"…I want you, Tomozaki-kun."

And it was just like that time.

But this time, she took my hand.

"Please let me choose you, too. This is the one thing that I think was missing."

Yes, that was…not me, stuck at a dead end and tangled up in contradictions.

It was her decision and her will.

"But…I don't deserve to be chosen …," I started to say.

But Kikuchi-san cut me off. "Nanami-san told me that you were trying to change."

"!"

Her voice was lonely, still chilled by the cold air. "She said, 'Brain's doing this thing, and it's probably for you.'" She spoke fervently, shoulders trembling. "'So I want you to know how hard he's trying.'" I sensed a hint of jealousy, but most of it was gratitude.

"Over the course of a year, you changed yourself and expanded your world…and your world became so colorful. And then you were willing to throw that away… You were trying to change for me, weren't you?" She brought my hand up to the level of her heart. "…I thought that was really amazing."

And then she took that hand and wrapped it in her warm, white hands, which were so dear to me.

*   *   *

"You're so like Poppol, you would even throw away *being* Poppol."

Those words were contradictory, celebrating me for trying to change myself from being a person who changed himself.

"...Kikuchi-san," I lowered my voice, and she nodded in acceptance.

"That's...my ideal person. Almost too much so." She slowly released my hand and touched her hands to her chest. "So, Tomozaki-kun. Please don't force yourself to change."

She looked into my eyes—and kindly smiled, exactly like a real angel.

"You tried to change for me when the person you've become is so important to you—that's enough for me."

Each and every one of her words was validating my actions and my thoughts.

The more I studied her, the more precious she became to me.

"...Huh?"

Before I knew it, I was holding her hands and drawing her close—I was embracing her in both arms. "Sorry... Thank you."

I was even surprised at myself for doing this. But it seemed like the natural thing to do for how I felt.

Yeah, this time for sure, we had really and actually—

—become a couple who had chosen each other.

"Oh, no... I'd like to thank you."

The both of us expressed our gratitude.

From just a few centimeters away, I couldn't tell what her expression was, but her body heat, her heartbeat, and her words communicated our feelings better than that.

I heard the cool river rushing. Some insects I didn't know the name of were buzzing. The glow of the headlights passing by were probably different ones from before.

It was like everything I saw and heard was unimportant. Just standing here like this, the earlier conflicts and anxieties all melted together when we had no distance between us. I could stay like this forever.

Eventually, we drew apart at about the same time, and with my hands still on her shoulders, I looked into her eyes. I didn't embarrass her by getting all flustered, although it's really nothing to be embarrassed about anyway. But both of our faces were still bright red.

I came away to stand at her side. Then I took her hand and said jokingly, "I'll walk you back."

She giggled. "Tee-hee... It's really close, but please do."

And then like that, still holding hands, we started to walk from the middle of the bridge the few dozen meters to her house.

Without even being aware of it, we were stepping in sync. The heat in our hands was the same temperature. I don't know what she was thinking, but I felt like I got everything.

In my mind right then was the fact that Kikuchi-san had chosen me now.

"Hey, so," I said in a conspiratorial voice, "doesn't that mean that you and I just chose each other based on feelings, and there's still no special reason?"

Kikuchi-san blinked awkwardly. "W-well..."

She looked and acted just like a little chipmunk. The tension had seeped out of both of us, and we had no more resistance to showing our weaknesses.

That's why I immediately killed my own trick. "...Sorry, I was just giving you a hard time. Actually...I already know the answer."

"Huh?"

Seeing her confused, I smiled at her mischievously.

I'd listened to a lot of people talk about relationships, and I'd learned many important things.

Sometimes there's nothing you can do but face each individual source of anxiety; there's plenty of things you can only talk about after you start dating; starting a relationship isn't the final goal of love.

And I'd learned that the old school badges of destiny, and any "special" thing was just a *formality*—created by an accumulation of stories.

That was why...

"This isn't a rom-com anime or a dating sim—it's just life," I said.

So then here, where we were—was not the finish line where two people, who were brought together by love, had arrived at a "Mission Complete." This was a starting point for both of us.

"From now on, let's do it all together—worrying, struggling, and putting our heads together to come up with solutions... We might sometimes hurt each other and make each other anxious, but let's do what we did when we made the script for the play. Let's search for that special reason together."

I could feel Kikuchi-san's hand squeeze tight in response.

"I think that's probably what it means to date."

It was like being minor accomplices; the goal was not to monopolize each other.

It was okay for it to start with feelings. Maybe there was no special reason to it.

But even if that was how this relationship started, even if it wasn't special, we would search for a reason it had to be the two of us.

"I mean, that's something that you can't do alone. It has to be two people, right?" I said.

Maybe I was just making up the logic as I went. Maybe it was a lie made to get through this one time.

But in this game of life, where nothing is absolutely correct and there's no magic, I think this counts as our special reason for dating.

"...So how about that?" I asked her shyly.

Kikuchi-san looked up at me like she was startled, and then eventually—

＊　　＊　　＊

—she gently released my hand.

Surprised, I looked at her. "Huh…?"

With her back to me, Kikuchi-san took a few steps away from where I was standing and stopped.

After some time, she spun around to face me and giggled mischievously.

The hem of her skirt fluttered as she slowly twirled in a dance.

It was just like that scene that had played so many times in my head.

"Do you remember when we saw those fireworks in the sky? They turned the gray sky all different colors. They were so bright and beautiful."

That caught my attention—that was from the secret ending Kikuchi-san had written just for us.

"It was a little humid since it was by the river, but the reflection on the water was so pretty. I'd never seen anything so beautiful in my life."

I didn't have to listen to know what Kikuchi-san was going to say next.

That was the line that I'd read I don't know how many times.

"But you know what?" Kikuchi-san looked up at me with an innocent smile like Kris. "Just like you taught me, the most important thing is that…"

It even felt like she was faintly glowing in my field of vision—she really was just like a fairy.

"…you don't need to force yourself to change to be together with someone you care about."

But Kikuchi-san wasn't calling out to Libra—she was talking to me.

"I wrote these words, but I haven't been able to say them. So please let me say them now."

* * *

And then mischievously, this time she smiled just like an angel.

"I love you, Fumiya-kun."

Kikuchi-san always goes just a little beyond my expectations.
"Y-you said *Fumiya-kun...!*"
As I flailed, she pouted sweetly. "I mean, um...that girl at the meetup was calling you that...um."
"Urk..." It was just so charming, and her jealousy was way too powerful for my heart.
Maybe it's weird to say so at a time like this, but her expression, the things she said—my feelings were ready to go out of control.
It was basically like—when I'd seen Kikuchi-san over the video call, or that itchy feeling Rena-chan had given me, and when she'd said, *"You haven't gone that far with your girlfriend yet, have you?"*
All that suddenly rushed at me to combine with my peaking affection for Kikuchi-san.
And I moved forward.

"—!"

All my senses but one fell away. Mine and Kikuchi-san's lips became the whole world.
If my thoughts and feelings that couldn't be put into words were to exist in reality, then would they be soft like this?
For a few seconds more, everything was frozen. My thoughts, time itself—
"Ah..." The sound that slipped out of her lips when we pulled apart would normally have been an unbearable magic spell to me, but right now, I was beyond that.
That sensation was just too sweet, and the comfortable aftertaste of her feelings against mine still lingered there.
"Umm..." As I was hesitating long enough that I couldn't even remember why anymore, Kikuchi-san was staring at me open-mouthed.

"U-um..."

And then with tears welling in her eyes, she said:

"...O-one more time."

"Huh?!" I yelped.

Kikuchi-san's eyes widened with a start like she was snapping out of a daze. "Oh, n-no, um, never mind!" She blushed beet red as she waved her hands aggressively. She really was going past angel and past human, and then coming back around again to angel.

"U-um..."

"Ah...ha-ha."

Though I felt weirdly shy and embarrassed, at least we were embarrassed together.

So our racing hearts, the body heat, and her asking for more all felt sweet to me.

Eventually, holding hands, we arrived in front of her house. As usual, the light seeping from her windows was warm.

"Um..." But Kikuchi-san still held on to my hand and wouldn't let go. "Before we say bye...there's something I wanted to ask."

"What?" I tilted my head.

In a charming voice, she said, "M-maybe...I still don't know you better than Hinami-san..."

And then touching her pale-pink lips with the pad of her index finger, she said:

"But I'm the only one...who knows, um, what it's like to k-kiss you... right?"

Those heated words and their mingled jealousy completely knocked me out.

7

You can't change your base stats so easily

"Why do you guys have such dramatic fights over every little thing? Are you guys crazy?"

We were at a restaurant in Omiya. Mizusawa was in front of me, leaning on one elbow as he listened with a smirk.

"Hey, I really angsted about this! Don't write it off," I argued back.

Mizusawa chuckled. "Fights can be like foreplay, so that's like another kind of experience."

"Hey…" After all my struggles, this high-ranked dater was cutting me down to size. Maybe everyone just went through the same thing. Wait, maybe they really do.

"Well, it's like unlocking a new achievement," he said.

"Don't talk about it like a video game."

"How was it not like a video game?" he said smugly, like he'd said something witty. That jerk.

"Okay, but I feel like using that comparison for love is kind of gross."

"Fine, fine."

He had me by the nose for the whole conversation, but I managed to report everything to him.

Then as he was taking a bite of his extra-special large *ten-don*, Mizusawa frowned. "…But okay, I'm a little surprised."

"About what?" I asked back, eating a normal, regular-size *ten-don*.

He took a sip of water. "When it came to a choice between her and Aoi, you thought you could only choose Aoi."

"Well, um… Wait, huh?"

While I struggled to find words, Mizusawa smiled coolly. "What?"

"Did I say the other person was Hinami?"

He chuckled. "Heh-heh. Well, the only person who could rival Kikuchi-san for you would be Aoi. Though, I don't really know why."

"...Ah." I didn't exactly admit to it, but I had basically given in.

Mizusawa didn't press the matter, which was very like him. "But— Oh, huh. This time, Fuka-chan chose you. She wanted to continue the relationship and said it's okay for you to be involved with Aoi."

"...Yeah." That was right. At the current stage, this was still not a complete resolution.

Honestly, my guess is that so long as you're two different people, there is no complete resolution to love.

I'm sure Kikuchi-san would still sometimes feel anxious about Hinami and me in the future. She'd feel lonely about me being Poppol sometimes, too. She'd also sometimes get hurt by my karma.

But she told me she was okay with that.

"...That's why I want to find a special reason for us while we're dating."

Mizusawa's hands stopped for a moment to pick up a piece of deep-fried eel with his chopsticks. "Hmm...I see. I get it." It would have taken me three bites to eat that, but he took it and tossed it into his mouth all at once, then pointed at me with his chopsticks. "So you think you can accept the old school badges."

"...Yeah. Since you guys did go to the trouble of asking us."

Mizusawa nodded *mm-hmm* and made another joke. "So then I don't have to invite Aoi anymore."

"You were serious about that...?"

"Of course I was. You know I like her." He said it so casually. This sort of confidence is what makes Mizusawa come off like a top-tier character, more than his communication skills and stuff like that...

I was still reeling while Mizusawa looked straight at me, pulling up the corners of his lips in a grin. "Once you figure out where to find a relationship you think is really special, let me know." He said it so smoothly like it was nothing, then looked down again.

"...Okay."

"All right, then... That was good."

"Huh? You ate so fast."

Didn't he get a large? How could he finish faster than me with a regular?

"You're the one who's slow. C'mon and hurry up."

"O-okay..."

So I rushed to bolt down my regular normal-sized *ten-don*. Hmm, even after all these different experiences, I guess I can't beat Mizusawa-sensei in life or fast eating, huh?

* * *

"Thank you to everyone from the beautification committee for their entertaining play."

A few days later, we were in the gym after noon.

The send-off that had started about an hour earlier was nearing its end, and the voice of Izumi, the organizer, rang out from the speaker. Perhaps thanks to her experience being on the cultural-festival committee and other things in these past few months, Izumi had become completely used to emceeing, and she hardly looked nervous at all anymore. An environment really does cultivate a person.

To my left, Takei was applauding with satisfaction for the play that had just ended. "Man, that was hilarious?!"

"You were laughing so hard, I couldn't hear half of it, though," I teased him.

"Lay off, man!" he cried, and Tachibana and the guys nearby all laughed.

I was taking the initiative to communicate and enjoying the atmosphere of the send-off with everyone. Spending this time being outgoing and fooling around with everyone isn't necessarily the right thing, and it's not like it's the only correct option.

But now that I could do something that I couldn't not so long ago, I was changing myself and broadening my world. In other words—I was being Poppol, or the Pureblood Hybrid, which Kikuchi-san and Mimimi had said they liked.

I happened to remember last year's send-off.

Back then, I'd just made myself invisible and sat in the corner, thinking only about *Atafami* to speed up my internal clock. I'd experienced a startling amount of change compared with how I was then—enough to call a character change.

But that was neither positive nor negative. I think it was just change. Chatting a lot made the time pass quickly, and eventually, the moment came.

"—And next, the presentation of mementos from the representatives of the current students."

That broadcast caused a bubbling of hushed excitement here and there in the gym. Though it was well-known among the students, the tradition had been passed down secretly without letting the teachers know. Well, after this much time, I figured the teachers kind of knew, but the secretive excitement was strangely more thrilling than just everyone going wild.

Kikuchi-san was sitting right behind me in the girls' seats.

"Representative of the third years, Mitamura-kun and Toda-san," came the call, and two students sitting a little ways from the exit stood up. The first was a tall jock-type boy with short hair, and the second was a model-looking girl with her hair beautifully curled. They suited each other, and according to Izumi, they were going to be living together after graduation.

"Representative of the current students, Tomozaki-kun. Kikuchi-san."

When our names were called, we stood, too. I looked back, and when my eyes met with Kikuchi-san's right behind me, I smiled and nodded. Though her expression was a little stiff, she gave me a couple little nods back. Well, I'm not good at this sort of thing, either, but I should be taking the lead here. I would show as much composure as I could.

The two of us walked side by side, and then right by the stairs to the stage, we took the plaque and bouquet. I went first up the podium and faced the two older students.

"From the current students, we offer a plaque and bouquet in commemoration of your graduation," Izumi announced. I handed the plaque to Mitamura-senpai, while Kikuchi-san handed the bouquet to Toda-senpai.

"Congratulations," I said as smoothly as possible.

"...Congratulations," Kikuchi said a little nervously but politely as we offered them out with both hands.

That was when I felt something cool at my fingertips.

"Thank you... This is for you," Mitamura-senpai added in a whisper. I glanced at him to find a dully shining bit of metal was touching my hand, hidden behind the plaque. So that was...

"Thank you very much, I'll take care of it," I replied to him quietly as I accepted it.

Lowering my hand like nothing had happened, I glanced at the thing he'd put in it. What I saw between my fingers was an old, rusty, common school pin with a cherry-blossom motif.

You could see the passage of time on the little badge. It felt packed with history, being passed down beneath the teachers' noses through every generation. How many of those people really had managed to get a special relationship, and how many went back to being strangers? I'm sure that had nothing to do with the romantic story that kept being told.

"...Thank you very much. I hope you two are happy," Kikuchi-san said to the graduating students quietly—she must have accepted hers in the same way.

The students below the stage watching must have confirmed that the badges had been handed over, as there was a stirring of whispers all around again.

The four of us smiled at one another conspiratorially, then came down from the podium as if nothing had happened. Once we were in the two seats that had been left open at the end of the girls' row so we could sit down smoothly, we sneakily checked each other's badges and gave each other shy smiles.

"We got 'em," I said in a warm voice.

Kikuchi-san smiled in satisfaction. "...We did. It's amazing that they've been passed down for ten years, isn't it?"

"Yeah." I nodded.

Her gaze went up like she was thinking. "But, Fumiya-kun," she said, using my new name, "is it all right for me to be a little mean?"

"...Hmm?"

Examining the old school badges, she teased, "These are the old school badges of the old school building. Doesn't this really...seem like they were made just for you and Hinami-san, after all?"

"Urk... Was that revenge?"

"Tee-hee. Yes," she said with a mischievous smile. It seemed like her reasoning went back to the time I'd touched on our "special reason" in Kita-Asaka.

It's true that most of that secret half year's worth of time with Hinami had been spent in Sewing Room #2—in the old school building from the same era when these badges had been in use.

That place and that time were unquestionably special to Hinami and me.

"It's true that we did go there every morning...," I said.

The specialness between me and Hinami had been brought up many times. And if you added the old school building and the old school badges on top of that, then it wouldn't be strange to feel like it had been made for us or like there was something fated in it.

I imagined Hinami and me putting on these badges, meeting together in the school building where they'd originally been used; as I pictured it, it did seem like these badges had been made for that purpose all along.

When I was awkwardly not sure what to say, Kikuchi-san giggled. "Kidding, I'm sorry. The truth is...I've thought of another answer."

"...Another answer?" I asked back.

Her eyes dropped to the badges. "Fumiya-kun...how about something like this?"

Then she slowly lifted up her fingers—

—and she gently brought a *flowery acessory* with a cherry-blossom motif up by her ear.

"Oh..."

And that's when I got it, too.

So then I—just like how Kikuchi-san had told me those words that she could only say in a story—

—I put that up by my ear in the same way and said, "I've always wanted to wear matching accessories."

Those were also words from that final scene.

But this time, the one who was saying it was not Kikuchi-san, but me.

"We really could make these our special thing," I said.

And then Kikuchi-san smiled innocently, just like Kris. "Tee-hee. But that line isn't Libra's. It was Kris's."

"Oh, you could tell?"

"Yes. I wrote it, after all."

They were just badges with no power. A story had been put onto what were just some lumps of metal, and someone had found reasons to carry them and to pass them on.

"You could say these are just old school badges…," I said, "but because everyone believed in them—this rust and these marks really did become special."

That was no doubt the power of those accumulated stories.

"So I'm sure our relationship will, too."

After I'd said that much, Kikuchi-san also nodded gladly, studying that school badge intently.

And then she traced those nicks, that rust gently with her fingers as if stroking something dear. "Our conflicts and contradictions eventually… become like these nicks," she said with a smile, her eyes looking straight ahead.

And I'm sure our time smiling at each other like that—

"Yeah… Let's make it special."

—was weaving a story that would paint our future in our colors.

* * *

And so the third-year send-off ended without a hitch, and school ended that day.

I'd come to Sewing Room #2.

It wasn't like I was leaning on the story of the old school badges that we'd inherited, but I just wanted to go someplace fitting the occasion. I wanted to have another important conversation there. I could feel the old air and familiar sights here as I gazed at the rusty glint.

Our falling-out had ultimately been resolved by forcing Kikuchi-san to suck it up, in a sense.

Our relationship as boyfriend and girlfriend would continue, but I also wanted to be involved with Hinami. We'd settled down on that selfish relationship because Hinami was important to me, and it was a line I wouldn't back down on.

It was irreplaceable enough to me that once, I'd been ready to give up my relationship with Kikuchi-san.

And Kikuchi-san had chosen me, that part included.

If a story woven from feelings and time together would make even rusty metal something special…then surely that could make my relationship with Kikuchi-san as special as mine with Hinami.

What rose in my mind was Alucia from the two stories.

Because she was bloodless, she could learn every skill, but she couldn't appreciate it down to her core.

That's why in her place, she trained up Libra and wanted him to master those skills.

Having no blood, she'd etched her experience of blood into Libra.

It was her fight against her fate, as someone bloodless who could never become special.

She was just like me, and individualist.

And more of an extreme realist than me.

*　　*　　*

Hinami lived like she was trying to prove she was right, but the life coaching was the one thing she did that seemed pointless.

But what if it wasn't pointless?
What if, in fact, it suited her motives more than anything else—?

That was when it happened.

"...So what is it?"
That familiar unreadable voice rang out in that familiar place.
When I turned around, there was Hinami, looking extremely inconvenienced.
"Hey...you're late."
Hinami furrowed her brow like she was annoyed and tap-tapped on the floor with her toe. "I have a lot of things to manage around the send-off, too, being on student council. Maybe show some gratitude that I even came here?"
"Ha-ha-ha...you haven't changed."
Normally, I might have felt amused about Hinami's reaction, but I wasn't in the mood right then.

"—Hey, Hinami."

I called out her name with feeling. Hinami was sensitive to subtleties like that, and she stopped a little and turned around with visible exasperation and some caution. "What?" Her short and cold reply was so direct, rejecting my determination to bring this up.
"I've always wondered..." But even with that stabbing me, Kikuchi-san had given me the determination to proceed. "I thought NO NAME couldn't stand anything pointless... I thought you had reasons for everything you did, so why would you be this involved with me?"
Hinami's eyebrows gave a tiny twitch.

"Why would you spare this much time to help me out strategizing for my life?"

"...Uh-huh. I assume you have an answer?" she said coolly with her arms folded.

Watching her like that, I slowly got out the words. "At first, I thought it had to do with *Atafami*. The only time you act natural is when the game is involved, which was why I thought something might be hidden there."

"Hmm..." Hinami's expression was composed, arms crossed. That was no different from usual.

"But then, talking with Kikuchi-san...and thinking a lot about you, I realized one thing." One by one, I carefully recalled all my conversations with Hinami, as well as Alucia's motivations. "Before you took me to your room. Do you remember what I said?" That was when Hinami—more accurately, NO NAME—and I first met. "That you can't change your character in the game of life."

"...Yep." Hinami nodded.

Everything had begun then, and now we were here.

"So many times after that, you said you wanted to prove that you can change your character, even in life. So I thought you were just being competitive, like you just wanted to argue me down for saying that life sucks as a game and that you can't change characters and stuff...but I was wrong." She was a gamer who hated to lose, and that's why she wanted to beat nanashi as NO NAME—those reasons had been convincing to me before.

"What you call a character change is actually something else."

Remembering the depiction of Alucia in *Pureblood Hybrid and Ice Cream*—

With no blood of her own, she'd taken in the knowledge of many different races to survive.

The way she offered that same knowledge to Libra—that was just like a character change.

"The point wasn't to change me, was it?"

Then I fixed a direct look on Hinami.

"—It was for you," I declared.

Her eyes widened, and the lips that had been pressed together parted just slightly.

And then looking at my hands—

—aware of the sticks and buttons under those fingers—

"In your mind...Aoi Hinami as a player was changing *the character you control.*"

Her folded arms twitched, and her lips closed firmly this time, as if trying to protect something.

"You always looked down over this world as a player, holding the controller to plug it into yourself," I continued.

Hinami's worldview was one step removed. She was seeing from a higher perspective, one above feelings or enjoyment as a player. I'd witnessed it during the camping trip and also during that good-bye afterward.

"So you took the port from the controller in your hand—the character you control—and switched it from Aoi Hinami to me."

It was an idea unique to Aoi Hinami, who lived purely as a player.

"You were starting over your life challenge from a level-one character with the same methods."

It was a way you'd do things if you craved your own correctness over everything else.

I'm sure that was a ceremony for filling up her bloodless and empty self with that correctness.

"You wanted to prove that even changing the character you're challenging life with—even using the bottom-tier character Fumiya Tomozaki, you could replicate the results."

That was exactly why it could be so cruel, lacking any warm-blooded emotion.

"It was to prove that how you do things is *correct*—that's all."

*   *   *

I laid it all out.

It was simple, patchworked together carefully from all her values and the principles behind her actions.

Aoi Hinami believed only in correctness, and that was her main support in life. That was why every day, she used those methods to produce straightforward results and prove that correctness, in which she found value, over and over.

Her studies, club, friendships, dating.

By analyzing them all to "completion" and reaching what could be called first place, she felt a stability in their value.

The more correct she was, the more value she had, and she became eager to prove that.

The more correct she was, the more she could be secure, and then she could seek out even more correct procedures.

As she was doing this over and over, she must have eventually hit on this idea:

Would this "strategy" of hers really be right if someone else was to use it?

I remembered that she'd mentioned the results being replicable. If you could produce the same results through the same method, even in a new environment, then it had high replicability, and you could say that it was even more correct. Be it in chemistry or math, the only thing that could logically guarantee that something was correct was if it was reproducible or not. To use that in life was a truly Hinami-like proof.

"You used a spell on me that changed the world I saw, but that wasn't to save me or because you wanted to beat me, either."

And then I—exactly like proving a conclusion from a hypothesis—

"You just wanted to prove that the strategy guide you came up with for the game of life was accurate."

Most likely, for everyone aside from herself.

If I had to say, then probably—to the world.

Hinami unfolded her arms and let them fall. "...As expected of nan-ashi," she said.

And she didn't deny it.

"So...that was it, after all." It was a saddening thing to hear. "I was able to come this far in just a little over six months because your way of doing things works. But enough is enough." All the time we had spent together was gradually fading into black and white. "Enough of using people like this. You'd even use my life to prove that you're right." I wasn't hiding my overflowing emotions.

As you'd expect, Hinami must have felt bad, as she averted her gaze, eyes sliding down and to the side. "I figured you would be mad."

That was when—

Perhaps because I'd talked on too long, the first bell rang. Since we never went to the classroom together, Hinami had to get back soon, or she'd miss her moment. "I'm sorry... Then I'm going back first."

"Ah..." I'd almost never heard Hinami apologize before.

Now I was left all alone in Sewing Room #2.

The usual classroom, the old sewing machines, the dusty air.

The random dates written at the edge of the board.

Having spent this space with her over the past six months, I'd come to like it. We'd made this room irreplaceable, something special. It was my place.

But the meaning and the memories packed in it were scattering like the air coming out of a balloon with a hole.

The chair would creak loudly just from putting a little weight on it, but I leaned my whole body on it. The lonely groaning was too quiet to drown out the solitude.

"...I wish she'd gotten mad," I muttered, then walked out, dragging my heart behind me.

* * *

A few minutes after Hinami left, in a hallway of the old school building.

Standing in the sun that was streaming in through the window, clouded from dust and limescale, I was thinking.

Maybe I was still a loner, in the real sense.

Being a loner means having responsibility for yourself.

To connect with another is to entrust each other with that responsibility.

But I still hadn't managed to fully surrender responsibility for myself to another, or to shoulder theirs—even with Kikuchi-san, with whom I'd talked so much. I was taking advantage of her kindness in saying that my attempts to change were enough. It had taken the positive form of *"Then let's search for a special reason together"* but that was ultimately an extension of associating as individuals. Of course, I don't think that's a bad thing. In fact, I think recklessly handing over responsibility and winding up with a dependent relationship would really be the most thoughtless and foolish thing. I'd even call it irresponsible.

But is this really enough for me?

For example, Tama-chan and Mimimi. I think because Tama-chan respects the individual like me, she won't easily pry into other people's business. But if she senses that Mimimi is in trouble, she'd try to save her, even if it was going too far to take responsibility in the real sense. She had the strength to believe in the mistaken logic of doing something just because you want to and taking responsibility by force.

Mimimi, too—she turns the weakness of not being able to live alone into flexibility, and she could entrust responsibility to another. I think that's why she accepts responsibility that she fundamentally doesn't need to carry when it's directed at her.

Nakamura and Izumi. I'm sure they don't think about responsibility or independence or dependence or whatever—they simply join hearts because they like each other, because they're sure it will lead to good places. They're running with their feelings. Takei's the same, too; he sympathizes with everyone around him, which leaves openings to sympathize with him, too. As you can understand from how quickly I started teasing him, he'll easily allow intrusion to important places from any kind of weakling. Mizusawa is like me in that he won't quickly try to pry into people, and he won't let them get so close easily, either. But there was that expression he showed Hinami during the camping trip, and the way he'd briefly taken off his mask. He'd been ready get close, going past the line where you could take responsibility. Since then, the way he connects with people has been slowly changing, and I'm sure that eventually, his desire to have the character-eye view, and his own adeptness and cleverness in turning the feelings he wishes into reality, would actualize that.

And even Kikuchi-san. She's shy and isn't good at involving herself with people, but she's strong at her core. As I've stubbornly refused to abandon my individualism, she's tried to come closer to me many times. I'm sure that if I just didn't refuse her, then she would slowly take away that line, and we could have a relationship where we're not separate people.

So what about me and Hinami?

I hold respect and esteem for other people. I care for them; I like them. I think that's completely normal.

But when Kikuchi-san showed that she didn't like me going to the meetups, I valued my own choice, and the only path I could go down was different from Kikuchi-san's. Now that I think of it, not so long ago, I'd even played with the "magic of words" that I'm so good at in order to escape from the responsibility of choosing another. I hadn't been able to handle the burden of the responsibility for anything other than what I levied on myself, or the fear of entrusting myself to another.

I've been getting through life by shutting myself up—

No, by shutting up the world and locking it away from myself.

Hinami believes only in correctness, and nothing else—not even herself.

She only finds meaning in what's easy to understand, like first place or winning a prize, with no foundation there for her own desires. Proving her correctness is the goal, and she was even using me as a "character" to manifest that. That's why she can't do anything without a reason, and she will firmly reject mistakes.

In a way, this is an ideology of extreme personal responsibility, and that's precisely why she never has expectations for anything outside her control, and why she's never let others into her world.

I have the baseless confidence that she doesn't, but we both conform to the fundamental principle of individual competition: I am me, and others are others. We believe in the results of our own effort more than anything else. We have faced *Atafami*, clubs, studies—the game of life—that was our battleground.

But we both ultimately saw that as a single-player game.

Me, as a character. Her, as a player.
Me, as a person acting on feelings. Her, as a person acting on logic.
I might be a top-tier character...and she might actually be a bottom-tier character.

I thought we were the same type, but the truth is that aside from being gamers, everything about us was different. But just one thing connected the two of us.

There was surely just one thing that defined us both.

Yes. I realized there was just one more thing we had in common.

Aoi Hinami and I—

We were alone, in the real sense.

Afterword

It's been a long time. I'm the official writer of Saitama Prefecture, Yuki Yaku.

By the time everyone is reading Volume 9 here, the TV anime will have begun broadcast, and its influence will cause the whole population to want to move to Omiya, so I think Omiya might functionally become the capital. Since it had the chance to appear in the *Anitamasai* held by Saitama Prefecture the other day, next stop: the world.

Anyway, ever since I was a newbie, I've gotten more fans, and more passionate fans, and more people who have followed this guy here—who's always going on about Omiya or *Smash* or self-Googling—and spreading the series for me.

It really took time until the initial reprint of this series, and the truth is that it's gotten big thanks to all of you.

No matter how much I thank you, I can't do it enough—and that's why now, there's something that I must absolutely tell you all.

That's about "the roundness expressed in elements other than the line of the leg," which is on Kikuchi-san's left leg in the cover illustration.

First of all, please pay attention to the lower area of the two legs that are together, to the central area of Kikuchi-san's left thigh. Can you see that leg showing its roundness toward us, the direction she is looking?

However, there is a mystery here. The lines that make up the leg are above and below, but there is only a roundness expressing the leg's outer edges, and no symbols used express the roundness, which is facing toward us.

Well then, why does it look as if it's rounded? Here, there is the magic of two kinks.

First, there is the exquisite painting of her skin color, with a contrast of a texture like marshmallow.

And the other is not the leg itself, but the curves of the skirt that decorate it.

Regarding the painting, that goes without saying. The part that is rounded is white and bright. The parts that aren't are painted in a dimmer color. That softens the otherwise flat image. In other words, this is love.

What is most important here are the curves of the skirt. The skirt comes toward us in three dimensions, lying against the leg in a curve, and from there, we indirectly can know the softness and the swell of the leg. However, this is ultimately not a leg, but lines that express the skirt. Essentially, since Fly-san's picture is reality, it also connects everything aside from her body to the world to express the character. Using "something on to the leg" and not elements that express the leg, it expresses the kink of the leg itself—in other words, it really is love.

Now on to the acknowledgments.

To my illustrator, Fly-san. The anime is finally here, huh. That's the one time I will be prepared to endlessly drink sake. I'll be counting on you, too. I'm a fan.

To my editor, Iwaasa-san. This time, I wound up living together with you at Shogakukan, huh. Next volume will wind up like this, too.

And to all my readers. We've gotten an anime, but of course, I'm aiming for a second and third season. I would be glad if you would continue to push forward with me. Thank you as always for your support. Well then, I would be glad if you would stay with me in the next volume, as well.

                                                    Yuki Yaku